BLADE KILLER

A chilling crime thriller with a stunning final twist

EMMY ELLIS

DI Bethany Smith Book 8

Originally published as *Blood of the Raven*

JOFFE BOOKS

Revised edition 2024
Joffe Books, London
www.joffebooks.com

First published in Great Britain in 2020
as *Blood of the Raven*

This paperback edition was first published
in Great Britain in 2024

This book is a work of fiction. Names, characters, businesses, organizations, places and events are either the product of the author's imagination or are used fictitiously. Any resemblance to actual persons, living or dead, events or locales is entirely coincidental.
The spelling used is British English except where fidelity to the author's rendering of accent or dialect supersedes this.

Cover art by Dee Dee Book Covers

ISBN: 978-1-83526-165-1

PROLOGUE

They cry. They scream.
Those dolls are rarely quiet.

Anne stared across the desk at her colleague. If Jolene asked her one more time what to say to a customer with a blocked drain, she'd reach over and punch her bloody lights out, sod the consequences. She didn't need this poxy job anyway, not now she had a new one, a lucrative scheme on the side, something she did at night. Maybe that was why Jolene was getting on her nellies. The lack of sleep was too much. She stayed up late, talking on WhatsApp to all the others in the group. The four of them stood to make a packet.

"You send out the appropriate tradesman and log it in the customer's file," Anne said, her smile fake as you like.

Jolene, thick as shit, probably thought it was genuine. She'd hadn't been here long and clearly hadn't listened during her training. Anne was meant to be mentoring her, but she couldn't be arsed. Jolene was a bit of an airhead, not Anne's cuppa at all.

"Thanks." Jolene tapped her keyboard and grinned as though the customer could see her through the phone line.

"Okay, Mr Bolton, I'll arrange for that to be fixed within the hour. Will you be at home?"

Of course he will, you divvy cow. He's standing there now in his loo, crap all over his nice floor tiles, not to mention his brand-new Reeboks from Sports Direct, forty-five quid, and his wife will go spare when she finds out they're ruined. They were a birthday present.

Jolene had shared that bit of info as well while Bolton had been on hold, and Anne had secretly hoped she'd forgotten to silence her head mic so he heard her laughing about it. Shame she hadn't, but you couldn't have it all, could you.

The flashing green light on Anne's dashboard heralded a new call. She sighed and answered. "Good afternoon, Franklin's Insurance Services Limited, how may I help you?"

"Oh, thank God you answered quickly. I've got a burst pipe under my kitchen sink, and it won't stop shooting water everywhere. I can't turn the stopcock off. It's stuck."

A baby cried in the background, and Anne's interest perked up. Talk about an omen, fate dropping things right on her doorstep.

"Aww, is that a little one I can hear?" she said.

"Yes, she's hungry, and I can't get to the fridge for her milk because there's too much water all over the floor. The towels I put down aren't doing anything. They're sopping and—"

"What's your name and address, please?"

"Fifty-one Galbraith Drive. I'm Vicky North."

"And your policy number?"

"EV19-20-32."

"And your date of birth?"

"January seventeenth, ninety-one."

"And your secret word?"

"Elephant."

Anne stifled a chortle at that. Some of the secret words people had were hilarious. Maybe Anne should change hers to murderer.

"Okay, Vicky, one second while I request an emergency repair." Anne put in the details and actioned a freelance worker to go there now. "He'll be with you in two minutes. His log says he's just up the road, so that's lucky."

"Thank you so much!"

The baby's wailing increased.

"How old is your nipper?"

"Maisie? Four months."

"Aww, that's lovely." *Perfect. Near enough the right age.* "In the meantime, go and tie a tea towel around the pipe if you can. Stem the flow."

"I already tried that, but it's spraying out. Every time I open the cupboard door, I get soaked."

"Okay, best to stay out of there then. We wouldn't want you hurting yourself, especially when you have Maisie to look after." *And we wouldn't want your baby to go hungry when you're sparko from slipping and banging your head. Babies need to be cared for at all times. They're a wonderful commodity.*

"Oh, the doorbell," Vicky said. "That was quick."

"Like I told you, he was close by. Happy to be of service," Anne said. "Bye now!"

"Bye!"

Anne drew her notebook towards her and wrote down Vicky's address. Her evening boss, Zooby, would be well happy she'd found another shipment. They called it that so people listening in didn't get what they were actually talking about. All his employees met up at the Purple Grape for updates on how the first job would go down, and sometimes they gathered at HQ. The Grape was a new wine bar in the high street, bang opposite the Flapping Crow pub, which had set off a stupid rivalry war, with each place making offers of cut-priced drinks on blackboards propped outside. Anne preferred the Crow, to be honest. People weren't so up their own arses in there. They were normal, her kind. Still, the Grape sold some nice wines, a few glam cocktails with rude names like Cockscrew instead of Corkscrew, and her boss paid for everything, so who was she to complain?

Free booze wasn't to be sniffed at.

She jotted down the baby's name. Maisie North. Was Vicky married? Or did she have a live-in boyfriend? Shit, Anne had forgotten to ask that question, or rather, steer the conversation that way. Bumholes. She'd messed up there.

She took two more calls, one regarding a woman smelling gas, another for a fridge that had broken down. God, it was all so boring. The trials and tribulations of other people's lives did nothing for her. Anne wanted danger, something to give her a thrill. Tomorrow night would give that to her, although . . . if she played her cards right, tonight would be exciting.

Jolene took her headset off, placed it on the desk, and winked at Anne. She got up and walked off, likely for her umpteenth fag break.

Anne grabbed her chance. Putting a call through to Vicky on Jolene's line, which she had control over while she mentored her, she cleared her throat, preparing to be nice. It was answered after the second ring. "Oh, hello, it's Jolene from Franklin's Insurance. Just a courtesy call to make sure it was our plumber at the door."

"Hello! Yes, he's stopped the water already and is using a machine to suck it up off the floor and from inside the cupboard. You can probably hear it because it's loud."

"Oh, I bet your husband or boyfriend will be pleased the leak has been fixed." *Wait for it . . .*

"Maybe he would if I had one," Vicky said, glum.

"Your parents then?"

"No, no, it's just me and my baby. That's why I panicked. I have no one to ask for help."

Chuffing hell, can this get any better? "Okay, well, so long as you're all right." Anne spotted Jolene coming back, so she'd better hurry up in case Vicky asked her to repeat her name or something. Anne had pretended to be Jolene so this wouldn't come back on her.

"I'm fine. Thanks so much for calling."

"All part of your insurance service, madam. Bye now." Anne cut the call and switched back to her own line.

Jolene plopped down into her seat. "There were loads of people out there fagging it. Bargain. I bummed drags off everyone's ciggies. Saved me smoking one of my own."

Cheapskate bitch. "You weren't gone as long as usual." Anne filled in the job sheet as if Jolene had taken the call. She doubted the dopey cow would even notice when she looked at the screen.

Jolene rubbed her arms. "Nah, it's too cold to hang about out there."

"I suppose it is if you don't wear a coat when there's frost on everything." She reckoned her sarcasm would be lost on this silly bint. It usually was.

"I suppose. Anyway, time to go home soon." Jolene rammed her headset on.

"Hmm."

While Jolene took a call, Anne thought about tonight. She had a job with the new gig, even though tomorrow was meant to be the first. Until now, it had been all about the planning, but she'd get to pay her part at last, and she was excited. She imagined what it would be like, creeping inside the house in the dark, staring down at the people sleeping. One would remain alive, and the other would be dead by the time she walked out again. That wasn't in Zooby's plan, but she was sure it was better to do that. You know, kill the witness. Zooby would realise that once she explained. Once he found out what she'd done.

And if he didn't? Well, she might just have to kill him an' all.

CHAPTER ONE

Vicky sighed. She'd had one hell of a day, what with the pipe springing that leak. Thank God the bloke had sucked all the water up. Her private landlord didn't need to know anything about it now his floor wasn't wrecked, but it had been touch and go there as to whether she phoned him or not. While he was a good sort, she didn't think he'd have taken kindly to shelling out more money. Not after he'd thrown a load of cash at the recent bathroom renovation because the last suite was old-fashioned, the sink unstable. She was just grateful she skinted herself to have home insurance.

Still, it was all over now, the catastrophe, and Maisie was in bed. She'd sleep through, bless her, and Vicky was well aware she'd got lucky. The other mums who met up at the café by the health centre after weighing-in day all had shadows beneath their eyes and complained of crappy nights.

Vicky wrapped her hands around her mug of hot chocolate and settled farther back on the sofa beneath her plush pink blanket. She'd got it from the catalogue last week, as affording things out of her Universal Credit was a nightmare. There was a documentary series she wanted to watch, eight o'clock, something about an old granny being mean to kiddies. She loved a good bit of crime, and this seemed right up her alley.

The programme lasted an hour, and the woman on it had frightened her silly. Such a creepy cow, and the things she'd done to the children . . .

Vicky got up for a wee. It was chilly in the hallway with the heating turned down, and she shivered, being quick about her business, returning to the living room to peer out of the window. It was bloody cold out there, she knew that from taking her rubbish into the back garden and dropping it in the green wheelie bin earlier, but it seemed more so with the sparkling of frost blanketing everything from car roofs to the pavement, even the edges of the leaves on her front hedge.

No one stood out there, as she'd convinced herself they were while she'd been in the loo, so she made a cup of tea and watched another episode of that series. By the time she'd finished it, she was jumping at every small sound and even had to go upstairs and check on Maisie. Her little love slept soundly, rosebud lips pursed as if she sucked on a bottle in her dreams, cheeks flushed. Vicky kept the radiator on low in there so her baby stayed warm.

With the time well past ten, she went round the downstairs ensuring everything was locked, then picked up her phone so she could browse social media until she fell asleep. Mind you, she had a Kindle app on there, so maybe she'd buy a new book and dive into that, seeing as she wasn't sleepy yet.

She hunched beneath her covers — a quilt and two blankets; no rad on in here for her, heating twenty-four seven was too expensive — and bought *Sin, Repent, Repeat* by someone called AJ Harlem. The blurb had sounded good, and with it being ninety-nine pence, it was well within her budget.

She read with one of the blankets over her head so she'd stop trembling faster, and seven chapters in, she was even more nervy than earlier. The creepiness in the book hadn't helped calm her nerves. Pulled from the story by a noise, she frowned, her heart banging. She strained her ears, and while the blanket muffled things, yes, something was tapping.

Blanket pushed down, she listened again.

Fuck.

She folded her bedding back and stood, the floor icy against her feet. A glow partially lit up the landing, a night-light she plugged in for if she ever had to go in to see Maisie. Ah, that was what it'd be. She'd probably woken up and was whacking a rattle on the cot bars. Maybe she was having a rare bad night.

Relief pouring into her, Vicky padded to the door opposite, which was half open. That wasn't right. She always left it ajar so the heat didn't come out. Had she forgotten to pull it to when she'd checked on her earlier?

She moved into the room, turning left, and faced the cot.

Someone stood over it, a black figure.

Momentarily stunned, Vicky was then flooded with the need to protect her baby. She screamed and dashed forward, gripping the person's jacket collar at the back and wrenching them away. They shook her off, and she stumbled, bashing her hip into the chest of drawers behind, a stack of children's books falling and fanning on the surface. She straightened to dart at the shape again, but they moved forward, stepping into the faint shaft of light coming in from the hallway.

A clown mask. A hood pulled up. "Stay the fuck away."

Adrenaline thundered through Vicky at the sound of a woman's voice. "What do you want?" She panted and glanced at Maisie, who slept on, arms up by her little head.

"Your kid, but that's none of your business."

The voice seemed familiar, but Vicky couldn't place it for the life of her. With her thoughts whirring, the need to get her daughter to safety uppermost in her mind, she took one pace forward, scared on the one hand, bold on another.

"I *said*, stay the fuck away." The woman had growled those words, and she came closer, raising her hand, a knife held tight in her fist.

"Oh God . . ." The mask was so scary, so horrible.

Vicky leapt forward, reaching the cot and dipping her hands in, needing to scoop Maisie up, get her out of here. A sharp crack on the back of her head meant her brow almost touched the baby's stomach, then she was dragged away again, thrown towards the door. Vicky struggled to remain upright and came to a stop by the jamb.

"Leave the little one alone," the intruder rasped out. "She's not yours anymore."

What? "She *is* mine." Vicky staggered towards the cot again, hands out ready.

The knife entered her stomach, the woman's fist punching into her, and there was no pain of the slice, just the dull ache of the thump. Vicky stared down, blood oozing onto her pyjama top, the stain so dark against the white fabric. Then agony speared with her acknowledgement of what had happened, and she whimpered. A fresh need to save Maisie swamped her, so she pushed the figure on the chest, hard, the blade coming out as she moved, wet heat seeping. Vicky hit out at her, palms connecting with the bitch's hood-covered head, and then came another punch-stab to her gut, followed by a slice of copper-smelling steel at a crossways angle on her face, temple to jaw.

Vicky screamed from how much it hurt.

"Shut up, you noisy bitch," the woman snapped.

Warm blood dripped into one eye, Vicky's sight impeded, and the pain was immeasurable as her skin parted on both cheeks and over her nose. She air went through the gaps and into her mouth, her face so open, so wrecked. Her whole face was hot, on fire.

Her attacker paused, knife midair. "Say goodbye now."

Vicky covered her face with her hands in an attempt to close the wound. The blood was slippery beneath her palms. *Why do I know you? Why can't I remember who you are?* She sobbed, trying to work out what this fucking cow meant. Say goodbye?

"Didn't you hear me?" the figure asked.

Vicky stretched her arms out, planning to dig her thumbs into the eyes in front of her, fight for her life as well as Maisie's.

"Your loss." A shrug. Then . . .

The knife bit into Vicky's neck and slashed right across. For a moment she just stood there, knowing what had occurred but unable to fully compute it, or the scorching blanket of blood drenching her chest. Her legs weakened, and she thudded onto the carpet, her knees hurting upon impact.

"Thanks for the baby," the woman said. "But not for the mess. I'll have to clean myself up before I take her now. That's inconvenient, you selfish tart."

Vicky pitched forward, landing face-first. And then she knew who this was, who had come into her home. It was Jolene from the insurance company.

One second later, she blacked out.

* * *

Anne was pissed off. She'd got blood on her gloves, and some of the splash had landed on her jacket. Good job it was a waterproof one. She used a sponge that was in a wire rack over the bath and cleaned it off, nosing in the mirror above the sink to ensure she didn't have red on the white of her mask. A quick scrub got rid of that, and she left the pink-stained sponge beside the soap. Something for the coppers to mull over.

Back in the baby's bedroom, she stepped over Vicky and the mess she'd made by bleeding out onto the pink carpet. Anne had shit a brick when Vicky had screamed — twice, for Pete's sake. What if one of the neighbours came knocking to see if she was all right? What if they called the police?

Best she get a move on.

She picked Maisie up, wrapped a blanket around her, and the kid stirred but soon settled, snuffling a bit with a scrunched hand to her mouth. Downstairs, Anne peered through the gap in the living room curtains. No one was about, so she moved into the kitchen. Back door open — she'd got in that way by jimmying the lock; Zooby was a great teacher — she crept along the garden path and left via the side gate. Down an alley she carried the shipment, glancing back at the houses. No one at the windows. No lights on. That was what being out after midnight did for you.

Her car was parked close by, away from any streetlights, shadowed beside an evergreen tree. She strapped Maisie into the pre-bought safety seat, blanket on top, and marvelled at how she still slept. Did Vicky drug her with that Phenergan stuff or what? Zooby had a supply of it for when the babies were in residence, going to several pharmacies to pick up bottles on the pretence it was for his kid's car sickness or hay fever so the cashiers didn't get all suspicious and shit. It wasn't meant to be given to children under two years old, but they only used small doses, enough to do the trick.

She drove towards her destination. Zooby would be there, although he wasn't expecting her to have a shipment so soon. She was due to go out tomorrow night to collect a baby, easy pickings because the mother was a bit of a slag and was too busy screwing blokes to be bothered about her child.

Anne didn't care either way. She collected the shipment, she got paid, simple as.

On the outskirts, past Wind Energy and those creepy turbines, she turned onto a track that led a mile or so behind Shadwell Hill, to a disused area that was home to a decrepit warehouse and another building that used to be the steel mill. All the rooms were empty now — well, the ones without the customers in them at any rate — the place perfect for what they were doing. No one to hear a thing, see a thing, or suspect a thing. Zooby said he hosted mass parties there sometimes, and she'd warned him he'd better be vigilant in case someone came along, expecting a disco and booze. They didn't need that sort of shizz going on.

In the courtyard, she parked outside the mill next to Zooby's car, and it looked like Joseph Hunt was here an' all, that geezer who'd set up the website and did the documents. His motorbike leant against the wall. He was a clever bastard, knew all sorts of stuff, but Anne didn't trust him as far as she could throw him. Not since he'd given her a funny look that time when she'd suggested burning off the babies' fingerprints to scupper identification purposes. He'd called her a stupid, demented cow and said they'd do DNA tests anyway if ever the shipments were discovered with the customers. Fair enough, but there was no need for him to be so abrasive about it, was there?

Anne took the blanket off Maisie, dropping it on the back seat, and lifted her out and held her against her shoulder. She walked towards the main door, her face sweaty from the mask, and Zooby appeared in his fake beard and glasses, staring at her like she was off her rocker.

"What the fucking hell have you gone and done?" he said, scratching his floppy-haired head. "This is a day early."

"It's a different kid." Anne brushed past him, into the mill, and placed the baby in one of the cots to the right. She covered her with a new fleece blanket and peered over at her boss. "Shut the door, will you? You're letting in a cold draught." She pushed the mask up on top of her head.

Zooby did that and strutted towards her, finger pointing. "You don't get to tell me what to do. I'm the one in charge, not you."

She sighed — he was such a stickler for the rules — and peered around for Joseph. He sat in an armchair in the top-left corner, on the edge of the seat, as if he was poised ready to come to Zooby's defence. A halogen heater turned one side of him orange, his clown face creepy in the light, and she reckoned it was typical of him, hogging the heat.

"I know that," Anne said to Zooby, "but if we have customers waiting, what's the problem?"

He stared into the cot. "Where the fuck did you get her from?"

"Look, it's a single mother, no bloke, no parents around — I checked. None of her neighbours even came to see what was going on when she screamed. There's only one house attached to hers anyway, plus, there's an alley between her place and the one on the other side."

"Screamed?" Zooby slapped his forehead. "What do you mean, screamed? Didn't you steal the kid when the mother was asleep? We talked about this — every night we met. The mothers aren't supposed to know the babies are gone until the morning. God!"

"I was about to take the baby, but the mum woke up." Anne shrugged. "Something was tapping, maybe a branch on a window, whatever, and she came in to see the sprog. She screamed, so I punched her in the stomach."

Zooby sighed. "Did she see your face?"

She saw something all right, but that's for me to know and you to find out. "Nah. Had the mask on, didn't I." Another shrug. "Are we cool or what?"

Zooby nodded. "I suppose so. And you're right, if we have customers waiting . . ."

Anne smiled. She knew he'd see sense. "Brilliant. She's called Maisie, by the way, not that it matters. Four months old."

"Four? Fucking hell. She's meant to be six. How did you know about her?"

"Through work. And before you say anything, I covered my tracks. I'll be leaving there soon if this gig keeps up. I can't do both jobs at once." She thought she'd better make herself useful, get back in Zooby's good books. "I'm going to see the customers. Saves you doing it. You look tired."

"Cheers."

Anne lowered her mask onto her face. She waited for Joseph to pipe up with something or other that would have her wanting to poke his eyes out. He kept quiet, though, so she moved on through the doorway and entered the mill's old office corridor. So many rooms, but only a few were being used at the minute.

Anne crept into the first one and stared at the woman on the sagging camp bed. Her surroundings were pretty grim, the walls stripped back to the plaster, which had gone grey and mouldy with time. The floor appeared black from the sticky stuff used to hold down lino, which had been ripped up long ago. A halogen heater hung on the wall in each room, otherwise it'd be freezing. The electricity hadn't been turned off, so whoever owned the place would notice his bill go up after the next quarter.

Customer One stirred in her sleep. Anne stepped closer, to the cot at the bottom of the bed, and peered over the edge. A doll rested under the covers, its eyes staring, its blonde curly hair all matted where One kept stroking it. All customers were kept semi out of it with the drugs Zooby gave them, and they actually thought the dolls were alive, their babies, the ones promised to them by Zooby. Their time here with the dolls was a 'bonding period', when in reality, it was a fake set-up until the real kids were snatched.

Well, this bint here would get her wish sooner than she thought, what with Maisie being collected. In the morning, Anne suspected Zooby would switch the doll for the real thing, and One wouldn't notice the difference. Hopefully. The dolls were the sort used for young women to teach them what having a baby was like. They cried, whimpered, screamed for milk, and the customers thought they were their new children.

Dopey shits.

Customer One had paid a lot of money for a kid. Once she took Maisie home with her fake birth certificate and passport, created by Joseph, Zooby would share out the cash. Anne's portion was large, considering she was the one taking the risk by stealing the shipments, so she'd be quids in soon. She'd worked out that if she could take five babies, she wouldn't have to work for ages if she was frugal.

Anne rubbed her hands and laughed. She'd get to kill again, too, and that was the main reason for doing this. Death. She loved it.

Roll on the next one.

CHAPTER TWO

Carla's head hurt. It was always foggy since she'd been here, same as the times she'd been out drinking in her early twenties, the effects of alcohol lingering, reminding her of the fun she'd had. Well, that fun was paid for by the hangover, but here, she'd hadn't *had* any bloody fun.

She couldn't complain either — she'd agreed to this, desperate as she was to have a child. After a car accident had mangled her abdomen, she'd had her womb and ovaries removed. The news that she'd never have children had shattered her. Years had gone by, her in some kind of no-man's land, incomplete without a baby. She'd always wanted one, but the crash had stolen her choice. She hadn't told her parents the severity of what had happened; they thought she could still have kids.

If only she hadn't had that abortion in her early twenties, she wouldn't be doing this now. The fear of what her parents would say about her being pregnant back then had played a huge part in her decision, and wasn't that ironic? She'd have to tell them she had a kid anyway. All she'd done was delay the inevitable.

Liam had walked out on her shortly after she'd returned home from hospital. "What's the point in being together if we can't have a family?" he'd said.

She'd begged, said they could adopt, or he could donate sperm and they'd employ a surrogate, but no, he wasn't having any of it. He hadn't loved her enough to stay. She was defective, useless to him, and the bite of that had sent her into a downward spiral.

So the hangover feeling was also akin to the one she'd experienced while taking antidepressants. Lethargy, apathy, the desire to do nothing but dwell on her losses, how life could have been if that drunk bastard hadn't run her off the road. How wonderful things would have panned out if Liam had stayed, they'd got married, and they'd found a baby some other way. It didn't matter to her that she hadn't given birth to it. She'd love it, adore it, and build a bond that could never be broken.

Her new baby cried in the cot, and she worried that being in this place, with its damp air and unsanitary conditions, was having an effect on the child, the same as it was having on her. Carla got up in a daze and scooped the baby into her arms, rocking her, soothing her with a song. If only she could feel normal, she'd take more pleasure from this, but right now, all she wanted to do was sleep.

Lily, that was what she'd named her, and the man who'd arranged this would give her a birth certificate and passport, and one of those books you get from the health visitor after you give birth, complete with NHS number. She'd have to fill it in with fake moments: first smile, first time of rolling over, first whatever. But that was okay. No one around here would know her anyway. Carla had moved to Shadwell to receive her baby, as instructed, and her home waited for the pair of them to create a new life inside it for the six months she had to stay there.

It was in the contract to do so.

The door opened, and the man stood inside the frame, the one with the beard, long fringe, and weird glasses.

"I need to take Lily for a bath," he said.

Carla handed the baby over, wishing she could bathe the little one herself, but Weird Glasses had said she couldn't, and that was that. She'd do whatever he said if it meant taking Lily home, and besides, she could do everything for her once she was out of this place.

He left, and she sat on the bed, rubbing her head. She didn't understand why she felt so shitty and blamed it on the damp. They reckoned mould was a stealthy bastard that made you ill.

What if it makes Lily ill?

She panicked, thinking of having to take her to the doctor. Weird Glasses had assured her that all documents looked genuine, and his associate, a young-sounding bloke in a clown mask, had even got into the system and put Lily in there so it appeared she'd been born at the John Radcliffe in Oxford. But she couldn't see a doctor until she'd left Shadwell.

It would be okay. Everything would work out.

She flopped down and slept for a while, waking when Weird Glasses came back and handed Lily over. She was warmer than usual, and her skin didn't feel the same. It was softer. Carla stroked her head and gasped.

"What have you done to her hair?" She pressed her daughter to her chest. The scent of baby products wafted up. How lovely to smell it on a real child instead of just sniffing the bottles and imagining.

"You're leaving today, Customer One."

She didn't like being called that but acknowledged it was necessary. No attachments, even by name. He was anonymous, but she wasn't — he knew who she was from the survey she'd filled out. She'd paid cash for Lily so didn't even have any bank account details of his to go on. He was just a fella, one who had changed her life.

"Today?" she said.

"That's why her hair's been cut. She's from here, so someone might recognise her."

"Oh." That made sense. Lily keeping her blonde curls wasn't wise. "Will you be taking us home?"

"I'll drop you off close by, but you'll need to walk the rest of the way."

"I don't think I'm very well, though. I feel like shit." Her head pounded.

"That'll pass. It's this place. Gets me like that, too. Once the fresh air is in your lungs, you'll liven up. Come on. We're off."

What, now? So quickly? Carla stood, her legs wobbly, and glanced around the tatty room. "Her bottles, her blanket . . ."

"She's just been fed, so no worries there. She has a new outfit on, fresh from the packet. And as for her blanket, no. It's a tie to here. You know the rules. You signed the form knowing you just took the child and whatever she's dressed in."

Carla nodded. How could she take care of Lily in this state? "Will I feel better once I'm home?"

"Yep, give it a few hours and you'll be good as new."

He held the door open for her, and she walked down the dingy corridor and into the big room she'd entered when she'd first arrived. It held two cots, a chair in the corner, and the man in a clown mask sat on it — the document fella.

He got up, took a few things off a table in the middle, and handed them to her. "Everything you need is there. Enjoy the kid."

She took them and blinked at him, the mask so freaky. Then she peered round. "My handbag?"

"Oh yeah, here you go." Weird Glasses passed it over and beckoned for her to follow him outside.

She did, and the air was so cold, the sky pitch-black, no stars twinkling. She hadn't seen the outside of the place before, she'd been blindfolded, but it was decrepit, and ahead in the far distance was a hill, some trees on top.

Lily, thankfully asleep, squirmed, and Carla wanted to get her home into the warm. She buckled her into a car seat and sat in the back beside her while the man got in behind the wheel.

"Put this on." Between the front seats, he handed her an eye mask, the sort you put on in bed, and she slid it on, recalling this part of the deal. She wasn't allowed to know where she'd been kept or where it was in relation to her house.

The engine rumbled, then the car set off. She plugged her seat belt in by feel alone, excitement flickering in her belly. This was really happening, she had a baby, and no one would know she wasn't hers. Well, no one she'd be involved with anyway while she lived in Shadwell. Since moving here, she'd only spent one night in her house, and she'd arrived during the dark hours so no neighbours spotted her. That was part of the deal as well: *Don't be seen until you have the baby. The sudden appearance of one will ring alarm bells. We don't want that, do we?*

What she didn't get was why she had to live in the same area the baby had been taken from. Wasn't that asking for trouble? She was permitted to move away after six months, and at no point during her time here could she go to the health centre for Lily to be weighed. The baby would be recognised if the birth mother had taken her there.

She didn't understand why that was an issue if the baby was being adopted.

Carla, desperate as she was, had agreed to everything, no matter how odd it seemed. She had money, given to her by her parents, so didn't need to work — working would increase the probability that a childminder or nursery would spot the child as someone else's. There were so many rules that she'd written them down in a notebook.

She regulated her breathing, reaching out blindly to cover Lily's hand with hers, comforted by the soft, podgy fist beneath her palm, something she'd wished for but had never thought she'd have. She was so lucky to have a baby at last, despite the strange hoops she'd had to jump through to get her, and somewhere out there, a mother had given her child away so Carla could bring her up. It was incomprehensible to her, but she understood the woman had encountered hard times and hadn't bonded with her daughter. She'd apparently been relieved to give her to Carla.

Poor Lily.

Well, Carla wouldn't ever let her know about her origins. She'd give her all the love in the world. Her baby would never want for anything. Carla hadn't told her parents about this. She'd devised a plan to turn up on their doorstep one day soon, saying she'd kept news of Lily from them through fear of being judged as a single, unmarried mother. Her mum and dad liked things done the 'right' way in that respect, but Carla needed to give Lily grandparents, so receiving their initial scorn would be worth it. She just had to hope they took to Lily as soon as the shock wore off.

"We're here," the man said. "Take the blindfold off."

Carla removed it and glanced around. He'd parked by an alley, one she didn't recognise. She'd had no chance to explore her surroundings when she'd arrived in Shadwell.

"Where are we?" she asked, unbuckling Lily's straps.

"Go down there, and you'll be in your street."

She fumbled inside her bag for her keys, wanting to have them in her hand so Lily didn't get too cold if she searched for them at the front door. The baby cradled in one arm, she scooted across to the door and opened it.

"Thank you, for everything," she said.

"Here, take this an' all." He chucked a carrier bag into the back. "Clothes for the baby. The ones you bought might not fit her. We thought this one would be six months old, but she's four. You'll have to pretend to people she's six because of the birth certificate."

That was odd. She now noticed Lily wasn't as chunky as she'd been before he'd taken her for a bath, nor as long. That mould had a lot to answer for, tricking her into thinking Lily was bigger. Already she felt marginally more clear-headed.

"Right. Okay." She grabbed the bag and got out, the cold wrapping around her, her handbag bouncing on her thigh. Conscious Lily had no blanket, she rushed down the alley, not daring to look back. And there they were, in her new street, her house just down the way a bit. She dashed to it, glancing about to see if any lights were on in other houses. None. She dropped the carrier bag on the step and inserted the key, taking Lily inside to place her in the pretty Moses basket she'd set up.

"There. All snug." She drew a blanket over the little girl.

Back at the front door, she picked up the bag and brought it inside, locking up, more conscious now than ever to ensure the house was secure. She had another person to protect, not just herself. Heating turned up, she put the bags on the sofa, checked on Lily, who still slept soundly, then ran up to have a shower. She had to get the smell of that room off her. While she soaped herself, she stared at her arm. It had several small holes on the skin at the inner elbow.

What?

Maybe she'd scratched herself in her sleep or something, or a bug could have bitten her. It wouldn't surprise her if that camp bed had fleas in the thin mattress.

She dried, slung on pyjamas, a dressing gown, some slippers, and went into the kitchen to make a cup of tea. She'd bought some dried milk with her and had taken the kettle and other things out of packing boxes, but the rest were stacked up. While the kettle boiled, she considered breaking the agreement.

If she left the country, they wouldn't find her. She'd tell her parents she'd was doing it so the father didn't find her. A few lies would help: he was abusive, controlling, she'd left him to save hers and Lily's lives . . . She could move to France, using one of her parents' many holiday homes.

This house was rented, a stopgap for the required six months she was told to stay. But why had they stipulated that? It didn't make sense.

Tomorrow, she'd visit Mum and Dad. They were loaded, dealt in property, and she'd live on the trust fund money they dished out to her on a monthly basis. She'd arrange for a firm to come and collect her things, move them to the place in France. No one would recognise Lily in another country. Carla could get her weighed and whatnot without panicking.

Tea in hand, her mind made up, she nodded to herself.

She'd be gone from Shadwell by tomorrow.

* * *

Joseph took his mask off and shook his head at Zooby. "I can't believe you let Anne get away with what she did. She broke all the rules. What's the point in making them if she can just flout them like that? Not to mention she came here in her car. She admitted she'd forgotten to change the number plates, for fuck's sake."

Zooby glared as if he contemplated having a go at him, then lowered his gaze. "I know, and I'll remind her to sort the plates next time, but this saves us having to find a kid for Customer Six, because we only had five lined up. Maisie has filled a slot."

Joseph huffed. "Things go wrong if you don't stick to the plan."

Zooby walked off and busied himself with changing the cot sheet.

Joseph had an uneasy feeling. He'd had it right from the start, to be honest, but the pound signs had swayed him. Plus, he'd known Zooby for years, trusted him, but Anne? He hadn't known her from Adam until she'd turned up at the Grapes that first night they'd all got together.

She'd applied online, answering that freakish questionnaire Zooby had devised, one that was supposedly anonymous, but the IP address showed up. That was where Joseph came in, finding out the location of whoever took the test, which was titled: COULD YOU BREAK THE LAW IF YOU KNEW YOU'D GET AWAY WITH IT? Zooby reckoned only nutjobs or those who weren't afraid to do bad shit would come forward, and depending on their answers, he'd chosen those most likely to commit crime without being bothered they had.

Anne had been the top scorer and, like Natasha Otter, the other person on their team, she happened to live in Shadwell, the reason they'd been picked.

From there, armed with Anne's home address, Zooby had put on a fake beard and a nasty pair of glasses, and visited her. He'd told her he'd found her via the questionnaire, and she hadn't batted an eyelid, which was fucking odd. Why hadn't she questioned him about it? Why let him in and offer him a cuppa like he was a mate? If Joseph had been approached like that by a stranger, you could bet he'd tell them where to go.

Anne had been eager to join them, even after Zooby had told her what they'd be doing — stealing babies, giving them to desperate women for a while, then stealing them back and selling them on to the next one. Eventually, once the kids grew, they'd get to stay with one lucky purchaser. After all, babies could be passed off as anyone's, but older children couldn't. They could speak, could say, "Where's my mummy?" Babies were mute, the keepers of secrets.

Customers had to sign a contract saying they agreed, at any point, that the baby may be taken away if Zooby didn't feel they were with the right mother. No refunds.

All eventualities had been covered.

"Is Natasha popping round to Customer One tomorrow to see how she is?" Joseph asked. "Or is that plan going by the wayside an' all?"

"Look, fuck off with your gripes, will you?" Zooby bundled the cot sheet up and stuffed it in his holdall. "Yes, she's going round there. We need to make sure One is okay and not still out of it, although she seemed more with it when I dropped her off."

"Yeah, the shipments are our top priority, our cash cows. If the new mothers are still fucked up from the drugs, we risk the babies being harmed. Dropped, not fed, drowned in the bath if the women space out." That was what bothered Joseph the most, the customers being in charge of the kiddies when they weren't compos mentis. His suggestion of delivering the babies to the houses once the 'mothers' were lucid had been stomped on. Zooby hadn't wanted any of the group to be seen by nosy neighbours.

Fair enough, but that didn't ring true for Natasha, who'd be going round there anyway. Joseph had backed down and put his worries aside, concentrating on the money, anything to get him through this. If he kept thinking of the innocent children, he'd torment himself and end up backing out.

And that wasn't wise. Zooby was friends with people who were good at making you disappear.

"Natasha's reliable," Zooby said. "And if Lily isn't being looked after properly, Nat will stay there until One is behaving normally."

Joseph plonked himself on a chair at the table and accessed their website. It hinted at adoption as an alternative for childless couples, and many women all over the country had sent in enquiries. Once again, with their home addresses given when they'd filled out the forms, Zooby had donned his disguise, which he kept on all the time now, and turned up on the doorsteps of the ladies who'd clicked 'ten' to a certain question: *On the scale of one to ten, how far would you be willing to go to have a child — could you break the law?*

A third of them had clicked ten, but after he'd told them they had to move to a specific location and stay there to bond, several had declined to continue. Zooby had driven away in his resprayed car with the fake plates, only continuing with those who'd agreed that the bonding period was fine — they wanted a baby in whatever way they could get one.

Six women with no morals, as far as Joseph was concerned.

Six women who'd admitted they were prepared to put another through pain by taking their children in order to assuage their own.

When the customers had arrived here, Zooby collecting them one by one in his car, Joseph had been hard pressed to look at them — mainly because they were the proof of his own involvement. *He* was prepared to ruin women's lives by helping to steal babies, too, therefore, *he* had no morals either.

Yet he did, and now they were in the thick of it, he wished he'd never joined the group.

Shit.

"We have another potential customer," he said, navigating with his mouse so he could look up their address on Google Maps. "She's only thirty miles away." He scribbled the location on a pad.

"Okay, I'll get hold of her, see if she wants a visit."

"When will she be brought here if she agrees to everything?"

"A couple of weeks. We'll get Anne to take Lily back off Carla. The new customer can have her."

Joseph stared at the face mask on the table. As a gang, were *they* the real clowns, thinking they could pull this off?

Only time would tell.

CHAPTER THREE

Carla jumped at a rapid knocking on the front door. She peered out of the living room window, and someone stood on the step in one of those awful clown masks. It was a person from the adoption organisation. What did they want? She'd done everything asked of her, yet they were here to what . . . harass her? Check on her? Was this how it would be for the six months if she stayed?

Having people turn up in masks would tip the neighbours off to things being dodgy — the visitors would get noticed *more* by wearing them. Well, it was a good job she was leaving then, wasn't it. She couldn't be doing with this. Her nerves were in shreds.

She glanced at the baby asleep in the Moses basket. While Carla had brightened up after a good sleep, almost her normal self now, Lily was still out of it. She'd roused for a bottle an hour ago but hadn't come fully awake. Was she coming down with something?

All the more reason to visit her parents. She could see a doctor there.

Taking a deep breath and smoothing her hands down her top, she walked to the front door and opened it. The person was short, so it couldn't be Weird Glasses or the document man. She vaguely recalled someone else coming into her room at that place during the night, but they'd been taller than this one here. How many worked for the outfit?

"Hello. I've come to check on Lily." It was a woman, her voice kind. She sounded young.

No one other than Carla and the organisation knew Lily's name, so this lady *had* to be from there.

Of course she bloody is. No one else galivants around in a mask.

But should she let her in?

"How do I know who you are?" She felt stupid saying that, what with the clown face, but Lily was so precious, she had to be extra careful.

"Because I've got this." She took a birth certificate out of her pocket.

Carla stared. It was Lily's, the same as the one the man had given her. Why did they have a copy? "Oh. Okay. Come in."

She stepped back, and the guest entered, going straight into the living room to the Moses basket, bending over it. Carla joined her, desperate to pick her daughter up so the woman couldn't. Instead, she got ready to pounce the moment the guest made a grab for her, if that was what her game was.

"Has she slept okay?" Clown Face asked.

"Yes, quite a lot actually."

"Good. She was dosed so she didn't cry when you walked down the alley. She'll come round eventually. You know, actually wake up properly."

Dosed? Carla remembered the dots on her arm. Had they done the same to her? Was that why she'd felt so out of it at that place? Had Weird Glasses lied by saying it was the building that made her ill?

"What did you give her?" Protectiveness surged through her. Lily was an innocent. These people had no right to give her anything.

"Don't panic. Phenergan. It doesn't do any harm if she only has it sporadically. Did you want her crying from the cold once you got out of the car? Did you want your neighbours to wake up and look out of the window, seeing you carrying a child during the night? It'd look well suss."

Carla wrung her hands. "When you put it like that . . ."

"Exactly. And how are you feeling?"

"Brilliant now I'm home."

"Yes, you seem perky enough. Right, well, she looks fine to me, too, so I'll be off. Back tomorrow, though."

"Pardon?"

The woman stared, the eyes inside the mask holes wide and creepy. "Best you don't question me, considering I know you've illegally adopted a baby . . ." She gave Lily the once-over.

"Right. Right." Carla's stomach rolled. *Illegally? What about the paperwork I signed? That was real enough.*

Clown Face nodded. "Glad to see you understand. I'll see myself out."

Once the front door closed, Carla rushed to the window to nose outside. The woman removed the mask when she stepped onto the pavement, but Carla couldn't see all of her face, just a cheek, the corner of an eye, and the tip of her nose. She waited for the visitor to disappear down the street, then dashed upstairs to grab her suitcase. This wasn't on, being monitored. Okay, it could be seen as nice that they wanted to ensure Lily was looked after, but Carla would *never* hurt her. And that illegal business . . . Bloody hell!

She'd leave now, not this afternoon.

She lugged her case downstairs and placed it on the sofa, adding the carrier bag containing Lily's clothes. Next, she packed a baby bag, putting in a couple of boxes of milk she'd bought a while ago and a few bottles, then shoved the microwave sterilising unit inside, too, along with some little toys and wet wipes.

She'd already put the car seat in her Kia, so all that was left was to switch the heating off and take Lily outside. Another check at the window proved the woman had definitely gone, but what if she was sitting in a car, watching?

Well, there had been no specification in the contract about not leaving the house, so for all Clown Face knew, Carla could be taking Lily to the supermarket. After all, she had a limited amount of clothes for her.

That reminded her to get the packets of nappies out from the cupboard under the stairs, and she carried everything outside in two trips, storing them in the boot beside the brand-new pushchair. Then she returned for Lily, who'd not long had a bottle — she'd guzzled five ounces, the greedy little scamp.

Carla took her baby to the car and strapped her in, then went in to get her handbag containing her passport and Lily's documents.

All set for her escape, she got in the driver's seat and drove in the opposite direction to the one Clown Face had taken. Regular checks in her rearview showed no one followed. On the main road, she relaxed, wanting to cry at how she was acting like a thief in the night, but wasn't that what she was by proxy? Yes, the birth mother had handed Lily over, but it still felt like stealing. The woman's comment about illegal adoption sat as a lump in Carla's throat.

Stuffing those thoughts to the back of her mind, she continued on, tension leaving her muscles the closer she got to her parents' town which was in the same county. There'd be tension of a different kind when she arrived, but that was preferable to anything she'd experienced since beginning this baby-getting journey.

At last, Carla pulled up onto her parents' expansive gravel driveway. The large house had been her childhood home, and she'd never been so glad to see it. Dad's car was parked out the front, which meant he wasn't at work. That brought Carla up short. Was he having a day off? How long had she been at that place?

Shit, she had no idea.

She cut the engine and grabbed her phone, switching it to life to check the date. God, she'd been holed up in the mouldy room for over a week? She'd had several messages and missed calls. Bloody hell.

Deep breath sucked in, and a long, slow one released, she gathered her mettle and got out, going straight to the back of the car to take Lily's seat out. She carried it to the front door, ringing the bell with a shaking finger, and prepared herself for battle, for recriminations, for her mum and dad to frown at her and tell her how stupid she'd been having a baby like this, and why had she left it so long to tell them? A whole pregnancy and four months later? Why hadn't she mentioned it during phone calls?

The door opened, and Mum stood there, smiling wide at Carla. "Oh, thank goodness you're okay. We've been trying to get hold of you with no answer." A frown wiggled her forehead once she spotted Lily, and her eyebrows scrunched. "And who is this?" She pointed at the car seat.

"I need to come in." Butterflies raged in Carla's tummy. This was going to be harder than she'd imagined. Just seeing her mother's expression change from relief to stern showed she'd have a battle on her hands.

"Of course. Silly me. It's so cold, and there's us on the doorstep." Mum moved back.

Carla went inside, struggling a bit with the car seat. It was cumbersome and difficult to carry with Lily's weight in it — the bloody thing banged on her leg with each step. She walked into the kitchen, the place they always gathered for family chats.

Dad sat at the vast marble-topped island in the centre, a newspaper spread out, a coffee to one side in his favourite Best Dad in the World mug. He wasn't the best, he was a bit of an ogre at times, moody and unyielding in his beliefs, but the mug was just something you bought for Father's Day, wasn't it? Everybody did it.

"Ah, Carla. Where on earth have you been? And who's this?" He stood, holding his arms out. "Looking after a friend's baby, are you?"

"Ah, yes, *that's* what it is." Mum sounded relieved that he'd found the solution to why their daughter had turned up with a child. She took a china mug out of a cupboard and poured coffee from the almost full carafe.

Carla put the car seat down and went to Dad for a hug. He squeezed her tightly, his aftershave the same one he always splashed on, and for a moment, she was comforted by the familiarity.

The calm before the storm.

He let her go, and she sat on a stool at the island, feeling all kinds of awkward. How to begin? Concoct a long story and tag Lily onto the end . . . or just come out with it? Mum interrupted her thoughts by placing coffee in front of Carla, then she sat.

Carla blew out a long breath. "The baby is mine." God, she'd said it, just jumped right in. Her heart thundered, and her stomach clenched.

Mum blinked. Dad stared.

"I didn't tell you at the time I got pregnant because I know how you both feel. About unmarried mothers. And single parents. I thought you'd be ashamed of me. That's why I made so many excuses not to come here. So you wouldn't know I was pregnant."

Silence. Then . . .

"How old is she?" Mum must have clocked the pink outfit Lily had on.

"Six months. She was premature, which is why she's so small for her age."

"So you held this inside, this secret, for over a year?" Mum frowned the same as she had on the doorstep. "You went through this *alone*?"

"I thought . . ."

Mum stood and came round the island, crouching to unbuckle the straps and take Lily out. She held her to her chest, eyes closed, and a tear fell. "You should have let us help you." She stroked Lily's back. "Oh, you precious child."

Carla, stunned, looked at Dad, the lump in her throat getting bigger. "I . . . I don't understand . . . You both said—"

Dad coughed and got up to stand beside Mum. He studied Lily's cherubic face, and a small smile tweaked his fleshy lips. "Now you're a parent, you'll understand why we said what we did. You'll want the best for Lily, just as we do for you. You'll say things to sway her mind, in the hopes she'll listen. But if she's like you and *doesn't* listen, then that's okay, too."

Carla couldn't believe this. All her life she'd had it drummed into her that being a single parent was bad, frowned upon, yet here her parents were, fawning over a baby they'd vowed never to take to if it was born out of wedlock. And what was with Dad being nice? Where was his grumpy facade? Had Lily stripped it away?

Carla had been lied to, duped, and while it hurt, while she wanted to shout at them, seeing Mum and Dad accepting Lily meant more than giving them a telling off. Besides, she was also duping.

"I'm so sorry you did this by yourself," Mum said. "Gosh, she smells delightful. It brings back so many memories. And she looks just like you at the same age. The same nose and everything."

Heat flushed Carla's cheeks. Mum was seeing what she wanted to, and for the first time, Carla fully acknowledged that from now on, everything was a deception. If she answered that yes, Lily looked like her, she'd be lying, because she didn't resemble her at all. In fact, Lily was blonde and Carla was a brunette. She'd have to pretend the 'father' was fair-headed, another lie for all she knew. Lily's birth mother might be blonde.

Fucking hell . . .

But her need for a baby trumped everything, and if it meant lying to keep her, then she'd do it. Just like her parents had lied to her, she'd do it back to them.

It didn't feel good. But Lily gripped Dad's finger then, and Mum patted the baby's bum in rhythmic taps. It had already gone too far, so Carla just had to make the best of it.

"Do you want to talk about her daddy?" Mum asked.

Carla shook her head. "No. I need to move out of the country. He's . . ." She couldn't bring herself to keep on with the abusive fib. "Lily is a new start."

"If he's not a nice person and you need to leave the UK, you have to report him," Dad said. "I'll get Pete to look into it."

Pete was his friend, a copper.

Carla's nerves stretched thin. "No!" That had been too abrupt. "No. I'll just move. He won't find us."

"This is awful." Mum kissed Lily's head. "To think you've been suffering. Is that why you didn't answer your phone recently?"

"Yes. I'd left him. I needed to hide, to get away."

And the lies will just keep on coming.

She thought about how Mum and Dad didn't even know about the removal of her womb and ovaries. She'd kept that from them as well, and she wondered now, whether all along she'd subconsciously held that part back, knowing she'd be doing this, parading someone else's child in front of them, passing it off as their grandchild.

Christ, this is hateful.

Lily opened her eyes, and Carla's heart melted. Mum *oohed* and *ahhed*, and Dad got a bit choked up.

"Would you look at that," he said. "She's smiling at me. This is Carla all over again."

"It is," Mum agreed.

How could something so wonderful as having a baby in her life feel so bad? But it did, right in this moment, her secrets squirming inside her, waiting on her tongue to come out. Carla bit her lip, tears stinging. She'd definitely move to France soon. She couldn't bear watching these people bonding with Lily when she wasn't theirs to bond with.

Wasn't even Carla's.

Yet despite that, she blurted, "She's due a bottle soon if you want to feed her."

Mum's face lit up. "Oh . . . Well, that would be lovely."

"I'll just go and get my bags then." Carla left her coffee untouched and stood. "Assuming I can stay for a bit?"

"Of course you can," Dad said. "We have a granddaughter to get to know. You stay as long as you like."

Carla managed to hold back the tears until she got outside. They fell, hot, burning, and she couldn't see for the life of her until the stream had cleared. She swiped her cheeks and collected the suitcase, the baby bag, her handbag, and locked her car. Back inside, she left the case at the foot of the stairs and took the bags into the kitchen.

Lily smiled up at Mum and Dad, gums on display. Love shone from their eyes, and Carla stared, jealous that her daughter had smiled at them first, before her, but at the same time disgusted with herself, with her desperate need for a child, that she was willing to trick these people.

God, what have I done?

CHAPTER FOUR

Bethany and Mike stood side by side just in the doorway of a baby's bedroom. A woman, dead on the floor, her face sliced open, her neck gaping, was suspected to be a Miss Vicky North, estranged from her family after she'd become pregnant, so her diary said. It made for sad reading, a young woman ousted from everything she knew into Shadwell, miles from her childhood home, not knowing a soul. She'd made a few friends at the baby clinic, though, so at least she'd had some joy since moving here.

Now, whatever joy she'd had was gone.

A cot stood empty, the imprint of a tiny body left behind where the child had slept. A search of the house had shown the baby wasn't there, and going by the state of the mother, if indeed it was her, the infant had either been taken or left with someone else.

"We come back from holiday to not only frost but this," Mike said.

"Hmm."

Their trip to Spain had been wonderful, a chance to recharge and forget things like this existed. They'd touched down in the UK yesterday, complete with nice tans, walking into the station this morning and collared by Rob Quarry, the daytime front desk sergeant.

A murder. A possible abduction. Full steam ahead.

Fran, Leona, and Tammy were hard at it in the incident room, doing their thing, while uniforms had the arduous task of going door-to-door out in Galbraith Drive, the street where this house stood, the peaceful road twisted up with a killing, neighbours out in force having a nose. Upon her arrival, Bethany had scoped out all the people in their front gardens and on the pavement. Sometimes a killer returned to watch the fallout, perverse bastards that they were. Hands were wrung, faces pinched, mouths flapping with supposition.

The usual shit.

Bethany sighed. Fran had sent a message earlier to report that the father of the baby lived in the next town over, and he'd been staying in a bed courtesy of the NHS for the past week, suffering from appendicitis. He'd had an operation recently and would be released today.

No suspect in that direction then.

Fran had contacted Tracy Collier from Serious Crimes to go and speak to Vicky's mum and dad, seeing as they lived where Tracy worked, asking if they could identify their daughter via an image taken of just her face. No parent, despite not being in their kid's life, wanted to see bloodstains on her pyjamas and a couple of slits in the fabric where a knife had gone in, or her face all but carved in half, her neck gaping. That kind of thing tended to jar a bit. Still, her face was all they had to go on, and despite the cut in a diagonal, despite the blood, she resembled the woman in various pictures around the house.

She hoped the parents didn't have nightmares over it.

Isabelle, the lead SOCO, came in after yet another tour of the house — she'd gone off to find the knife used to stab the victim. "Nothing, so they must have taken it with them, although we'll take the knives that are in the house in case the killer decided to wash it and put it back in the drawer. Some people are sick like that."

Bethany thought about the bathroom. "Just as they're sick in cleaning themselves after getting blood on them. The sponge . . ."

Isabelle nodded. "Yep. Fancy being that blasé that you had the time and inclination to wash up. Maybe they didn't want to get the baby dirty."

"So you reckon she was definitely taken then?" Mike asked.

"Don't you? Vicky didn't get involved with her neighbours so had no one to babysit the kiddie. Uniform have established that by asking around."

That was true. Tory Yates and Glen Underby had nipped in with their initial report — no one really knew Vicky — and had gone back out to question other residents. So, with a lady and child living here, and no one who had anything to do with her, finding who'd done this was looking like it'd be a mammoth task if family members were ruled out.

"Presley will be here in a minute." Isabelle peered into the cot, her eyes narrowed above her face mask.

The ME was a no-nonsense sort who Isabelle verbally poked every time they met up. Bethany braved herself for the usual snipes, planning to stay only long enough to get an estimated time of death.

The man himself came up behind Bethany, and she stepped aside to allow him entry. "Hi, Pres."

"Ah, speak of the Devil and he shall appear." Isabelle straightened and turned to face him. "Better late than never. I've been here for two hours, Bethany and Mike one."

Presley placed his bag down on an evidence step. "Not that it's any of your business whatsoever, but I was at the scene of an RTA, so while this lady here is out of sight, I felt it more pleasant for those drivers going past to remove bodies that were in full view inside mangled cars." He sniffed in disdain and took his clipboard out, adding the stab marks to the shape of a body on his sheet of paper.

Isabelle waggled her eyebrows at Bethany, clearly gearing up to say something else.

Bethany shook her head: *Please don't.*

"Right, can we have the temp done then so Bethany and Mike can move along?" Isabelle asked.

"All in good time," Presley said.

Bethany held back laughter. He was making her wait as punishment.

Bethany's phone beeped, and she took it out.

Fran: YES, IT'S VICKY NORTH. TRACY COLLIER WAS GOING TO CONTINUE QUESTIONING HER PARENTS FOR YOU WHILE SHE WAS THERE, BUT SHE'S BEEN CALLED OUT FOR SOMETHING ELSE IN THE MIDDLE OF IT. HER WORDS WERE: FUCK, I NEED TO LEAVE THE NORTHS' PLACE, SO TELL BETH TO GET HER ARSE ROUND HERE SOON.

Bethany: OKAY, WE'LL GO THERE NOW.

She laughed. Tracy was an acquired taste, someone she hadn't liked at first, but since she usually kept her nose out of Bethany's cases, the woman had grown on her. "Okay, this is Vicky, confirmation just came in, so we'll go once we know the time of death."

Presley took his temperature gadget out, ignoring Isabelle's huff that said: *Oh, so you'll do it for Bethany but not for me?* Bethany shot her a warning look, and Presley got on with the job at hand.

"She's stiff," he said, "so we're talking hours ago. Hang on . . ." He peered at the reading. "Right, around one a.m., maybe up until two."

"Thanks." Bethany smiled behind her mask. "We'll be off then."

She left the room and went downstairs, her mind straying to where the baby could be. A little girl, four months old according to Leona, who'd looked it up. Maisie North, born here in Shadwell. Was she still here? If she'd been taken, who the hell had her if her mother didn't really know anyone? They'd have to visit the health centre and see if any mothers there recognised Vicky. At least they had a few first names from the diary.

On that note, she went into the living room to take a picture using her phone — a studio portrait of Vicky and Maisie on the wall. She sent it to Rob for him to distribute to patrol in case they recognised the baby on their travels. You never knew if you'd get lucky.

At the front door, she removed her protective clothing, as did Mike, and handed them to Penny Dickens who served as the one in charge of the log. They signed out, and in the street, Bethany walked over to Tory, who was closest.

"Anything?" she asked.

"No one I've spoken to has heard a thing." Tory sighed. "Surely there'd have been some noise if she's been stabbed. The neighbour directly next door said she'd slept through and only knew something was wrong when she knocked to ask Vicky if she'd like a bag of baby clothes her daughter needed to get rid of."

"So Rob said. Comes to something when you peer through the letterbox and spot a scuff of blood on the newel post."

"I know. She's shaken up, but I think she'll be okay. Thank God she called it in, though, eh? God knows how long Vicky would've been there otherwise."

"Yep, and the longer she was, the farther away the killer could get with the baby — if they took her."

"I'm thinking they did." Tory rubbed her temple.

"Same here, unfortunately. Do you think I need to speak to the neighbour? Only, we need to visit the victim's parents really."

"No, read this. That'll get you up to speed." Tory handed over her notebook.

Bethany scanned it. The neighbour was no use to them regarding the murder. She'd taken a sleeping pill at ten and conked out. Bethany gave the book back. "You're right. No point in getting her to go over it again when she has nothing to say about the time in question. Did you offer her some counselling if she needs it?"

Tory nodded. "She doesn't want it."

Bethany shrugged. "You can't help some people, can you. Tara for now." She checked in with Glen down the street. "Any luck?"

"Someone heard a car come down around half twelve, but they didn't bother getting up to look," he said. "Who'd want to climb out of a warm bed and get cold?"

"True. Not many people would, unless they live in the arse end of nowhere and it's unusual to hear a vehicle." She thanked him and met Mike at the car. "Off we go then."

She drove to Vicky's parents' house in the next town over, the pair of them throwing scenarios about. They did this to get their minds churning in order to work out what had happened. In this case, it sounded as if someone had arrived in a vehicle, killed her, then left with the baby. With Maisie North's father out of the picture, who else would want to kidnap her and kill Vicky, a woman with no known enemies?

Another baffling puzzle, but then her cases usually were.

She parked outside a modest house with empty flowerpots beneath the window beside the door, looking forlorn without their flowery enhancements. Cold fully had its feet planted in the early winter season, the grass rimed with sparkling frost.

At the front door, her ID in hand, she knocked. Mike stood just behind her.

A black-haired man answered, his face ruddy, perhaps from the excessive heat that bathed them from inside. It was clearly warm enough in there for him to go about in a white vest, which showcased his chest hairs that were going grey in patches. An anchor tattoo had pride of place at the top of one arm, barbed wire going around the other. Greasy hair was slicked back with comb lines present, although that could be from some kind of product. Whatever, it gave him a dirty air, like he needed to jump in the bath and stay there for a month. The smell emanating from the house plus the shoes in a haphazard pile by the stairs gave credence to her initial impression — these people weren't particularly clean.

She held up her ID. "DI Bethany Smith and DS Mike Wilkins from Shadwell. We'll need to come in."

"We've just had a copper here," he said. "Bolshy sort. Ginger. Quite rude, if you ask me."

Bethany hid a smile. "DI Collier is very forthright, yes. Shall we?" She gestured for him to move out of the way.

He did, and they followed him into a cluttered living room that appeared to have a pile of crusty shit in front of the TV unit. How lovely. A cat sprang up from its curled position on the windowsill and darted out into the hallway. A woman, Vicky's mother Bethany presumed, sat beneath a heap of ratty, multicoloured, filthy crocheted blankets, just her head visible. She, too, had greasy hair that hung heavy and coiled on her shoulders, the blonde strands dull under the main light bulb, the shade a blue glass ball that had a thick layer of dust on it.

The odour was revolting. The shit, fag smoke, old food, and BO.

"Have a seat," Mr North said.

Not on your nelly. "We'll stand, thank you." Bethany remained by the door.

Mike did his usual and stood near the window, notebook and pen out.

"When did you last see your daughter?" she asked.

Mr North plopped onto the magazine-strewn sofa. "Months ago. Before she had the nipper."

"We know you weren't happy about her pregnancy. How unhappy?"

He bristled, squaring his pasty, flaccid shoulders. "She'd got knocked up by that fucking twerp who sells drugs. Of course we weren't happy. But if you're implying, like that other copper did, that either of us had anything to do with

Vicky's murder, you can piddle off to Fuckyouville and don't come back."

Mike cleared his throat and wrote on his pad. Probably the word 'Fuckyouville' so he didn't forget it.

Bethany gave a tight smile. "I don't know where that is, sir, but regardless, we have to ask these questions. Where were you last night?"

"Down the pub playing bingo," he said. "Didn't we, love?"

He glanced over at the head in the chair. The woman nodded, her hair writhing.

"Which pub?"

"Our local," he said.

"And what's it called?"

"Oh, the Frog and Toad. Got a new name. Used to be the Swan. It's had a makeover." He hawked up phlegm.

Dear God . . . "Right. What time did you leave there?"

"Dunno, about eleven."

"And what did you do after that?"

He grinned, showing rank teeth even a dentist would shy away from fixing. "We went to Flossie's for a nightcap."

"Where does she live?"

"Fuck me. It's like being on a game show here. Do I win a prize if I get them all right?" He belly-laughed.

Bethany didn't find him amusing. A man roaring like that when his daughter was dead? She took back her earlier thought of no parent wanting to see blood on their child. It seemed it wouldn't have bothered him. Vicky was right to have moved away.

"Flossie's address, please." She tapped her foot.

"Next door at number fifteen."

"What time did you leave there?"

He stared at the ceiling.

"Five past two," the head muttered.

Bethany turned to her. "Thank you. Mike, can you go and confirm that, please?"

He nodded and left the house. She didn't want these two having a chance to contact Flossie and cook up an alibi.

They remained in awkward silence until Mike came back. He dipped his head once to confirm their story.

Bethany pushed on, wanting to get out of this gopping place. "Do you know whether Vicky had any enemies?"

"Well, there was that bint who got arsey about her seeing the kid's father. What was her name?" He glanced over at Head in Blankets. "She threatened our Vic, didn't she."

The woman yawned. "Said she'd bottle Vicky if she kept on going out with him, but we soon sorted that."

"Karen!" Mr North shouted.

Bethany raised her eyebrows. "How did you 'sort that', Mrs North?"

"We went round to her house, told her to fuck off. Said if she touched Vic, we'd have her. It's what you do, looking after your own."

"Like you looked after her when she got pregnant?" Bethany's temper rose. "Maybe if you'd been more concerned about her then, she'd still be alive."

She shouldn't have said that.

"You're no better than that Collier woman," Mr North barked. "She said the same damn thing, but it isn't our fault Vic's been stabbed."

"How do you know she was stabbed?"

"That copper told us." He reached over and brought out a bottle of beer from behind a manky cushion, downing the contents. A burp and a full body shiver followed. "Look, Vic left after a row. She'd been planning to move out anyway, saving up her wages for a deposit, so her going wasn't anything unusual, just brought forward like." He shrugged. "She made her new bed, and look where it got her. Dead."

Bethany didn't even thank them for their time. She walked out, using her sleeve to open the front door, then stomped to the car and shut herself inside. A deep breath calmed her somewhat, but Mr North's attitude rankled, and she had nothing but extreme sympathy for Vicky. Living with them must have been a nightmare. Vicky's house was tidy, clean, and although she had minimal furniture, what she did have was decent. She clearly hadn't wanted to follow in her parents' footsteps with regard to living in a shithole.

Mike sat beside her and sighed. "What a pair. And that cat shit on the floor . . ."

Bethany held back a retch. "Don't."

Mike chuckled. "Fuckyouville, though."

"Bloody twat. He's revolting. Poor Vicky. No wonder she kept the baby away from them." She took her phone out to search for the postcode of the hospital. With it plugged into the satnav, she drove towards it. "While the ex may not have done it, that girl they mentioned might have. We're going to speak to him, see if he can remember her name. Him being in hospital could also be convenient. What if he sent someone to nick the baby?"

"True."

While that scenario wasn't nice, they had to look into it.

Someone, somewhere, had to know where Maisie North was.

CHAPTER FIVE

Anne stared at Jolene. What was this woman on? Yet again, she'd asked what to do about a leak.

"Plumber," Anne snapped. Fuck, she was so tired. She'd stayed awake for ages once she'd got home from HQ, reliving the murder, watching herself from the outside in so she got a proper view of everything. She was the star of the show in her own film.

With any luck, Vicky having no one, her body might not be discovered for ages. She'd bloat, all her fluids seeping out, and unless someone noticed the smell, she'd be left to rot all by herself.

That'd be nice.

"Cheers, me dears," Jolene chirped, bright and cheerful.

Anne gritted her teeth and imagined holding Jolene's head under water until she drowned.

She brought up Notepad on her monitor and tapped out her resignation. If she handed it in today, she'd only have to work a week's notice. Someone else would then take over mentoring that scrag-end opposite, and Anne could sleep all day and work at night. She'd even offer to sit with the customers at HQ so Zooby and Joseph got some proper sleep.

It couldn't be easy taking it in turns to kip in the chair for three-hour stints.

Happy now she'd made a firm decision, she put her name at the bottom, hit PRINT, and got up to take the letter out of the machine tray across the room, ignoring the green flashing light on her dashboard. There were enough people working here to take the call. She didn't have to be the first one to pick up anymore — they got bonuses based on how many enquiries they dealt with, hence why she grabbed all the ones she could. She didn't need them now. Zooby had dished out her cut of the money for Maisie/Lily prior to Anne leaving last night, so she was minted.

Folding her letter in half, she walked to the manager's office and tapped on the door. He was a right fucker, always letting out snide remarks, so she'd give him one of her own in a minute if he snarked at her. Nothing left to lose and all that.

"Come in," Mr Knight called.

She entered, and he indicated for her to sit in front of his desk.

"Come to give your report on Jolene, have you?" he asked. "I suspect she's picking it up a bit better now you're on top of it, keeping her in line."

"Er, no. She's slow to learn. Keeps asking which tradesman goes to which job all the time, even though she had her initial training, and it's common sense, *and* I wrote it as a list so she could check that first before bothering me."

"Oh dear. Can't you cope?"

Anne resisted the urge to kick his shin under the desk. What a gimp. "Yes, I can cope, but when someone's either dim or being lazy by not bothering to learn, it gets a bit much, considering I have my own job to do as well. How often does someone need to be told something before it penetrates their thick skull?"

"I see." Knight winced. "She's the sister of my daughter-in-law, so it's a bit awkward for me to have a word with her. Will you do it?"

Anne nodded. She'd love to, and she'd do so on her last day, give Jolene both barrels. Verbally cannon-blast the woman.

"It's also a tad awkward regarding her probation period," he said. "Letting her go afterwards isn't an option. Family ruckus if I did that."

"Hmm."

He gazed off into space. "I need to take a week off to look after our grandchild," he went on, as if she gave a toss about that.

Then again . . . "How old is it?"

"Five months. Little Dominic. Such a lovely lad. Always smiling."

"Ah, that's sweet." She knew where her boss lived because of his constant bragging, just not the number of the house. It wouldn't be difficult to spot it if his Merc was outside. Customer Three wanted a boy but had agreed to a girl if lads weren't available. Dominic would do nicely. Who said fate didn't lend you a helping hand, eh?

"He arrives this evening. Me and the wife are looking forward to it. Now then, did you want anything else?"

She pushed her letter across the desk. "I'm handing in my notice."

His cheeks reddened, and he spluttered out a cough. "Oh. Well. I hadn't expected that. You're my top target-hitter. Anything I can do to help? Make your workday more enjoyable?"

So he was nice now he was losing her. Typical. "No, I've made my mind up."

"Okay, so that's a week left for you here then, unless you want to forfeit your final wage and go now?"

What a bargain. "Yes, please."

"Oh. Right. Well then . . ."

"Have fun with Dominic."

It'll be the last night you have him.

She smiled and left his office, marching over to her desk. Bits and bobs swept into her bag, she leant over and glared at Jolene. "The boss asked me to talk to you as I just gave him your weekly progress report. Apparently, he can't let you go after your probation period because you're family. Well, I have no such worries about that, so let's make it simple. You're shit. You're thick. You're the most bugging person I've ever had to work with. You stink of fags — and just so you're aware, you can have a break in the morning and one in the afternoon to smoke, not nip out there at all times of the day, you skiving prat. I dislike you, can't see how anyone would want to be near you, so buck your ideas up if you want to get anywhere in life. No one likes a Bubbly Betty like you, they're irritating. Now, bad day to you, shitface, and don't have a nice life."

Jolene blinked, tears spilling, and her bottom lip wobbled.

God, that had felt good to say that to her, and Anne didn't feel one ounce of guilt. More people ought to say what was on their mind instead of hiding it away if it meant being on cloud nine. She flounced away, her grip on her bag tight, and once outside, let the laughter free.

If only Jolene had a kid, Anne could kill her.

One day. If anyone even went near the stupid cow's fireplace. That was the joke about sex with ugly people, wasn't it? Poking the fire.

She drove off, pleased as punch with herself, and went straight to bed once she got home. She had a baby to snatch after midnight, and she needed sleep to ensure she had the energy to do it.

And tomorrow night?

She was going after Dominic.

* * *

Her dreams were usually nightmares, full of shadowy spectres that hung back at the recesses of the scene, waiting in a curved row to devour her, ominous mist floating up behind them. The scene was always grey tinged with blue. In front of them stood her godmother, a woman who looked after her while her mum worked. Raven, she was called, a pretty name for a wicked woman, who smacked Anne more often than not and threatened to kidnap her one day and dump her in the woods at Shadwell Hill with the rats.

The idea of rats scared her. Raven said they attacked you in swarms and chomped your eyes out, choking you with their oily fur.

"What are you looking at?" Raven snarled, blood dripping down her chin.

Anne had watched Raven bite the head off a small rat and chew on it, the crunch of the bones loud in the silence of the woods.

"I . . . I don't know." Anne twiddled her fingers.

"What, no sarky comeback? No: Dunno, doesn't have a label on it?"

Anne had wanted to say that, but to speak to Raven in that way wasn't wise or clever. Raven would only slap her anyway — and force her to eat some of the rat. She usually did in this dreamscape, mimicking real life.

Anne suspended her nightmare, pulling back as she sometimes could, and thought about Raven, the twenty-something who hadn't grown up enough to watch eight-year-old Anne properly. Mum was older, thirty-two, and she'd met Raven years ago through another friend.

"Don't you fucking zone out on me," her godmother said.

It snapped Anne back into the woods, with the figures in the mist, the rat's body on the ground, blood staining the crispy brown autumn leaves beneath it. She stared at Raven, sending hate towards her, but Raven only laughed.

"You're pathetic," she said. "Your mum would have a much better life without you."

If Raven ever took Anne into the woods to let the rats feast on her, she'd get away somehow, and kill Raven. Raven's baby would be left with no one, be taken in by strangers, and Anne would feel better knowing she herself had nothing to fear.

One day she'd make all mothers of babies pay.

It'd give her something to focus on until she got older.

It always helped to have goals.

* * *

Joseph browsed the Shadwell Community page on Facebook while Zooby had a nap in the chair. It was best to keep an eye on what was going on, even though there was no way they could be caught for abducting the babies. He'd put up a special firewall to stop anyone visiting the site finding them, so even if the police searched for any reason, it wouldn't even show up unless they thought to access the Dark Web. At least he didn't think it would.

There were the usual posts.

Anyone got a fridge freezer I can have for free? Skint.

Can someone give me a quote to paint my hallway, please?

Who does pet sitting? Going away for work. Dog needs feeding and walking.

Then there were older links to the *Shadwell Herald*, one with the headline of NEW WINE BAR OPENS! and another: RECENT BUTCHER KILLER DECIDES TO REVEAL ALL. God, he'd been a right nutter, some bloke who lived in the back of his lorry, going about killing people, chopping them up, then putting them in graves after he'd nicked the women out of the coffins. Who did bad shit like that?

He swallowed. He was being bad. Even though he hadn't taken Lily, he'd been a part of it. Several times since last night he'd considered telling Zooby he couldn't do this, that he'd made a mistake, and he wouldn't tell a soul what they were doing, but each time, the courage had failed him. Zooby would get his dodgy mates to follow him to the ends of the earth if Joseph ever walked out on this.

He snapped out of his head and concentrated on the screen.

Teddy bear found outside the gym in the high street.

Did anyone else see Specsavers is shut?

I'm disgusted by some of the people around here. I got spat on when a car drove past me. The passenger opened the window and gobbed. Get some manners, you lot!

WOMAN FOUND MURDERED. CHILD MISSING.

"Oh, Jesus . . ."

He clicked the link, heart thumping, skin breaking out in the cold sweat of fear.

WOMAN FOUND MURDERED. CHILD MISSING.

PETER UXBRIDGE — REGIONAL CRIME

Today, police were called to a house in Galbraith Drive, where a neighbour had raised the alarm. Vicky North had been found stabbed, her face and throat slashed. Her baby, Maisie, has either been abducted or is safe with someone Vicky had asked to look after her.

If that's you and you have Maisie, please contact the police immediately.

However, if she's been kidnapped, we need all eyes on alert. Let's get the community spirit going and band together on this.

A source close to the police said: "Maisie is four months old, blonde, and weighs fourteen and half pounds. We don't know what she was wearing at the time of her mother's murder or, in fact, whether she was at home during this terrible incident."

The saddest part of this is, Vicky had only been found because the neighbour was passing on some unwanted baby clothes. As Vicky kept to herself, had the neighbour not gone round and seen the blood inside on the newel post, Vicky's death would have remained undetected for some time.

Someone out there would have had blood on them, although they cleaned themselves at the scene using a bath sponge. The blood has been sent in so Forensics can determine who it belongs to. Did the killer cut themselves? Will the blood be theirs, Vicky's, or both?

A vehicle had gone down the street after midnight, reported by a resident. Was that the killer/abductor? Was everyone sleeping soundly in Galbraith Drive while poor Vicky lost her life?

We need to find out. If you know anything, however insignificant you think it may be, contact either me at the Herald, the Shadwell police, or phone Crimestoppers anonymously. This is a wicked act, and a baby is missing. Whether she's dead or alive remains to be seen.

Keep a watch out, folks!

Joseph swallowed the glut of bile that flooded his throat and burnt it. What the fuck had Anne done? Why had she killed the mother and not said a thing about it?

He thought back to when she'd brought the child into HQ. He hadn't noticed any blood on her, but then he hadn't been looking for it, had he. This was supposed to be a simple abduction, not a murder inquiry.

Fucking hell's bells.

Zooby snorted in his sleep, the sound bringing on more panic. When he found out what Anne had done, he'd go mental.

Joseph got up and went over to the sideboard to make a coffee. The halogen was doing jack shit in warming the room up, and he shivered, the rumble of the kettle somehow portentous beside him. Zooby stirred because of it, so Joseph sorted an extra cup. They could both hash this out over a brew, decide how to handle Anne.

Drinks done, he took them to the table, placed them down, and moved to Zooby in the corner. Joseph would love nothing more than to leave him be, pretend this hadn't happened, but Zooby would check the internet anyway at some point, see the news, then have a go at Joseph for keeping it quiet if he let on that he already knew.

"Zoobs." Joseph shook his shoulder. "Zoobs, man, wake up."

"What?" Zooby flapped a hand at Joseph, sitting up and rubbing his eyes. "I've never had three hours already, have I?"

"No, an hour, but there's something you need to fucking see. I told you Anne was a liability." He went over to the table. "Park your arse and get a load of this." He scrolled to the top of the article.

Zooby shuffled over, yawning. "What are you on about, you sodding douche?" He sank onto the chair and slid a steaming cup towards him. "Let me just wake up first, will you?"

Joseph sighed in frustration and walked away, clutching at his hair. And he remembered what else Anne had done. She'd used her own number plates when collecting Lily. What if CCTV spotted her? The police would find her, and she'd take them down with her, he didn't doubt that. They'd all agreed to remain silent on anyone else's involvement should any of them get caught, but seeing as how the stupid cow had taken matters in her own hands and stabbed some poor bitch, who knew whether she'd stick to the rest of the plan?

He paced in front of the halogen to get some heat back into his bones from where his body had gone so cold after he'd read the article. He didn't reckon he'd ever be warm again. Not until everything was behind them, but when would that be? With all six customers having babies, the next wave would begin with them being taken away and handed to someone else. How many rounds of that deceit would there be? There had to be a point they'd stop, surely. They couldn't kidnap kids here indefinitely.

"Fuck me sideways," Zooby said.

So he'd read it then. Now for the eruption . . .

It didn't come.

Joseph went over to sit beside him. A few sips of coffee later, and Zooby hadn't said anything else. He was still scouring the article. In the past he'd have gone off on one, so why not now?

"What the chuff do we do?" Joseph asked to chivvy Zooby's anger along. "She's lost it. Who goes in and kills a woman?"

Zooby cradled his cup. "Shut up, I'm trying to think what she told us." He shook his head. "Right, she said she was getting ready to take Lily, then the mum came in. She didn't say anything about killing her, though. What if Anne forgot to close the front door and some other nutter went inside and offed this Vicky slag?"

"Oh, behave. What are the chances of that?" *He's as deluded as she is!*

"Fact is stranger than fiction."

"You're just making up excuses because you don't want to admit we have a mental tart in the group — someone *you* vetted. I said it was weird how easily she accepted what we were doing. At least Nat had reservations, same as me." Joseph drank some more to stop himself saying shit he'd regret, like Zooby being the biggest twazzock ever. Then he thought of something. "Anne said she punched the mother. I assumed she'd blacked out and Anne left her there. But what if she did kill her? A slit face and throat. What the hell? How do we deal with that? Or trust her on the other jobs? She might kill the next mother an' all."

"Does it matter?" Zooby asked.

No, he hadn't just heard that, had he? "You what?" Joseph slammed his hand on the table, and their cups jumped, liquid sploshing. "I can't believe you said that. Does it matter? Yes, it fucking does! She's been driving around in her car, for God's sake. She didn't change her plates."

"Oh yeah."

Joseph frowned. What was up with Zooby? Normally he'd go ape at this sort of thing. He hadn't even really pushed it with Anne about the mother being awake either, just offered some lip service. How come he wasn't steaming angry?

"Look," Zooby said. "Before we start throwing accusations around, we need to talk to her. Get hold of her on WhatsApp and tell her to come here."

"She'll be at work."

"So? Say it's important."

"WhatsApp is a stupid idea, by the way. I said that at the start." Joseph took his phone out then thought better of it. Why use his? Why implicate himself if the police twigged it was them and went through their digital footprint? He didn't know if anyone had noticed, but he hadn't written a word on that group when everyone discussed the plan. Fuck getting blamed for this. "You message her. I don't want any part of her now she's done this."

Zooby sighed and fired off a message. "Right, now we wait." His mobile chimed, as did Joseph's. "There you go, she's on her way."

"Probably still with her original plates. God, she's such a dickwad."

Zooby tapped out another message. "I've told her to switch them out."

On WhatsApp. Where it's easy to see what you said. You utter knob.

The wait for Anne seemed to take forever, then the crunch of her tyres going over the debris in the courtyard got Zooby off his arse and to the door, mask firmly in place. He let her in, and she took her mask off, letting it dangle around her neck from the elastic cord.

"What's going on?" She cocked her hip.

"You, that's what," Joseph snapped, pointing at the laptop, which had gone to sleep. "Have you even seen the bloody news?"

"I was in bed. Zooby's message woke me up." She pranced over to the table and sat, stroking the touchpad to bring the screen to life. Her smile spread so wide it created apples out of her cheeks. "That's a bummer they found her so quickly, but you can't score all the time, can you."

"Score?" Joseph's ire writhed about inside him, hot and fierce. "Score? Like this is some kind of *game*?"

"Of course it is." She sounded bored. "Life's a game. You either play by the rules or break them. I broke them. Because I could. Because I wanted to. And who's going to miss her? She had no one. So would you rather I knocked her out and risked her telling someone a woman was in her house wearing a clown mask?"

"How would she know you're a woman?" Joseph asked.

"One, I have tits, which were obvious despite my jacket, and two, I spoke to her." Anne got up and walked over to the heater, rubbing her hands, her back to them.

"You *spoke* to her?" Joseph couldn't get over this. What planet was she on? And why wasn't Zooby giving her a bollocking?

"Yes, I did." Anne nodded. "I told her to say goodbye to the kid."

"Why?"

"Reasons."

"And they are?"

"None of your business." She turned to face him and warmed her hands behind her. "Is that money nice and hot in your pocket? You know, the money you got paid for your part in this?"

And that was all she'd needed to say to remind him he was in the shit just as much as her. All right, he hadn't killed anyone, but him being a part of the group, him being the one to set up stuff online to lure women in . . . He'd go down for a long stretch if she chose to open her mouth and drop him in it.

And he believed she would. Maybe that was why Zooby was being so accommodating. He'd sensed she was unstable, and their stack of cards could come tumbling down if he got heavy with her.

"Hmm, thought so." She smiled smugly. "Let's all keep our gobs shut, yes?" She looked at Zooby. "Unless you think otherwise?"

"Just don't do it again," Zooby said. "Tonight's mother has family nearby. She *will* be missed."

That was it? That was all the dressing down she'd get?

Joseph stomped to the door and grabbed his helmet and jacket off a nearby pile of boxes containing Pampers.

"Oi! Where do you think you're going?" Zooby called.

"Out. Away from her. I'll be back later. Maybe she can help you look after the customers, seeing as she's all but taking over the way things are done around here." He jammed his helmet on, thrust his arms into his jacket, and zipped it up. Outside, he climbed on his bike and revved the engine in anger. Fuck Zooby, and fuck Anne for muscling in.

The pair of them were welcome to each other.

* * *

On the way to Natasha's, Joseph had done something he never thought he would. Now, in her living room, he shuddered from that act, plus at what he'd told Nat.

"She did *what*?" She stared at him. "Shit, this isn't just an abduction now. It's us in hot water, that's what it is. We need to get Carla and Lily out of Shadwell, because they'll be even more intent on finding the kid now her mum's been killed." She paced in front of the three-bar electric fire, one of those ancient fuckers from years ago.

He rubbed his eyes. "Yep. Anne isn't right in the head. We need to be careful. That's why I came here to tell you, so you're aware of how much trouble we could be in. Zooby just told her not to do it again. I mean, what?"

"D'you think he fancies her or something? Is that why he's not threatening her like he would if it was us? Or is he shagging her, and they're keeping it quiet? Or is he scared of her, especially now he knows she's murdered someone?"

"I don't know, but whatever it is, we're at risk of being nicked. We need to get going to Carla's."

"Give me a minute. I need a wee."

He waited for her outside on his bike, and she used his spare helmet, getting on the back behind him, her arms tight around his waist. They raced to Carla's, and Joseph waited at the kerb with the engine running while Nat knocked on the front door. She turned, and he couldn't see her expression through the visor, but she shrugged at him.

Joseph propped the bike up and legged it round the back, where he used a copy of Carla's key to get in. They'd had it made while she'd been out of it, finding her original bunch in her handbag. Easier to steal Lily back that way.

He rushed through the house, coming to a stop in the living room. The Moses basket was empty. In the kitchen, he poked around. No baby paraphernalia.

Shit. Carla must have gone, and she'd taken Lily with her.

CHAPTER SIX

Bethany and Mike stood either side of the hospital bed. Greg Walker, the occupant, was pale-skinned other than flush spots on each cheek. Bethany had introduced them, and Greg had acted nervy at first, probably thinking they were there about the drugs he peddled. While dealing them was an issue, Bethany had more important things to discover regarding him. She'd send Tracy a message about him, let her decide whether or not she followed it up.

Passing the buck was handy at times.

"We know of your activities," she said, "but we're not here for that. When was the last time you saw Vicky North?"

He frowned and ran a hand through his tufty blond hair. It appeared he cropped it to keep the curls at bay, which were just reappearing. He was probably due a cut. "Christ, that's got to be over a year ago. More than that even. She got preggers. I didn't want to know, so she fucked off. I'm not even sure if the kid's mine, to be honest."

Bethany thought about the diary. Vicky hadn't mentioned any other male in her life around the time she'd fallen for the child, so for now, they'd go with the idea she was Greg's. "Who is the woman who had a grudge against Vicky for seeing you?"

"Old What's Her Face? Um, she went to uni in St Andrews last year, a couple of months after Vicky moved away. Can't even remember her name. Why?"

"Have you had any TV on while you've been here? Accessed your phone?"

Greg laughed. "You're joking, aren't you? This lot in here, even though I was crippled with pain, decided my appendix wasn't the issue at first. Then they discovered it was close to bursting after finally doing a bloody scan, so no, I haven't wanted to watch telly in the slightest. Too busy curled up waiting for the next round of pain meds."

"No visitors?"

His cheeks pinked even more at that. "None I can mention, no."

"Well, you better had."

"All right, people who report to me about my business, d'you get me?"

"Okay. So no one's told you about what hit the news earlier today?"

That had dogged her off, Mike coming across an article in the *Herald* on their way here. Peter Uxbridge had struck again, the journalistic twat.

Greg frowned harder. "Eh?"

"Vicky was murdered during the night."

"Fuck off!" He guffawed, a tad nervously, though.

"This is serious, Mr Walker. The baby wasn't in the house."

Greg shifted to get more comfortable, cringing at the movement. "Hang on a sec . . ." He pushed his palms to the mattress and hoiked himself upright. "Vicky's dead and the kid's gone? Gone where?"

"We don't know. No one has come forward to say they're watching her for Vicky, so we're assuming she was abducted. We have officers out searching for her."

"Fuck me, that's a bit rough."

"A bit? I'd say a lot." She stared at him, working out whether his reaction was genuine or not.

"I knew nothing about it. And it's not like it's my problem anyway. I was only with her for about two months, and to be fair, she had a gut on her, so she was probably pregnant before she met me."

Was this bloke for real? It seemed so.

He closed his eyes as if none of this bothered him and let out a long breath.

"So how did you part ways?" she asked. "Amicably?"

"Something like that. I said I didn't want a baby until I was over thirty. She asked me to reconsider or at least spend some time with the kid. I said no, and that was that. I heard she moved to Shadwell, got herself a little house." He opened his eyes. "She was always banging on about saving a deposit, saying we could move in together. I didn't want nowt to do with that either. I live with a couple of mates. Why change what works?"

"Do you know of anyone who would want to do this to Vicky?"

"Nah." He shook his head. "Saying that, there was a rumour her dad went a bit mental when he found out she was up the duff."

"He has an alibi, as does her mother."

"If it's from Fucked-Up Flossie, she'll say anything if it means she gets bunged a few quid after. She's . . . an acquaintance. Likes a bit of sniff every now and then, know what I mean? The white stuff."

Bethany looked at Mike. He rolled his eyes.

"Thank you for your time," she said to Greg. "Hope you feel better soon."

"Cheers. Just so you know, if that kid does get found, I don't want her."

Bethany bit her tongue. What a bastard he was.

They walked out, and she drove to Flossie's. On the doorstep, they chatted to her, and she still maintained the Norths had been with her. Without any proof to the contrary, and no other names given of people who could corroborate this, Bethany made the decision to go back to Shadwell and see how things were going in the incident room.

Once there, she made everyone a coffee, handed them out, and stood in front of the whiteboards to get up to speed. "Okay, Leona, you've been on CCTV. As usual, no public cameras on Vicky's estate bar those outside the shops. They've been checked, and all cars have been signed off as not suspicious. CCTV elsewhere is the same, so the killer left in their vehicle and went wherever they went next, unseen. Vicky has Facebook and Instagram. Facebook is mainly memes about motherhood, being lonely, and wishing she had friends. That is bloody sad."

Fran nodded. "She has thirty-one on her list, most of them not interacting with her, although two, I assume from the health centre visits, are from Shadwell and leave hearts as responses. No commenting, though. As for Instagram, she puts up images of Maisie every day, and each one is labelled something like, 'One month old today!' Maybe it was her cataloguing her daughter's life so far."

"Sounds about right." Bethany nodded.

"I've found all the friends and where they live," Fran said, "so between me and Tammy, we've phoned them. Basically, no one from her old haunts speaks to her anymore and didn't much when she lived there anyway — something to do with her coming from a bad family — and the two from Shadwell only know her to have a brief chat with while they have a cuppa after weighing their babies. They did, however, tell us the name of a woman who seems more friendly with Vicky, so I phoned her. While she interacted with Vicky a lot over coffee, it didn't go beyond that, so no plans to meet outside of the times at the café for play dates for the babies. Sounds like Vicky was isolated, more than the memes expressed."

"She wrote as much in her diary," Bethany said. "Have you had a chance to go through it?"

Leona nodded. "I started it after CCTV threw nothing up. So it spans from when she started seeing Greg Walker to the day she was killed. She doesn't name the person who gave her hassle while she was with Greg. She calls her 'that thing'."

Bethany wrote that on the board. "Greg doesn't remember her name, or so he says, and he said she's at a uni in St Andrews, so Tammy, get on that and ask them if there are any students from this county there. Find out who they are. Once you know, get hold of the police up there and explain the situation. They can go to the uni and ask questions. If we're lucky enough to know who she is, her alibi will save her if she's been in Scotland all this time, but we may be looking at someone asking another to kill and abduct. If that's what we're dealing with, good luck to us in finding them." She paused for breath. "Fran, poke into getting clearance for us to have a gander at the main players' bank details. I'm specifically wanting large clumps of money going out, then into someone else's account. We need to know who that person is if they've been paid a huge sum, and why it was paid. Those people are . . ." She wrote them on the board as she spoke. "Mr and Mrs North. Greg Walker. The uni woman once we know who she is." She turned to face the team. "Any sightings from patrol on Maisie?"

Head shakes.

"Someone did ring in, though," Fran said. "I've yet to put it on the board because I just finished the call before you walked in, so here's the slip of paper it's on."

Mike took it and passed it over to Bethany.

"Oh," Bethany said. "A man claims he knows who killed Vicky. A crackpot or genuine?"

Fran sighed. "Hard to tell. He sounded like he was telling the truth but said he couldn't say who it was as it would come back on him. I pressed for him to elaborate, and he reckoned that even though he knew about Vicky's murder and was associated with the killer, he didn't know anything about the killing until after it was done. The call was via a burner, which is now switched off, and the ping was at the tower near the road leading down south, so he maybe stopped on the hard shoulder. His location during the call was in this area here." She got up and took a printout from the tray and handed it to Bethany. "We couldn't get any more specific than that."

"Right, so they likely went through the Ring Road Estate to get on that main road." Bethany pondered that for a moment. "Are they stupid enough to call in from near there if that's where they live?"

"Who knows, but I sent patrol over there anyway, and we're waiting on CCTV from the main road." Fran clicked her mouse. "Some uniforms have been drafted in from other places. Massive house-to-house going on at the minute, asking about the baby, plus a load of them in fields and whatnot, doing line searches."

The image of that, everyone pulling together to find a wee mite, saddened Bethany.

She sat on the edge of a desk and sipped her coffee. Where did they go from here? With uniforms doing a lot of leg work for Maisie, she wondered if she and the team were better off going down the killer route. After all, they'd had enough of them the past couple of years so knew what they were doing. If they found the killer, they found the abductor — and hopefully found Maisie alive.

Her phone rang, and she walked to her office and answered it. "Hi, Tracy." She sat behind her desk.

"How's it going? With the baby missing, I'll have to help you out here. What I'm going to do, as well as working the other case I'm on, *like* I can stretch myself that thin, is to question people here who knew Vicky in my neck of the woods. What have you done so far?"

"Firstly, thanks for the help. I'm going to need it on this one. Right, we visited Vicky's parents and—"

"What an absolute pair of goats," Tracy said. "The mother sits there under a heap of blankets looking like she's Jabba the Hut, and the father . . . Nice vest. Did you see the *stain* on the front?"

"No, I was too busy trying not to smell the cat shit on the floor."

"Ah, now I didn't see that but put the odour down to Mr North's backside."

Bethany heaved. "Pack it in. So, moving on. I spoke to the parents. They haven't seen their daughter since she moved out, didn't seem bothered she was dead or that Maisie is missing, and they have an alibi with a Flossie Hungerford. Greg Walker, the ex-boyfriend of Vicky and supposed father of Maisie, is in hospital recovering from appendicitis. We nipped to see him. He doesn't care about Vicky or Maisie either, and a woman who was iffy with Vicky about her seeing Greg may not be in the picture because she's apparently in Scotland. Fran is dealing with the latter now. While two of my team have rung some of Vicky's old friends, it might be better if you speak to them in person. I'll get Fran to send you the list of names, addresses, and phone numbers. Greg is a drug dealer, by the way."

"Oh right. I'll just have to pass that on to the drug unit then, won't I?"

"Thought you might. Much as he's a prat, I don't think it's him who did this. He said something interesting about Flossie Hungerford, though."

"What's that then?"

"That she'd give anyone an alibi if she thought she'd get cash for it. Now, me and Mike visited her again to chat about whether the Norths really were with her once they left the pub last night, and she insisted they were. You might get more out of her, seeing as you have a certain way with you."

Tracy laughed. "I'm trying hard to ditch my arsehole persona, but it won't hurt to get it back out on this occasion. Okay, we have officers here doing door-to-door regarding the baby, and I see you've got some drafted in to do the same in Shadwell. If we come up negative, we'll expand the search area. What's the deal on the murder side of it?"

"A vehicle was heard in Galbraith Drive around the estimated time of death, so we're taking it that the killer arrived in it. CCTV is a load of bollocks. Oh, but Fran did get a call from a man using a burner. Said he knows who the killer is but can't say because he'll be implicated."

"That tells me he's involved with the killer somehow, be it closely or not, sooooo." A pause. "Sorry, just needed to think for a sec. So, we assume he didn't give a name because his would crop up as a result. Now then, why would that matter if the killer was arrested and held in custody, unless the killer knows something about him and tells us so *he* gets in the shit? Sound about right?"

"Yep. There could be a few involved in the abduction."

"Exactly."

Bethany went on to tell her about the bank detail search they were putting into action on Vicky's finances. She accessed her emails on her computer. "Okay, info just through. Vicky's phone is with digi forensics. I have the first email open here. So far, they have the fact that her phone screen showed a page from a Kindle book when it was switched on, so she was perhaps reading in bed when the killer came in? Let's see what else . . . She made a phone call to a catalogue company last week, so I assume that was to order something or pay her bill. There's a call yesterday to an insurance company, and the same number called her back a bit later, but then there's nothing after, and the call before those was a fortnight ago to a play centre. Aww, the poor cow was trying so hard to make friends." She told Tracy about the diary and how lonely Vicky was.

"What are you trying to do, make me cry? Bugger off, Smith."

Bethany laughed. "Seriously now, if we're going down the route of more than one person being involved with the abduction, had Vicky been targeted *because* she didn't know anyone?"

"Good angle. But surely they realised this would hit the news."

"Maybe they don't care now they have the child. I'll get Leona to look into cases where women have stolen someone's baby. It might give us some kind of insight in how to proceed. To be honest, I'll try anything at the moment." A muted beep went off in her ear. "Give me a mo. I've got another call." She switched over to it. "Yep."

"It's Glen."

"Hi. Got something interesting?"

"You could say so. Vicky had a plumber around yesterday. A neighbour, who was out when we questioned everyone earlier, came back just as we were leaving. She told me a van parked up and a man went inside."

The insurance call? "Okay, house number and name."

"Twenty Galbraith, Helen Slocombe."

"Thanks, we'll pop to see her now." She swapped back over to Tracy and explained the latest.

"You had a previous case where that bloke gained entry by pretending to be a High Court agent. Reckon it could be the same deal, only a plumber?"

"No idea, but I'll have a good go at finding out. Catch up with you later."

Bethany left her office and touched Mike's elbow.

"Where are we off to?" he asked.

"Back to Galbraith. Someone saw a plumber entering Vicky's property yesterday." She told Fran to send Tracy Vicky's friends' details, and to Tammy, "Ring the insurance company Vicky phoned — I'll send you the email with the digi stuff on. We need to find out who the hell that plumber is."

CHAPTER SEVEN

Joseph stopped halfway back to HQ. He had shit on his mind and needed to talk about it with Natasha before he spoke to Zooby and Anne. Standing at the side of the bike, he lifted his visor instead of taking the helmet off. His phone call to the police earlier had got him jittery — there were cameras out here, and he'd only just remembered that *after* he'd rung them. A novice mistake. What a plankton. Good job he had fake plates, ones he only used when doing the gang's business.

Unlike Anne.

Stop harping on about that.

Natasha remained on the back seat and also raised her visor. "What's the matter? Why did we stop?"

"I dunno." He paced. "All right, I do. I can't . . . This . . . all of this is way more than I can handle."

Natasha nodded. "I'm just glad I'm only the one who visits the new mums afterwards. Taking a kid, killing a mother . . . no, I couldn't stand to do that."

"Why did you agree to join us? Was it just for the money?"

"Yep. I was skint, as in, at the point of having the bailiffs coming round, and that's the only reason I said I'd do this, although when Zooby told me what it was we'd all be doing, I was well shocked. But that first chunk of cash got the worst creditors off my back. One more payment, and I'm free of debt, although . . . that might not matter if I . . ." She shook her head, the helmet strap swinging beneath her chin. "Doesn't matter."

"What doesn't matter?"

She cocked her head and narrowed her eyes. "Can I trust you?"

He stopped pacing and stared at her, incredulous. "After I came and warned you what the fuck was going on with Anne, knowing Zooby could beat the shit out of me for it if he found out? Of course you can."

"Okay." She took a deep breath. "I'm just going to jump in and say it. Can you do me a new passport and birth certificate?"

Joseph's shoulders slumped with relief — he'd thought she was going to tell him something hideous, like killing the mothers was always in the plan and they just hadn't told him. "Thank God you said that. I was thinking of doing the same myself. Well, I already have new documents, made them once I knew what we'd be doing. Just in case. What I meant when I said 'Thank God' was me thinking of just fucking off. You feeling the same, well . . ."

She dug into her back jeans pocket. "I lied at my house, sorry. I didn't need a wee. I was getting this." She handed him a passport photo. "Just in case." She smiled at stealing his words. "I've got a wig on in the pic."

"I can see that. Black hair suits you. You going to dye yours to match this then?"

"Might do."

He got his wallet out and slipped the image behind the plastic pane. It seemed weird doing that, like she was his girlfriend, so he took it out and slid it into a credit card slot. "Where will you go?"

If she was getting paid half as much as him, she'd have enough to set up somewhere else if she kept the second payment and didn't clear her outstanding bills. With a new name, they wouldn't be able to find her to recoup the debt anyway.

She smiled sadly. "No idea. Want to come with me?"

He didn't think she was asking because she fancied him, more along the lines of them escaping together, having each other while they settled in a strange place. It saved them being alone, didn't it? It wasn't a bad idea, that. He had no ties to Shadwell and presumed she didn't either if she could just up sticks.

He asked her anyway. "Won't anyone wonder where you are?"

She shrugged. Stared over his shoulder. Maybe at the whooshing cars, maybe the bleak sky, or maybe the trees lining the other side of the road with their shivering, empty limbs. "I'm out of work at the minute, apart from this job. Been doing some thieving jobs to get cash. I have people, family, but they won't care whether I'm gone or not. If I leave a note saying goodbye, that'll be enough. They'll probably be relieved I'm out of their lives. Same for you, I reckon. After all, what kind of people are we to be doing this shit? Who'd want deviants like us around? We're lowlifes, aren't we."

"That's the thing. I thought I *was* that sort of person, and now . . ."

She nodded absently, still staring. "Now you know you're not. I've kind of got the same thing going on here."

"Yeah, sounds like it."

"So, what's the plan at HQ?" She focused on him again. "How do we get it across to Zooby that Anne's going to bring the whole thing crashing down? And if she's still there with him, it'll be hard to say what we want with her earwigging."

"You know, I was worried about him having a mare at me if I told him I was backing out, but seeing how he was about Anne, I don't know. *Would* he just let me go now with my promise to keep my gob shut? We've been mates for years, and not once have I grassed on him." That was also why he'd refrained from telling the police Anne's name when it came down to it. It'd get his old pal right up turd creek. There was respect among rogues, so Zooby said, lines you just didn't cross no matter what.

Natasha sighed. "I say we back off on Anne until the second job is done. It's tonight, so we're not waiting too long. Once the new mother has left HQ with the kid, been taken home, we leg it. I need that second payment. It's enough to last me months, as well as sort a deposit for a flat. If you go in with me . . ."

He thought about what he'd do for wages once the money ran out. How he'd have to establish himself as the fake documents man elsewhere, although, with his knowledge, his access to the Dark Web, he could do it all online, open a new bank account in his next name, and get people to stump up the cash through PayPal or whatever.

"When will we leave?" he asked.

"Customer Two will be allowed home tomorrow morning, won't she, and Zooby doesn't need to know I didn't go and pay her a visit. So, say, one o'clock? He dished out the last lot of money just before that."

"Yep. I'll have to take my laptop from HQ then. No way can I leave it there. It's got all my contacts on it."

"Won't Zooby ask questions about that? He said we need it to monitor the website."

"My fucking laptop, none of his business. For all he knows, I'm doing work at home — actually, I'll tell him that." He mentally worked out how much he could fit in his saddlebags on the bike when they scarpered. The empty passports — he had about two hundred of those, same with the birth certificates. Then there were clothes, although he could take the bare minimum for now and use the second cash influx to buy new ones once they got to wherever they were going.

"S'pose," she said.

"Try to get all your main things in a backpack because we'll take my bike. I have more dodgy plates. I'll sort the docs for it so it looks legit. Maybe spray the bodywork tonight after Anne's brought the new nipper in. She can sit with

Zooby after." He rubbed a hand around the back of his neck. "Where shall we go?"

"We'd merge better in a city."

"Not London. It's too expensive to live down there. North/south divide and all that."

"York?"

"That'll do. Cheaper rent. Food." He rolled his shoulders, easing the tension out of them. "So, we're going to HQ now but we're not saying anything about Anne, just that Carla has gone?"

"Well, we won't say anything we wouldn't normally say. If you've already had a mare about her and stormed out, stick with that attitude. Zooby will think it's weird if you're suddenly amenable. I'll make out I know nothing about what she's done, then you won't get in the shit for telling me."

"Agreed. I know we've just come from there, but we'll go back and check on Carla again, see if she's come home. If she hasn't, we tell Zooby she might have legged it with the baby. That'll take his mind off me — he might be watching me closely otherwise, what with me kicking off earlier."

"Good call. Come on then." She snapped her visor down.

Joseph did the same, then climbed on the bike and drove back to Carla's. Once again, she wasn't answering, so he trooped inside and did another scout. No Carla. No kid. Shaking his head, he left the house, jogging down the path.

Some old biddy came out and hung her tits over the dividing fence. "If you're looking for the new woman, she went out earlier with a baby. Took a suitcase and a few other bits."

He just about heard that, what with the helmet clamped over his ears. He raised a hand in thanks then sped them to HQ. The pair of them went inside, still with helmets on, and took them off once the door was locked. Joseph plonked his on top of the Pampers boxes.

"Ooh, look who's turned up again," Anne said from the chair. "Thought you'd gone off in a strop. Didn't expect to see you so soon."

Joseph almost ignored her, but his comeback was right there on his treacherous tongue. "I had to pick Nat up, so shut your fucking face." He was doing what Natasha had told him, acting normal, but now Anne had killed someone, he might be better off being politer to her in case she took it into her head to slice *his* face and throat an' all.

"You shut yours," Anne threw back.

What was she, ten?

"What on earth's the matter with you two?" Natasha said, acting all innocent.

"Ask that twat." Anne waved a hand in Joseph's direction.

"You really want her to know?" he asked.

Anne shrugged. "No skin off my hooter."

Did she not mind Natasha knowing, or did she not mind *anyone* knowing? If it was the latter, she was a psycho. Wasn't it better to keep the knowledge of her killing ways to the minimum of people?

Joseph looked around. "Where's Zooby?"

"In with the customers." Anne sniffed. "*Not* that what he's doing is any of *your* business. You're not his keeper, you know."

What the hell was up with her? Had becoming a murderer given her the green light to be a total bitch instead of a slight one? Bloody Nora.

"Anne, I'm not in the mood to argue with you." *I should have given the police your name then fucked off.* But there was his new bank account and PayPal to set up first. He'd do that now, right in front of the cow.

He sat at the table, opposite her, and pulled his laptop towards him. Turning it round, he brushed the touchpad. The news article stared at him, and his anger refreshed. And he got a thought. Zooby could come out from seeing the women any second and catch him sorting the accounts. Joseph would have to make up some bullshit story, and that was too much of an effort at the minute. He snapped the lid down. "I'm going to see how long he'll be. I have something to tell him and shit to do at home." He grabbed a mask and covered his face. Looked at Natasha to convey what he'd meant by that: *Your passport.*

She dipped her helmeted head imperceptibly, and he left the room.

In the corridor, he listened for where Zooby was. Three doors down by the sounds of it. Joseph moved along, catching low murmurs.

"Yes," Zooby said. "Not long, and you can go home with your baby."

"But she's always crying, and I'm so tired." Pause. "Can't cope . . . by myself . . ."

"Look, this mould in here is toxic, but you know why you're here. It's for the bonding period. She's crying because of the mould, you're knackered because of it. I swear, once you leave here, you'll be right as rain. Besides, did you forget what I told you just now? One of my associates will come and check on you once you're home, make sure you're doing okay. Like one of those health visitors. You're not alone in this."

She won't come and check . . . Joseph swallowed. How long would it be before Zooby cottoned on that they'd done a runner? Tonight was a stint in the Grape. Shit, they'd have to go and make nice. It'd be well iffy if neither of them turned up.

Joseph cleared his throat and reached out to knock on the open door.

"Yep?" Zooby said.

Joseph poked his head around the frame. The mother shrieked at the sight of him. Probably the mask putting the shits up her, although she'd seen it before. Maybe Zooby had upped the crap he was injecting into her. She might be having hallucinations.

"Quick word?" Joseph retreated.

Zooby came out, pulling the door to. It didn't deaden the woman's wails, and the fake baby was still blarting — the 'hungry' cry.

"See if it needs a bottle," Zooby shouted through the gap.

"But I'm so sleepy . . ."

Zooby rolled his eyes and scratched his fake beard. "Shit, this itches. She's becoming problematic, and the dolls all seem to cry at the same fucking time. Anyway, what did you want?"

"I've got passports and stuff to do for other people. I'm going home to get them done, so I won't be sitting here with you all day and night anymore. Anne can take my place. People are naffed off because they've paid and I haven't sent them the goods yet. I have to keep these people happy. This scam we're doing won't last forever, so I need my document job to pay the bills when the extra cash runs out. Plus, I have more info for you, so I can either tell you now or do it in front of everyone."

"Where's Nat?"

"Out there." Joseph thumbed in that direction. "I picked her up."

"Right, well . . . Does she know about Anne?"

"I never told her, and if she's read the news, she hasn't said jack to me."

"Should we tell her?"

Joseph was surprised at that, Zooby asking his opinion. "We shouldn't really discuss this here." He glanced at Customer Three's door to make his point and walked off to room eleven, far enough away so none of the women would hear.

Zooby followed. He appeared troubled. "Look, I've been talking to Anne while you were gone. She's . . . she's not bothered she killed someone. Like, *really* not bothered."

"I told you, she's off her nut, but you seemed to think it was okay."

"I was shocked, to be honest. Didn't know how to deal with it so brushed it off. If I come down on her, she could kill me next."

"Then pack this in after Six has got her kid. Don't do the next few rounds. It's too risky. Tell Anne we're stopping soon because of the police being involved. I don't know. Just finish this. You do realise that because we know what she's done, we're accessories after the fact, don't you? Something like that. Even though we didn't do it, we'd go on trial just the bloody same. I don't want to go down for a stretch, do you?"

"No, I fucking well don't."

"Then tell her after Six is packed off home. If you do it before that, she's likely to do something weird."

"What if she kills tonight's mother?"

Joseph hadn't wanted to think about that too much, but there was a possibility she'd repeat last night's antics. "I don't know. Listen, Carla went to visit One this morning, per the plan. One was fine, chipper, but the baby was groggy. She told her the Phenergan would wear off soon. Anyway, when I went round Nat's for a chat, I said I'd take her to check on Lily again, just in case she was still out of it. We can't be doing with Carla going to the bloody doctors just yet. Carla wasn't in. I went inside, checked the house, and it was cold, like, no heating on, and all the baby stuff — bottles, milk, whatever — were gone. Some old bird came out and said Carla had gone somewhere with the baby and a suitcase. I reckon she's scarpered."

"Shite." Zooby played with the beard. "What the hell are we going to do if she's legged it?"

"Calm down. Think about it. If she's gone, that's a good thing. She's out of the area — and our faces. If we don't do the second or subsequent rounds, we don't need Lily anyway. Let the woman enjoy her new kid."

Zooby nodded. "You're right. Okay, you nip off to do your shit. We'll meet in the Grapes at eight."

"Maybe we should stop that an' all. Meeting in public now . . . Dodgy."

"Then come here."

Joseph patted Zooby's shoulder. "It'll work out. Just the six babies in total, right?"

"Yeah."

"I'll take Nat with me now, unless she fancies hanging around here. Want me to tell her about Anne?"

"May as well. She's going to find out anyway."

Joseph walked off, sickened at the sounds coming from the rooms. Snores, fake babies crying, some mothers sobbing, others singing lullabies. This was so wrong, all of it, and the sooner one o'clock tomorrow came, the better he'd feel.

He should never have agreed to do this. But hadn't he beaten himself up about that already?

Change the fucking record, mate.

He pushed the door open and entered the main room. Anne was on his laptop, poking around, Google on the screen. Thank God he'd decided not to get the bank page up. She'd be onto him if he had.

"Oi, get your manky mitts off my stuff," he said. "I've got loads of things on there that're private."

"So I saw." She scraped the chair back and stood. "Files. Lots of names and addresses. Cor, what I could do with those. As in, tell *certain people*, like the police, names and what their new ones are . . ."

"Look, you stupid heifer. If you do that, what's to stop *me* telling certain people what *you* did?"

She threw her head back and laughed, the mad bastard. "Like you'd do that."

"Don't test me."

She sauntered off to the corner chair and sat, sticking her legs out and crossing them at the ankles. Hands on the armrests, she looked as though ice wouldn't melt. Frozen.

Natasha, helmet taken off now, unpacked wet wipes from a cardboard box. "We go through so many of these. Such a waste when they're only being used on dolls. Have you ever wondered why the customers don't ask questions? Like, they don't ever have to change a wet or shitty nappy."

Anne roared with maniacal laughter again, eyes screwed up so tight the skin around them formed wrinkles. "That's because they're thick and doped up to the tits."

Joseph had had enough of being in her company. If he was so inclined, he'd stab the barmy bint and dump her body somewhere she'd never be found. That wasn't an option, though, and he *wasn't* inclined. That was the problem now. He wasn't who he'd thought he was, who he thought he could become if push came to shove. He was no killer.

"Nat, Anne can take over doing that. I need to go, and Zooby said for me to drop you off. We're due back here at eight, not going to the Grapes tonight, so I'll pick you up again about quarter to, yeah?"

Natasha nodded and reached for her helmet. "Fine by me."

"You what?" Anne shot out of the chair, hands on hips like she was their mum or something. "Not going to the Grapes? Fucking hell, I like it when we go there. I was going to try a Screw on the Beach."

Joseph ignored her, taking off his mask. He jammed his helmet on, grabbed his lappy and the power cord, and walked out, sliding his stuff into the saddlebag. Natasha joined him, and once she was on the bike behind him, he zoomed off. Instead of going into Shadwell, he took a left up the track to the woods and stopped in the tarmac car park at the top of the rise. Visor up, he turned to speak to Natasha over his shoulder, telling her everything that had gone on with Zooby.

"So we're still on for tomorrow, yes?" He prayed she hadn't changed her mind. "If you are, I'll do your passport and whatever once I get home. I'll give it to you when I come and collect you later."

"Thanks. And yes, I need to get out of here. Oh, and Anne was well weird while you were gone. She was talking about some woman called Raven who bit the heads off rats and ate them. Said she'd even done it herself."

Joseph shuddered. "Did you believe her?"

"I did. She said it with such conviction."

"Nutter, got to be."

"You're not wrong there."

He had to change the subject else he'd go loopy. "So, back to the other stuff. If Zooby asks you, I told you about Anne. What do you want me to say if he questions me on how you took it?"

"Say I agreed we ought to cut the job short after Six has her baby. It won't matter to us whether they carry on after tonight, because we'll be long gone. Sorry to sound harsh, but I need to compartmentalise, shove this crap in a box in my head, otherwise I won't be able to stop feeling guilty. I was so desperate for the money, I thought I'd be okay with all this. But I'm not."

"Don't beat yourself up. I feel the same. But we'll move on, become better people." He thought of the passports — he couldn't give up doing those. "Well, better people than we are at the minute anyway."

He lowered the visor and drove Natasha home. At his ground-floor flat, he locked the doors and pushed the catches in place on the windows, fretting that Anne would call round and do him in.

CHAPTER EIGHT

Anne sat on the sofa. Raven was in a chair on one side of the fireplace, feeding her baby. Mum had gone out to one of her many cleaning jobs, a 'posh nob' so she'd said, who always left her money on the worktop with a little extra because she knew how Mum struggled.

"That's it, get this milk into your fat gut, you little bitch," Raven said.

She didn't talk to the baby like other mums did to theirs, with that daft voice that sounded like singing. She was harsh instead. Anne didn't like the baby, but she thought Raven should. Weren't you supposed to love your kids? This one was better off with a new mother, one who actually cared.

"What are you staring at, shit for brains?"

Anne jumped and lowered her sights so she wasn't looking directly into Raven's scary eyes. She'd zoned out and hadn't realised the nasty woman had caught her watching.

"Well? Are you going to answer me?" Raven demanded, her cheeks going red.

Anne shrugged.

"You're such a dumb child. No wonder your mum goes out at all hours to work. Means she gets away from you." Raven narrowed her eyes, nose scrunching into the bargain. "You'll be filling your gut as well in a few, after this lump of lard has finished her bottle."

A shudder rippled up Anne's back, a violent one, and she clasped her hands in her lap. Raven wouldn't see them shaking then. Anne knew what she'd have to do, had known as soon as Raven had turned up with a bag the same as what doctors used. That shiny black thing she lugged about with her, a golden padlock on the clasp. She'd convinced Mum it was her baby bag, but it really wasn't. It had small holes punched in the sides so the rats could breathe. They scratched to get out, to find freedom. Squeaked. Raven said she had loads of rats, in several cages in her spare room, a floor-to-ceiling pet shop. She bred them, whatever that was, and people came from all over to buy the creepy things. That was how she made her money, as well as Mum paying her to watch Anne.

"Enjoy our dinner, did you?" Raven asked.

Anne nodded. Mum had made ham sandwiches with fluffy white bread, and Anne had been allowed a yoghurt afterwards for pudding. Strawberry, it was, with big bits in it. She didn't like the bits. The texture reminded her of rat flesh, except that was warm.

"Well, you'll soon be seeing it again when it comes back out." Raven chuckled.

Anne was always sick after eating rat, and Raven used a dessert spoon and scooped it up, feeding it back to Anne, who heaved and regurgitated, and once, Raven had slapped thick tape on Anne's mouth so she'd had no choice but to swallow.

Times with Raven were so hard.

She wanted Mum to come home.

"There, Tub Belly has finished, so I'll just burp the greedy cow, then we can get sorted. You're lucky a few of my rats recently had sprogs. I've brought one of the babies for you to try. It isn't big, hardly has any fur, so you can eat the whole thing in one go. Can you imagine the body popping between your teeth? Tasty little bastards, those babies."

Anne's stomach spasmed, her sandwich and yoghurt already coming up to say hello.

* * *

Anne stared at the main door. Joseph was pushing his luck, talking to her like that. Who did he think he was? She could slit his throat in a second, stopping him from spewing bullshit from his spiteful mouth. It'd be so nice not to have to listen to him.

She nosed at the things on the table. The passports and birth certificates were there, but there was one missing, the boy Zooby fretted they wouldn't find. But there was Dominic. She was looking forward to nabbing him so much. That'd teach Mr Knight for speaking to her all snarky for years, and the kid's abduction would upset Jolene as well, her precious nephew stolen in the night, oh my God, what will we do without him, he was such a sweetheart. So, two hits in one. Anne was the bowling ball, and all the people were the pins. She'd knock every fucker down one by one.

Zooby came in and frowned at her. "Um, what are you up to?" He seemed uneasy, his body movements stiff.

"Just looking at these." She stroked the top passport on the pile. "Guess what?" She was going to tell him her plans, see if he was on her side or Joseph's. God knew what that prat had told Zooby while he'd been here. She'd bet they'd had a secret conflab in the corridor, Joseph poisoning Zooby's mind with regards to her. "I can do two kids tomorrow night." She paused to study his facial expression.

A lift of the eyebrows, the widening of his peepers.

"And," she went on, "the second is a boy. I found one."

Zooby swallowed so forcefully his Adam's apple wobbled. He coughed. Had a frog in his throat, did he? "Where's he from?"

"Better you don't know really."

"Fair enough."

His answer was perfect. It meant Joseph hadn't got to him. Anne could have hugged herself at that. She was the one Zooby liked best, not that bloody gimp.

"Just one thing, though," he said. "Can you *not* kill any more mothers."

She shrugged. "I'll try." *But not quite hard enough. Damn, Zooby, I'm so sorry, but my knife slipped again . . .* She bit back laughter. Christ, it was a stubborn sod, pushing to come out.

"Like you said, tonight's woman has family, she'll be missed. Same with the boy, he has a big family. No promises, though. If they come in and catch me, there isn't much I can do but stab them."

Zooby closed his eyes. Let out a long breath. "Right. I suppose."

What a fella. Top-notch. Maybe they could become serial killer partners in the future. He could hold the women down while she slashed them silly. They could get Joseph to make them new documents, a few sets of them, and they'd tour the country, bumping people off for a laugh.

She decided she'd put doubt in his head, play with him for a bit. Boredom was getting to her. "So Joseph took his laptop. I assume he'll be keeping an eye on the website for new customers while he's at it."

"Yeah."

"How long have you known him?"

"Years. Why?" He frowned.

"Just thinking about trust, that's all. I mean, he was so pissed off I topped that bird. Who knows whether he can handle the heat. For all we know, he might crumble from the pressure."

"He'll cope. He's a good bloke."

"Right. His laptop files say otherwise."

Zooby reared his head back as if in shock, his eyes wide. "How do you mean? And what were you doing poking around on there anyway?"

"One, I was passing the time — that Natasha isn't the most riveting person of the bunch, and I tried talking to her, but she didn't seem to want to engage." That had pissed her off. Why hadn't the woman been more interested in the rat story? Who wouldn't find it fascinating that Anne had eaten some, alive? "And two, I don't trust him. He's iffy. So I poked about. I did it for *us*. Best to be prepared, to know what's coming our way, don't you think? So, those files. He's created over one thousand fake passports, loads of birth certificates, *and* there are cheques he's forged — God knows how he's done that — and credit cards, well, you have no idea how many numbers and CVCs he's got. I mean, he basically allows people to be fraudulent. From what I gathered, he sells card information. I suspect he got it from someone else. You know, bought it off one of those scammers."

"But that's why he's in the gang, because of what he does. Without him, the babies wouldn't have paperwork. He does that kind of shit all the time, has done for years. I know all about that stuff."

"Well, it was the Dark Web 'shit' that bothered me."

He stiffened even more than before. "What Dark Web shit?"

"There was a file called Hurters for Hire. Lots of names and email addresses of people you can contact to duff someone up for you. Kill for you. Why would he need that? Unless . . . He could be planning to eliminate us" — she almost laughed at using 'eliminate' — "after all this is over. Otherwise, why have the list?" There *was* no file, and she was proud of herself for thinking up this lie. Pinocchio had nothing on her.

Zooby appeared suitably startled, and Anne's work was done. She'd sown the seed, and it'd sprout in his mind, spreading its tendrils.

"I'll ask him about that," he said.

"But then he'll think *you've* been poking into his files — he already knows I have. Isn't it better we keep it to ourselves and watch him? Watch our backs as well? Who knows whether someone will be hiding in the dark at some point, ready to jump out and kill us." Laughter inside. Several LOLs.

"Okay." He shivered. "Okay. Um . . . I need a minute." He tugged at his fake beard and walked into the corridor.

Anne smiled and sat on the armchair. Closed her eyes.

She was good at this lark.

* * *

Raven had driven them to Shadwell Hill. It was so dark up here, the only light coming from the headlamps of the car. The baby, sparko in her safety seat, didn't know how lucky she was to be inside and warm. Anne stood at the edge of the parking area, by the tree line. Cold. Shivering. Wishing she was at home and that Mum didn't have to work so many jobs.

"The rats will be along in a minute," Raven said. "Then you'll believe me when I say I'll dump you here if you tell anyone what we get up to. I'll let the animals scoff you, and someone will find your body, all the flesh eaten off."

Anne shuddered, and her eyes stung, hot tears promising to fall. Raven hadn't let her bring a coat, and goosebumps had parked themselves on her arms. She didn't rub them, though. That'd show Raven she was suffering, and the woman would like that. She'd laugh and call Anne pathetic.

"I'll just go and see where they are," Raven said. "Shut your eyes, and don't open them until I say so."

Anne did as instructed. It sounded like Raven was opening the car door, and Anne's heart picked up speed. What if Raven had lied and was really leaving her here? What would Mum think when she got home from work and Anne wasn't there? Would Raven pretend she'd been kidnapped? The rats, they might come out and get her, their teeth so sharp.

She didn't dare open her eyes.

The closing of the door.

Oh God, the engine would start any second, Raven driving away.

The tears fell.

Footsteps. The skitter of small stones on the tarmac.

Anne relaxed. Raven must be going into the woods to find the rats. It was better to see them than be left here, alone. That was what Raven had said on the way — "I want you to actually see them so you know I'm telling the truth. I can call them from their hiding places. They listen to me because I'm the rat whisperer."

The scrunching of undergrowth. A thud. More footsteps, coming closer.

"Open your eyes."

Anne obeyed, staring ahead into the woods, and there, in the illumination of the headlights, rats, their eyes glowing red, some white. They paused as if struck by a magic spell chanted by Raven, who sucked her teeth, a strange sound emerging, and those rats, they darted forward, towards them, as if they were tame and that noise told them what to do.

Anne screamed. She couldn't help it. There must be about twenty rats, all big and fat, fur a dirty brown or black, ears pale, triangular flaps of sticking-up skin. They smiled, those nasty beasts, their two front teeth long, embedded in pallid gums. Shrieks came out of the monsters as they advanced, their pink, hairless paws digging into the mulch. And then they were there, right in front of her, crawling over her shoes, claws lightly scratching her bare legs above her ankle socks.

Anne wet herself.

"See?" Raven asked. "See what I said is true? And oh, you filthy little fucker. You've pissed." She stamped her foot, and the rats scattered, bounding off into the woods. "So now you know. I can command the rats. They'll do whatever I say. Tell your mum what goes on when I babysit you, and I'll bring you here again. Let them eat you like you've eaten them."

But you made me eat them. I didn't want to.

Her bottom lip wobbled. She wanted to cry, really cry.

"Now get in the car, you pissy wretch."

Anne sobbed all the way home.

But Raven laughed.

* * *

The past always got Anne riled up. She hated the way the memories popped into her head without ringing the doorbell first. They were rude, turning up the way they did on her mental doorstep, uninvited. Still, there was a good side to it. They fuelled her to continue what she'd started.

The plan, the call for employment, had been as if fate had directed her to fill out the questionnaire. For years, after she'd finally sorted Raven, she'd wandered through life aimlessly, her desire to kill there, but with no opportunity to execute it. This job had given her an outlet, a way to release the constant pressure inside her and get rid of mothers.

She told herself they were all the same as Raven. It saved her having to acknowledge that what she wanted to do was wrong, that the women didn't deserve what she had in mind for them.

They did deserve it. They had to.

Thoughts of Mum came then. The poor thing had died a couple of years ago — natural causes. Anne wouldn't have stooped *that* low, despite having anger issues regarding being left with Raven — Mum should have been punished somehow, but Anne didn't have the heart. She'd been left with no one whatsoever, her dad never a fixture, just someone she saw in town every so often, sitting on a bench, his clothes filthy, and he drank from a bottle enclosed in a brown paper bag. A tramp, an alky, so Raven had informed her. And after Mum's death, she couldn't even rush to Raven for some kind of warped comfort because she'd killed her. The baby, though, she hadn't touched her. She'd gone off to a better life with a better mother, just like the customers' babies would. Like that Maisie/Lily kid already had.

Zooby came back in with one of the dolls, its blue eyes creepy and staring, and this one didn't have a lot of hair compared to the one Carla had looked after. He held it dangling by the arm, and it looked obscene, as if the fake was real and he was abusing it. "There's something you should know."

Oh, so he was confiding in her, was he? That was a good sign.

"What's that then?" She folded her hands over her stomach.

"Customer One seems to have fucked off." He sat at the table and rested his brow in his hands.

How should she play this? Calm and collected? Panicked? She went for the former. "No biggie. I'll just get another kid, and we can do the rounds with that one instead."

He raised his head and stared at her. "What? Aren't you worried?"

"What about? Carla would have gone after we stole Lily back anyway. I think she's got the right of it, considering how much she paid for the kid. I mean, no offence, but having them hanging around Shadwell when they've been stolen from here . . . Stupid much? Better to have them far away so no one spots the babies. What with us recycling them, someone, somewhere is going to recognise them eventually. Why not just steal a baby each time for the new customers?"

"Hmm. You're right."

Blimey, he was really trusting her now. Maybe her serial killer couple idea had legs after all. She'd put the feelers out. "Want to come with me tonight? See how it's done?"

He blanched. "Err, no. We all stick to our own jobs. You've been employed to do the kidnapping. I keep track of the situation and look after the customers. Joseph sorts the documents and watches the customers while I'm sleeping, plus he mans the website. Natasha checks the customers and babies afterwards. Although . . . Shit. With Joseph busy on his normal job . . . Can you hang around here with me?"

"Yeah. I don't have another job to go to anymore. May as well. But I don't want to kip in that chair. Got a spare camp bed we can set up?"

"Yeah. And there's all those throw blankets we bought. Use one of them. Actually, I'm going to sort that now and get some shuteye first. You keep guard."

Anne had well and truly got her feet under the table.

Brilliant.

CHAPTER NINE

Carla had left Lily with her parents while she went upstairs to her old room. She had to unpack. Lily was asleep on Mum's chest anyway, and Carla didn't have the heart to disturb her. They wouldn't be able to bond for long, seeing as she was going to France, so what could a bit of coddling hurt?

She hefted the suitcase on the bed then took some hangers out of her pine wardrobe, the doors a little battered now but a stalwart in her memory all the same, despite the passage of time since she'd lived here. They'd once had posters attached with good old Blu Tack, all manner of men in bands or off her favourite programmes on the telly, striking poses, beaming smiles, perfect hair. She'd told herself she'd meet a great bloke like them one day, except she'd had dickheads breezing in instead, the biggest one Liam.

In her youth, apart from dreaming about her prince charming, she'd lounged on her bed thinking of nothing much more than what to wear to school the next day, or if she could get away with putting eyeliner on, hoping the head, Mr Barclay, didn't notice and give her detention. Or she'd get excited about spending her birthday money in Claire's Accessories, even getting her ears pierced in there.

Things had been so simple then, although at the time, she'd have sworn they were hard.

Funny how your perspective changed, how life threw unexpected curveballs that swatted you in the gut, literally in her case, and doubled you over with the pain of it. Never would she have thought a simple car journey would change her world to such a degree. The drunk driver had served three years for good behaviour, returning to his previous life, continuing as normal while Carla had dropped into a spiral of despair and a depression so deep it had engulfed any ability she may have had to claw her way out.

"Stop it," she muttered and swiped the tears away.

It didn't take long to hang her clothes, then came Lily's, so cute and small, so pink and white, the velvet of the sleepsuits so soft. The shop labels hung from the neck tags, a good brand, so Weird Glasses hadn't scrimped on the cost. She could hardly believe she was doing this for real, that it wasn't some figment of her desperate imagination. Next, she pushed the suitcase under the bed for now, thinking she could have a little lie down for a moment. Check her phone. Her emails. Any messages.

Her stomach didn't like that idea, tightening, squeezing. She'd put the mobile on silent since leaving Shadwell, not wanting to have her alerts going off while driving, and then later, with her parents. They'd have casually told her to answer, to not leave the person hanging, but the only people she'd get texts from now were those in the organisation. She'd cut everyone she knew off — they'd question her having a baby; they knew she'd had something happen in the pelvic region. Work colleagues tended to find these things out when you were signed off work for two months.

What if the organisation knew she'd left?

What if they sent someone to look for her?

What if they'd put a tracker app on her phone while it had been in her handbag?

They'd had access to it, could have done it easily, and she'd been none the wiser.

She'd check the Shadwell Facebook page, where they said they'd leave cryptic messages if they couldn't get hold of her any other way. She looked at her notifications. None. No missed calls, no texts, so maybe the woman hadn't gone to the house for a second time today and discovered her gone. Maybe she'd return tomorrow to check on Lily. They'd only find out then that Carla wasn't there.

She brought the Facebook page up anyway. Scrolled. Spotted a headline. Clicked the link.

"Oh shit. Oh fuck . . ."

All the blood seemed to drain out of her.

The words told her things she didn't want to know.

A mother, killed.

A baby, taken.

A picture of Lily, *oh my God, Lily.*

And then her phone rang, the tone shrill and frightening, cutting into her psyche, the bar across the middle containing the organisation's name, so stark and scary.

They knew. Oh God, they knew.

* * *

It took Carla a while to calm down. She'd taken the battery out, and the SIM, and thought up a plan: she'd leave Lily with Mum and Dad, saying she needed some supplies for Lily.

In the car now, she drove away, heading for the next town over. It took twenty minutes to get there, and she parked in the multi-storey. A quick walk took her to the shopping area, and she strode past a bin and placed the SIM inside. In the mobile shop, she bought a new SIM, pay-as-you-go like the old. She'd only give her number to Mum and Dad.

That sorted, she felt much better, and even managed a smile walking past the Oh, Baby! boutique. There were so many pretty things for girls in the window that she couldn't resist and went inside. Lily would look lovely in that lilac dress with tiny flowers all over it, and Mum, she'd approve.

She didn't hold with baby girls having leggings or jeans, or T-shirts and the like. Dressing them older before their time, she called it.

Carla browsed all the dresses, the two women behind the counter nattering away. It wasn't until she picked up 'murder' and 'kidnap' that she properly listened, her tummy protesting with the sharp spike of fear stabbing it, her heart hurting it thumped so hard.

"Absolutely heartbreaking," one said. "To think that poor woman put her baby to bed, and everything was fine, then she got up in the night to see someone in the nursery. I mean, that must have been what happened because she was killed in the baby's room."

"Oh, I know. Bloody tragic. Had to have been the father, don't you think? They say the parents are usually to blame, and what with one of them being dead, that only leaves him."

"Maybe he wanted access, she denied it, so he stabbed her. It said on the news she'd had her face slashed, her neck, too. Imagine bleeding out like that, knowing you're going to die, knowing your baby is left with a killer, and your last thought is whether they're going to kill your baby, too."

Carla couldn't stand it anymore. She grabbed three random dresses off the rack and approached the counter. Thankfully the women stopped talking about the murder, one of them ringing up the purchases, the other taking security tags off the clothes.

"Aww, got a little girl, have you?" one asked.

Carla nodded. "Yes, Lily." She was so proud to be able to say that, despite the mother being killed so she could have what she wanted. Was it bad for her to only be concerned with getting away so she could keep Lily to herself? Was she a wicked person?

"How old?"

"Six months," she said deliberately, not wanting four months known, that age being given in the paper.

"Oh, these won't fit her then, they're too small," the other one said, pausing the job of putting them in a bag.

"They're fine." Carla smiled — it was tight; it was *mind your own fucking business*. "She's tiny. Premature." How the lie tripped so easily.

"Ah, that explains it. That's thirty pounds then, love."

Carla paid using her debit card, the niggle of doubt creeping in that the organisation would know she'd spent money here. Like with her phone, they could have done something to track her expenditure, couldn't they?

You're just being paranoid. They can't get your bank details.

But they'd got a birth certificate, a passport, and they'd faked Lily's birth information at that hospital in Oxford so it produced a medical number. Hacking. What was to stop them doing the same in her account? Who knew how clever they were?

A cold sweat drenched her, and she took her card, the carrier bag, and left, calling a shaky thank you over her shoulder. She ran to Boots, busying her raving mind by dumping powdered milk, a rattle, and some Sudocrem in her basket, plus some of that teething gel in case Lily had trouble there.

While she stood in the queue, more people discussed the abduction, speculating as to where she could have gone and that they hoped she was found alive and not dead.

"That would be terrible, but what if the kidnapper is a paedophile? Imagine what they're doing to that kiddie *right now*."

Carla's world seemed to shrink, the shop narrowing around her into a rectangular tunnel, the edges fuzzy, a cashier so far away at the other end.

A customer sighed. "Doesn't bear thinking about, does it."

On and on it went, and by the time a cashier became free behind the long counter, Carla's view expanding once more, she was on the verge of having a panic attack.

She couldn't stay in the UK a moment longer than necessary.

If she did, she risked losing Lily, and that wasn't something she was prepared to do. She hadn't gone through all this for nothing. Moving to Shadwell. Meeting with Weird Glasses. The mouldy room.

The organisation had lied about where her baby had come from. The mother hadn't wanted to give her up at all. She'd *died* because of what Carla needed.

It doesn't matter. None of it does. I have a child, and that's the most important thing. Maisie is Lily. Maisie no longer exists.

She's mine.

* * *

Carla dropped the Boots bag in the hallway but took the other one containing the dresses into the living room. Lily was still asleep on Mum. Dad snored in a chair, catching flies.

Mum was reading on her phone, and she looked up, tears in her eyes. "Have you read the news?"

Carla shook her head. "I haven't had the time. Why?"

"There's this baby. She's been kidnapped. It breaks my heart — oh, the mother was murdered, the child taken. Dreadful."

"Oh, that's so awful." Carla sat beside her mother and checked Lily was breathing. God knew what that stuff the organisation had given her did to such a small person.

Mum went on, "She looks so much like Lily, too."

Carla's stomach knotted. "Aww, babies can look the same." She remembered stroking her curly hair, then Weird Glasses bringing her back in without it. There was no doubt in her mind that Lily was the child everyone was looking for.

"That's true enough," Mum said. "The kidnapped baby is called Maisie. Such a pretty name."

"It's lovely." Carla dug into the carrier bag, wincing. She'd forgotten to be quiet about it; the crackles could wake her daughter. She'd have to get a handle on that sort of behaviour, or people would think it odd that she clattered about as usual, as if she hadn't had a baby up until now. "Look what I got her." She drew the dresses out and fanned them on her lap.

"Oh, now they're gorgeous. You'll need to wash them first, though. The material has all sorts of chemicals in it, so I heard. It's not good for the baby's skin."

Carla hadn't known that, and there was Lily now, in one of the brand-new outfits Weird Glasses had given her. Were the chemicals keeping her asleep, not the effects of the Phenergan? A kernel of panic unfurled inside her. "Oh, well, I'll have to go and get her other clothes then. They're all new, too. I'll pop them in the wash."

"Why are they all new?" Mum frowned.

Carla had to think on her feet. "When I left in a hurry, I couldn't pack all her things."

"Oh, you poor thing."

Carla left the room, eager to get away in case Mum brought the abduction up again.

How the hell was she going to get through her time here without breaking down?

CHAPTER TEN

Helen Slocombe was an ancient sort, the kind with leathery skin and an old-fashioned tight perm, gunmetal grey, the hair coarse, wire wool. She sat in a floral-patterned chair by the living room window, and it reminded Bethany of the one in the back of the lorry in the evil butcher case. This one was in a prime spot for nosing out and seeing what the neighbours were getting up to. "Better than daytime TV," Helen had said.

They all had cups of tea in hand, poured from a 'proper pot' and 'none of this teabag business'. Bethany had to admit, it did taste good. She didn't have time to ponce around with a pot at home, though, so would just enjoy this drink while she could.

"So I thought to myself, who's that there then?" Helen gestured to the window in a queen's wave, the back of her hand liver-spotted, veins bulging. "We don't get many cars down here during the day. Mostly everyone works, except me, of course, and a couple of stay-at-home mums. Oh, and then there's Harry, off with his broken leg, and Mitchell, that fella who hurt his back from falling off a ladder. And . . . Okay, I was wrong. There are plenty of us around during the day, just not vehicles. Regardless, I wondered what a plumber was doing here, and I thought about burst pipes or boilers going on the blink, that sort of thing. Funny what you entertain, what certain events set off in your head. He got out of his van and went to that young woman's door. She's lived here for about fifteen months, rarely speaks unless you engage her. Always has a sad air about her."

"Did you get a good look at him?" Bethany asked.

"Oh yes. I have the perfect vantage point here, and there's a hole in my nets, haven't got around to sewing it up, so I was able to see him clearly through that. A spyhole." She tittered as only old ladies could. "Brown hair, and he must have been about thirty. He went in and came out again pretty sharpish, taking some machine or other out of his van. It had a wide hose, I remember that. And that van; Nigel's Waterworks Repairs was on the side."

Bethany glanced at Mike, and he took his phone out to message the team.

"What was he wearing?" Bethany sipped some tea.

"A white boiler suit, which I thought was silly really. He must get dirty in his job, being near all the dusty pipes. That's a boil wash every night with white vinegar if ever there was one. Good for stains, that is, *and* it cleans the drum at the same time. No need for that Calgon business."

Noted. "Did you see him come out again?"

Mike's phone beeped.

Helen nodded. "Yes. It was about an hour later, because I timed him, and he put his machine away and drove off."

Was it that van another neighbour had heard in the early hours?

Mike cleared his throat and waved his phone. "Well, we know he was a legitimate tradesman."

Bethany nodded to acknowledge that info.

"That's a relief," Helen said, "because I wouldn't mind using him to put in a new toilet. My one downstairs, well, it's leaking at the base of the pedestal. I think there's a crack inside the pan, which is a worry. Do plumbers fit toilets? Oh, I don't know."

While the message Mike had received had obviously confirmed the plumber was genuine in what he did for a living, it didn't mean the man hadn't returned later to kill Vicky and take Maisie.

"Perhaps try someone else, Helen," Bethany suggested. "We don't really know who he is yet, so hold off."

"Could he be the killer?" Helen waggled her tree-root fingers. "I haven't had this much excitement since my Bob took me to Blackpool thirty-odd years ago and we got drunk in a creepy little pub."

I wouldn't call murder exciting, but whatever. "We'll leave you be now. Thank you for your time."

"Oh, that's quite all right. Happy to have helped."

Bethany left the house, Mike beside her, and halfway across the road, her phone twanged.

Isabelle: ERM, STRANGE FIND ALERT. YOU MIGHT WANT TO COME BACK TO VICKY'S. THERE'S A PRESENT UNDER THE COT.

Bethany: WE'RE OUTSIDE. GIVE US A MINUTE.

"Isabelle's got something," she said. "Best we get suited up."

While they pulled on outfits from the SOCO van, Mike elaborated on the message he'd received.

"Leona said the plumber was called out by Franklin's Insurance. Vicky had a leaking pipe under her kitchen sink, water everywhere. The machine was used to suck it up, as a fair bit had got on her floor." He snapped gloves on. "The call was taken by Jolene Lyme, and she said the plumber is on their approved list, although she doesn't remember taking that particular ticket. He phoned in afterwards to say what work had been done, hence me knowing about the machine, and that was that. He's called Nigel."

"I wouldn't have known if you hadn't said . . ." She smiled.

"Well, no."

"You don't get it, do you?"

"What?"

"I was being sarcastic. The van had Nigel's Waterworks on the side of it. You must remember that because you sent the message about it to Leona."

"Shit, so I did." He popped a hat on.

Bethany did the same, tucking all the strands inside. "So did you message back asking for this Nigel's address and phone number, or did Leona already supply them?"

"She did."

"Bloody brilliant, that woman is. Get hold of him now — we can drive to wherever he's working. I'll nip inside to see what's got Isabelle's knickers in a twist."

She signed the log and went up the stairs, standing by the baby's bedroom doorway. Isabelle was staring out of the window — she must have opened the curtains since Bethany had been here last — while a SOCO dusted the wardrobe door for prints. Bethany hadn't noticed it before, but some books were laid out like a fan on the chest of drawers, as if a stack had been knocked over. Had there been a struggle?

"What is it?" she asked.

Isabelle turned to face her. "Bloody revolting, that's what it is. In that box on the floor there." She pointed to a plastic one, about the size of those used for packed lunches.

Bethany entered, walking on the evidence steps, ignoring Vicky's body as best she could. It'd be there for a while yet, until SOCO had finished with the room. She crouched to peer at the contents and recoiled, almost landing on her arse. "Um, a mouse?"

"I'd say it's a rat."

"With no head."

"Right. And it seems to have been ripped off rather than chopped."

The blood and flesh had dried, crusty from exposure to the air. Some carpet fibres had stuck to the fur. Bethany tried to imagine someone ripping the head off and couldn't. "Wouldn't it need quite a bit of force to decapitate it by using hands?"

"Who said hands? Look closer. You'll see one small, straight slice and the rest of the edges are ragged. Teeth?"

Bloody hell . . . "Someone *bit* it off?" Bethany retched and stood so she wasn't anywhere near the poor creature.

"I think so."

"So it must have been placed under the cot by this freak we're after."

"Unless Vicky enjoyed chomping on the little beasts and she put it there." Isabelle smiled. "I was joking, by the way."

"I realise that . . ." Someone walked over Bethany's grave, and she shook her shoulders to get rid of the sensation. "So the rat means something, but buggered if I know what that is."

"Vicky's a rat? As in, someone told her a secret and she blabbed?"

"That's a plausible angle, one we could look into, but with no real friends, it's hard to believe someone would entrust her with a secret anyway."

"I'm just miffed about all this blood." Isabelle pointed at the pool beneath Vicky's neck. "Some of it might be the rat's if they bit the head off in here. It's bound to have dripped. Aradul's got his work cut out for him — that's if he's on shift today. I forgot to ask him last night. We went to the Lamb Shank. That bloody barmaid, Rita, is a riot."

Aradul was Isabelle's boyfriend, and she usually used her charms on him to push for results faster. He was great at helping them out, nothing was ever too much trouble. He was the kind of fella you couldn't imagine being down. Always smiling, that one.

"Here's hoping he is. Have the blood samples been sent in already then?" Bethany asked.

"Yep. I felt the sooner the better."

"Makes sense."

"The killer might have nicked themselves with the knife, so some of that blood could also be theirs."

Mike appeared on the threshold. "So where's the fire then?"

"A dead rat under the cot, now in a box," Bethany said. "Isabelle thinks the head's been bitten off."

"You what?" He indicated with a wave for Bethany to come out so he could use the steps and look.

She stood in the doorway. "Honestly, who does that, though."

Mike approached the box and went down on his haunches. "Bloody hell. Imagine if they did it while it was still alive."

"I'm guessing they did." Isabelle grasped the end of the cot, her gloves squeaking on the wood. "Shit, I thought that was the rat then."

Bethany laughed.

"Not funny." Isabelle's forehead scrunched. "I'm going to move this now all the preliminaries have been done, and you'll see the patch of blood where the rat was. Also, there's a line of blood dots where the animal seems to have been thrown under there."

"How come you didn't see it when you first came in?" Mike asked.

"I did check under the cot and would have seen the animal had there not been a blanket on top of it. Well, half a blanket, as the other half was fed through the cot bars. Maybe it fell when the baby was picked up. There's blood on it as well, so the rat was bleeding out on the carpet, the blood still wet when the blanket landed. Here you go, see." Isabelle lifted the cot end and pushed the bed forward until it was well away from the main crime scene area.

Yes, the rat had definitely been lobbed across the floor, and Bethany imagined a killer getting down on their knees in order to throw it beneath. Why bite its head off, though? Why bring a rat here at all? There hadn't been a cage in the house when she'd done the walkaround earlier, so it wasn't

Vicky's pet, and the garden contained nothing but an old cracked patio chair and rotary washing line, leaning as if half cut. No hutch, nothing to keep a rat in. She thought about it being allowed to run around willy-nilly, like some people did with rabbits, but there weren't any food bowls on the floor, nor a litter tray, if one was even used to housetrain rats. She didn't have a clue.

"Forensics will soon know regarding the rat," Isabelle said. "Saliva will be present on the fur."

"What I want to know is, where's the head?" Mike scratched his with the heel of his hand, the suit hood rustling.

"We've been unable to locate it," Isabelle informed him. "So perhaps it was taken with them for whatever bizarre reason. Honestly, the minds of these people . . . I just don't understand their logic at all."

"Me neither. We'd better go," Mike said. "We're meeting Nigel Urba in ten minutes."

"Okay." Bethany sighed. "Well, keep us posted, Izz. If that head turns up . . ."

"Will do." Isabelle nodded. "Who's Nigel?"

"A plumber who was here yesterday," Mike said.

"Do me a favour and nab his prints for me then." Isabelle bagged the bloodied blanket. "Elimination purposes."

"I'll grab a machine from the SOCO van for that." Bethany smiled and walked downstairs. She signed out, left her protective clothes in a large evidence bag by the front door, got the fingerprinting kit, and waited for Mike in the car.

He flumped in, then plugged an address into the satnav. He leant his head back. "Now then, what's the rat all about?"

She told him Isabelle's suggestion and why Bethany had discounted it.

"Hmm," Mike said. "I'm inclined to agree with you. Who would tell her a secret if she didn't have friends, and again, for the same reason, who would she tell it to?" His message tone sounded, and he read the text. "Ah, that uni girl *is* in Scotland. Alibi in place — one of the teachers gave an evening lecture that went on past midnight, apparently unusual for it to go on that long, and he remembers her sitting there throughout."

"Right." She started the engine and drove off. "So the upset girl theory is out of the window, and with Maisie's father in hospital — d'you know, I've forgotten his name already — it wasn't him."

"Greg Walker."

"That's it."

"I've got another message. The monetary footprints came in on everyone. No large sums of cash in or out, nor was there a pattern of someone withdrawing cash to save up and pay a big kill fee. Vicky was pretty skint. Universal Credit, just the amenities, rent, and council tax going out, a payment to a catalogue of a tenner each month, and one to the insurance place. Asda online shop every fortnight, totalling thirty-five quid or thereabouts."

"So she'd survived on around seventeen a week for food? Fucking hell. Nappies aren't cheap, so they'd have eaten into her budget. Poor girl."

"I know. I always feel sad when I see their bank accounts. Like, they were living, you get a feel for their lives, then it's all gone. No more Asda coming to her door."

"When did that Asda money come out?"

"Hang on, Fran sent us an email with the info." He prodded his screen. "Here we go. Let me just see . . . Ah, there. Eight days ago."

"So it wouldn't be a rogue Asda bloke bumping her off."

"Unless he came back."

"There is that. Get Fran to find out who brought the shopping and look into whoever it is." She squeezed the steering wheel in frustration. "We're actually floundering, aren't we."

"Yep." Mike typed on his screen.

"Never mind. We're here now."

She glanced out of the window. A posh residential street, all the homes detached, large buggers with fancy lead-paned windows and shiny front doors with elegant knockers. Nigel's van was parked in front of her car, and it needed a good wash. Lots of filth on the back doors, clean stripes where he'd brushed it to touch the handles.

"He's in that one there." Mike pointed to number three. "I'll ring him, tell him we've arrived."

Bethany closed her eyes for a moment, but the image of the headless rat popped up, so she opened them again. A brown-haired man strode out of the house, phone pressed to his ear, so she waved, and he slid the mobile into his boiler suit pocket. It was white with streaks of dirt, and she wanted to pass on Helen's advice about white vinegar but reckoned he'd think her a right weirdo.

Out on the pavement, she introduced them and asked the standard questions first. With those over, she went on with, "Did you notice anything about Vicky that stood out?"

"What, apart from her panicking her landlord would have to replace the floor plus the cupboard under the sink? Nope. All right, she was fretting about her baby being hungry — couldn't get to the fridge without wading through water, see — so I sucked it up quickly, then the baby could have a bottle. I tell you, these landlords ought to be shot. That pipe was old as arseholes. The pipes were subpar and had corroded around the joint. If that had happened when the poor girl was asleep, she'd have had a bigger problem on her hands. The water would have ended up flooding the whole of the ground floor."

"Did you know Vicky other than for the callout?"

"Nah, I live in Farley, only come here for work. I don't socialise anyway. The missus says one bevvy with the lads turns into ten and me falling over from the drink. She's got a point — I can't handle the beer. I can't be gadding about like I'm in my teens anymore anyway. We've got a kiddie on the way."

"Have you heard the main news story today?"

"As it happens, I've been run off my feet since seven. Every call has been from Franklin's — greatest thing that happened workwise, me getting my foot in the door there. I haven't even stopped to eat, although the bird in that house there, she's rustling me up a sandwich. Bacon, she said. Brown sauce."

Bethany's mouth watered. "So you're unaware of what happened to Vicky and her baby then."

"Gawd, she's never had another leak somewhere, has she?"

"Um, no. She was murdered during the night, and her baby was taken."

Nigel staggered backwards, plonking his backside on the low brick garden wall. His white face said it all — he'd had a bloody good shock. "It was *her*?" He shook his head and rubbed his temple. "The customer here, she was talking about something like that, but she didn't mention any names. Stone me."

"So you understand why I asked if anything stood out."

"Yeah, I get it, but no, it was all about the water, the mess, and her littlun."

"Would you mind giving us a fingerprint sample? Only, yours will be in the kitchen, and we don't want to be chasing the identification of who they belong to. We can discount you right away."

"Of course, yeah, whatever you want." He stared across the street. "Bloody hell. That's knocked me for a hundred, let alone six."

Mike went off to the car then returned with the device. He got to work, and with the prints sorted, they said their goodbyes. Bethany left Nigel her card in case he recalled anything, but she walked off convinced it wasn't him.

"Where to now?" Mike asked as she drove them away.

"Where do you think?"

"Somewhere with a bacon sarnie."

"Yep. Damn that sodding Nigel. He's made me want one now."

She found a nice café, and they entered, choosing to sit in a corner at the back. It was waitress service, so they put in their order and chatted.

"Right, I need to say this out loud so I don't forget," Bethany said. "Unless something major comes up, the order for the rest of the day is as follows. We eat, then go back to the station. The crime scene photos have probably been uploaded by now, so we'll go through those. There's our paperwork so far that needs doing. There's umpteen other things on the whiteboard that Fran's probably added in our absence. Then there's a phone call to Tracy — I need to touch base and see if she's come up with anything. Oh, and a quick chat with Rob on the front desk — an update on the uniform situation looking for Maisie is in order. There's also the feedback regarding CCTV on that road where the phone was pinged when that bloke rang in about the killer. By then, it'll be home time, and if we haven't got anything at that point, we'll call it a day."

The waitress brought their coffees over then walked off. The sarnies must be coming soon — but not soon enough. Bethany was hungry.

"In the meantime, let's act like normal humans and take some time out."

Mike sighed and looked over at the large window. "Spain this is not."

"No, but what it is still begins with S."

"Yeah, Shadwell."

"No," she said. "Shit. It really is a big bag of shit."

CHAPTER ELEVEN

The afternoon seemed to float by in a haze of work, everyone doing their various tasks. Bethany had completed her statements for today, and she'd just finished writing to DCI Kribbs, shooting him an email rather than bothering him with a face-to-face meeting. He was busy with other people anyway and would appreciate her leaving him alone. If she remembered rightly, he had some top brass in to discuss costs and whatnot. So long as they didn't cut any funding for her team, she'd be happy.

She left her office, muscles aching from being hunched over in her chair, and joined the others in the incident room, just as Fran jumped up, punching the air.

"We have the still of a vehicle, a motorbike, parked up on the verge of that road where the call was made." She pointed to her monitor. "A man is beside it, see? No visual on his face as his back is to the camera, though. Okay, write this down on the board for me, will you, Leona? He's medium build, stands about five ten. The plates have been run, and it belongs to a Samuel Biggins, forty-two Gladstone House."

"Bollocks," Bethany muttered. "The Heights estate."

She hated that area. Uncle Crack, the big-time dealer the drug's unit hadn't been able to pin anything on, lived there — supposedly — in a high-rise, although he did have another, swankier property elsewhere in Shadwell. She suspected the high-rise was a base, filled with your average person's furniture so as not to arouse suspicion that he earnt a packet — she should know, she'd been in it on another case. He probably used it for when people came round to put in orders, then left there to go to the better house for the night. He had people outside on the balcony walkway of the high-rise at all times, young men on guard, watching for 'the feds' as they called them.

Since when had good old 'copper' not been a good enough term?

"Never mind. We're unlikely to see Crack anyway," she said, more to herself than anything.

The man unnerved her in every way, his eyes, so compelling, drawing her in. Whenever she was near him, she had to mentally pull away so he didn't lure her with his charm. She couldn't explain how she felt about him and hated what he did to earn money, but his charisma, that left her muddled.

She'd asked herself once if she fancied him, even if just a little bit, and she supposed the attraction was there, as it would be for anyone noticing someone was a bit of all right. But Vinny, her late husband, was the love of her life, and she didn't have any plans to start again with someone new, and especially not a *Peaky Blinders* Tommy lookalike who lived off the proceeds of selling drugs.

"So we'll nip to see this Samuel fella then, Mike." She smiled at him, sorry that they had to do this because he appeared tired. "Everyone else, carry on until five, then call it a day unless Samuel Biggins turns out to be the bloke we want. Then we'll need warrants and such to search his place for Maisie — I'm going on the assumption that if he's afraid of getting dragged into this because of his association with the killer, he may have something to do with the abduction. Crime scene photos still need looking at, so on you go."

Down at the front desk, she checked in again with Rob regarding the uniform search for the baby. As with his earlier report, nothing had come in. The outlying fields surrounding Shadwell were still being checked, as was Shadwell Hill itself, the woods in particular. So far, no clothing, no suspicious ground disturbance that could indicate a grave, and no body.

The kid was in a house or building, she had to be.

She thanked Rob and waved. Out in the car park, she drew in some fresh air, breathed it out slowly, and got in the driver's seat, thinking she still had to ring Tracy Collier yet. She fired off a message to her instead.

Bethany: ANYTHING?

Tracy: NOPE, SOD ALL. WE'LL KEEP PLODDING ON.

Mike sat beside her and sorted the satnav, then they were off to see Biggins. Her stomach cramped as she turned onto the Heights, the high-rises looming in the distance at the end of the long road that bisected the estate. Upon their arrival at the worst part, where poverty was rife and crimes rampant, she tensed, looking out for Crack's car. There had been a time he'd driven past her, and both of them had glanced in their rearview mirrors. Eye contact had been made, and she'd moved on quickly, wanting to get out of his orbit.

But his car wasn't anywhere, thank God, so she parked up on the rough tarmac area outside Gladstone House. Only cars were visible, no motorbikes. She cut the engine, working out where forty-two would be. The fourth floor, certainly, but which side? On this building, the balcony walkways went all around, so they took the stinky, graffitied lift to the correct floor and searched until they found Biggins' place. His bike wasn't outside his door either, like she'd suspected it might be, so perhaps he was out on it.

A possible wasted journey.

She knocked on the door.

It took about half a minute, and it was opened. The man who stood in front of them was neither five ten nor medium build. He must be five-four and was certainly rotund, nothing like the figure of the fella on the verge. His clothes, a tight fit, did no favours and showed every curve of his rolls, one of them flubbing out between the bottom of his grubby white T-shirt and his boxer shorts waistband.

"Samuel Biggins?" she asked, holding up her ID. "DI Bethany Smith and DS Mike Wilkins. We're here about your bike."

"Haven't had one for months."

"Oh, it's just there's one registered in your name that we're interested in."

Mike took his pad out and found a page. He repeated the number plate.

"Blimey," Biggins said. "That's the last one I owned. I sold it to a garage. That place on Parson's Lane. D'you know it?"

"Yes. When did you sell it?"

"Urr, got to be six months ago now. Hang on, I'll get you the receipt. I keep everything like that. Never trust a car dealer, that's what my old mum used to say." He vanished then reappeared, paper in hand, his breathing shallow. Exercise wasn't his best friend. "Here you go."

"Thanks." She stared down at the details. "Oh. This says it's a moped."

"Yeah. Bloody ancient, it was. Couldn't afford to get it fixed. Shame, because I nipped about everywhere on it. I bought a second-hand pushbike instead for thirty quid." He used his thumb to indicate a scratched BMX leaning against the hallway wall.

"I see. Well, sorry to bother you."

"No problem." He scratched his nuts and shut the door.

Oh . . .

Bethany and Mike headed for the lift.

"The plates have been taken, put on the motorbike," Mike said.

"Yep, sounds likely." She jabbed the lift button. "I swear, I get my hopes up every time, yet I know we're going to find dead ends."

Mike shrugged and held a splayed hand out for her to enter the lift before him. "Not to worry. We'll go to Parson's Lane, see what happened to the moped."

"He said it was ancient." She reckoned it was more likely broken up for parts.

Mike nodded. "But the plates would still be okay."

"Hmm."

The lift trundled downwards, a grating sound putting her on edge. It'd be sod's law that the damn thing broke down.

They stepped out, much to her relief, and walked quickly to the car. Bethany ignored the catcalls from unseen people — maybe she and Mike stood out as coppers and residents felt the need to heckle, thinking it was funny, and maybe it brightened an otherwise boring day. She got behind the wheel, Mike buckled up, and they nipped to Parson's Lane.

Ken Corby's Cars was a decent-sized effort, around ten cars on the forecourt, some newish, others not so much, one in particular with rusty arches and a busted headlamp — bad advertising or what. Better vehicles were inside behind the large showroom windows, gleaming, smart, the price tags far exceeding those outside. A sign proclaimed finance was available if a deposit was put down, and she dreaded to think how much that would cost out of a monthly wage.

They exited the car, and no sooner had her feet touched the ground, a skinny man in his fifties, monk hairdo alert, came out of the showroom and rushed towards them, his dark-blue suit fronts flapping, grey tie swinging. An eager beaver then. Well, he'd be disappointed, because no sale was in his future regarding them. Wounded.

"What are you looking for today, sir, madam?" He came to a breathless stop in front of them, beads of sweat on his vein-addled temples.

She produced her ID. "DI Bethany Smith, DS Mike Wilkins. Nothing to worry about. We're enquiring about a bike you bought from a Mr Samuel Biggins." She thought back to the receipt and told him the date. "You gave him fifty pounds, as I recall."

"I wouldn't know offhand, not that far back. If you'd like to come inside, I'll check the records on my computer."

"Brilliant."

They followed a rather crestfallen Ken Corby inside, his shoulders slumped with the burden of 'no sale this time', and waited for him to find the information they needed.

"Got it," he said. "Yep, fifty quid."

"What happened to the bike after that?" she asked.

"Now I've seen a picture of it on my screen, and it's a moped — you threw me off with 'bike' — I remember it well, and it's brought back a memory." He lifted his head and made eye contact with Bethany. "One of the strangest things really. I sold it to a man called . . ." He checked his screen. "Phil Vaughn, for two hundred pounds. Now don't you look like that, just because I bought it for fifty and upped the selling price. I'd sorted the brakes and whatever else was needed, you see — yes, says here it had a new carburettor and tyres as well. Anyway, he rode off on it, and later that night, while I drove home on the A1, bugger me, the moped was on the verge. Not kidding, it was right there on its side in the long grass. Except the number plate wasn't on the back."

So it was dumped after purchase? Interesting. "Oh, I see. What did you do about it?"

"Nothing, just carried on home. Not my business really."

She made a mental note to contact Fran to do a search on whether any bikes had been picked up by the police during that time. "When we did our checks, the bike was still registered to Mr Biggins. Why did you not register yourself as the owner after you bought it?"

"I didn't get the chance. I'd only had the moped around four hours — I'd propped it up in the forecourt after it'd been fixed up; I've got a mechanic who works out the back — and that Vaughn fella came in and purchased it."

Vaughn hadn't registered it either, so it seemed the purchase was solely for the plates. Why bother spending that much when you could just buy them online? Stupid question. That would leave a money trail.

"How did he pay for the bike?"

"Cash."

"Did he leave an address by any chance?"

"He did." Ken called it out.

Mike wrote it down.

"Do you happen to remember what he looks like?" She was asking for the earth after so much time had passed, but hope was always there.

"Err, about five-nine, average body. Brown hair. He had fancy trainers on, I know that much. Pure white. Noticed them when he came in. He drove the moped away, so I'm guessing he walked here."

"How old would you say he is?"

"Twenty-five, something like that. Oh, and he had a smart beard, one of those trimmed ones. Stubble."

"Thank you."

They said goodbye, then sat in the car. Bethany sent a message to Fran about mopeds found on verges and gave her the date.

Mike looked up the address Corby had given for Vaughn. "What a sodding joke. It's an old people's home."

"Hmm, and the man's in his twenties. Right. We won't bother going there. I'll give them a ring when we get back to the station."

She drove there, and the call proved fruitless. No one in residence was even related to someone called Phil Vaughn, so the fucker had just picked a random address.

You only did that if you had something to hide.

Didn't you?

CHAPTER TWELVE

In Natasha's living room, Joseph handed over her fake documents. He'd done a bloody good job and was proud of himself.

She took them, giving each one serious scrutiny. "You can't even tell they're not the real ones."

A smile lit her up, as if all the promise of a new life filled her. Had she been desperate to start again elsewhere for a while? How long had she drifted around Shadwell doing small crimes just to get by? It was clear she was after something more, otherwise she wouldn't have joined them on this. Maybe fate had stuck her in Joseph's path so he could help her achieve a better life.

It helped for him to think that, so all of this . . . this crap had a good reason and outcome.

"God, we've just got to get tonight over and done with, wait it out tomorrow morning, then go. I can't believe this is happening." She glanced around. "Kind of sad to be leaving my stuff in a way, though. All right, it isn't anything to write home about, and I got most of the big stuff from that charity warehouse place, but it's mine."

Joseph thought about his flat, his things, and yes, he related to what she'd said. It was home, where familiarity brought comfort. His furniture was a mix of Argos and IKEA, nothing fancy, but it was decent and looked nice. It was time to move on, though. "Maybe we can get a few bits together once we're settled. That or rent a furnished place."

But what about those checks they do?

For his place, he'd had to pay the estate agent to run one so the landlord knew he was an okay tenant. Neither of them had backgrounds in their new names. He didn't say anything — why shit on her happiness? — but maybe he could get someone on the Dark Web to create a fictitious life for them both. All right, he'd pay though the nose to get it done at short notice, but he had the funds in savings. He must remember to go to the bank in the morning and withdraw it all, then get hold of his contact. Until everything was sorted, they'd stay in a Premier Inn.

She eyed the wall clock. "Shall we go then? And a furnished place is fine by me."

He nodded, and the journey to HQ was over quickly, him belting along the roads, part of him wanting this over and done with as soon as possible, the other half wanting nothing to do with it at all. He wondered whether Zooby would tell him to take Natasha home after the meeting so she wasn't there when Anne barrelled in with the new baby. Time enough to find out.

In the main room, they settled at the table, while Anne slouched in the armchair, Zooby on a camp bed that hadn't been there earlier. Cans of Coke, some crisps and peanuts, and a few pre-packed sandwiches from Tesco were on offer in lieu of the cocktails, snacks, and chicken in a basket they were missing out on at the Grape. All in all, apart from the documents in a pile in the centre, it looked like a group of friends meeting for a laugh, albeit in shitty surroundings.

Zooby got up and scratched his head. "Glad you're here."

He seemed relieved, and Joseph wondered if Anne had acted weird or something while they'd been gone.

For the next couple of hours, they talked about tonight, even though they'd agreed how it would go long before now.

Anne announced she had a second kid to pinch, a boy, and Joseph kept his feelings about it to himself. The subject of Anne behaving herself came up.

"Look, if the parents spot me, what can I do?" she said.

"Take the babies and get out," Joseph muttered, earning himself the side-eye from her.

"I can't do that if they're fierce and try to stop me, can I. That Vicky woman was well protective and kept trying to grab the kid. She got on my tits, so I stabbed her, simple as. If tonight ends up the same, so be it." Anne shrugged. "Why does it bother you? It's not like I'll get you in the shit if I get caught, is it? I promised to keep my mouth shut, and I will." It was an easy thing to say — she probably didn't intend on getting caught.

Zooby sighed. "I'm bothered because you're killing, taking a life. Can't you see how that would upset me? Upset anyone?"

"Nope." Anne picked a hangnail. "Sorry, but I rather enjoy it."

Zooby rubbed one eye. "I don't get you at all. Please, just don't do it again. Joseph, mate, can you do a check on the customers for me. I'm not in the right frame of mind for some reason." He sent Anne a scathing look.

What the hell is she on? Who 'rather enjoys' killing?

Joseph took his mask out of his pocket and put it on, conscious, now more than ever, that he didn't want his face seen, even by drugged-up women. The feel of it on his face . . . God, he hated it, the coldness of the rubber, the smell of his dried breath from previous uses. The sheer weirdness of the clown's face and how it frightened the customers. If he were being totally honest, he'd got a kick out of it the first time, but now the enormity of what was happening — *that woman's dead, she's fucking dead!* — had taken any perverse enjoyment away, and he questioned every move, every thought.

Questioned who he was as a human being.

He shoved through the doorway into the corridor, thinking of whether to tell Natasha what he considered doing once they'd escaped — ringing the police on another burner and telling them Anne's name. He'd keep Zooby out of it, couldn't bring himself to dob him in now he knew his mate wasn't comfy with Anne being a killer. Would Natasha go for that, or was he better off just doing it and keeping it to himself? The problem was, he didn't want to do anything that would jeopardise her. Then again, they had new names, so the coppers would be searching for ghosts if Anne blabbed who they were.

One of the fake babies cried.

Sighing, his skin clammy beneath the mask, he pushed open the second door. Customer Two was co-sleeping with the doll, which stared at the ceiling, its manic eyes giving him the jitters. The dolls were well expensive, and Zooby had borrowed from a loan shark to buy them, hence why he took an extra cut of the 'adoption' money to pay it back. Anne had pointed out that he could sell them again afterwards, recouping the cash that way. Joseph should have known then that she was a wily bugger who didn't miss a trick.

He moved on to Three, who was also asleep, curled on her side, so young and desperate. He didn't want to know why she wasn't able to get pregnant — he'd feel worse than he already did — and where someone of her age had got the money to pay for a kid. The doll rested in the cot beneath a pink blanket, all tucked in like the real thing. Three was a nurturer, even while drugged.

Moving along. Four sat on her camp bed, feeding her 'baby' with one of those bottles that appeared to have milk in it — the white fluid was inside double-walled plastic — and he got to thinking.

How come none of them question why the milk doesn't disappear?

Aren't they worried their kids are going hungry if the milk's still there?

What is Zooby injecting the customers with?

Where did he get it from?

Another four questions he didn't really want to know the answers to.

He left her to it, going in to see Five. It was her doll blarting, and the cries had turned to piercing screams, a strain on the old ears. He winced, didn't reckon he could have a kid himself. They made too much noise. The customer was out for the count. Should they be trusting her with a live baby if she slept through its distress?

Fucking hell.

All these emotions, they weren't doing him any good, and the guilt was ripping into his heart. This job was a step too far. There was being a criminal, then being a *criminal*, the type who needed balls of steel. But after tonight, the babies or the women weren't any of his concern.

He crept towards her, angry at himself for even being here, and shook her. "Wake up. Your baby needs you."

Her cold shoulder beneath his palm created a coil of dread in the pit of his stomach. He shoved her again, and she flopped onto her back.

"Customer Five, will you bloody well get with it!"

She didn't.

His breathing harsh inside the mask, he knelt to put his ear over her mouth.

No warm air against his skin.

He jumped up, heart bulging with the stress of knowing he was involved with two murderers now. He was, wasn't he? Zooby was the one administering the drugs, so he'd killed her, right? She was dead, he knew it, but his mind couldn't quite accept it.

"Oh fuck, oh shitting hell . . ."

He backed up to the exit, legs weak, and barged into the corridor, running down it, the door to the main room seeming so far away, elusive, his means of escape kept from him by some strange time warp. At last, his palm met the door, and he pushed. A sense of being outside his body observing from above encompassed him, so eerie, and he had the bizarre thought that *he* was the dead woman, looking down at himself just leaving her there in the bed. A shiver spread and enticed goosebumps to flood every bit of his skin, the hairs on his arms standing upright, his scalp itching where the follicles seemed to shrink then expand.

At last, he was in the main room, his lungs tight, his throat closing.

Anne shot up from the armchair. "What the fuck's up with you, wombat?"

Joseph couldn't get any words out. They rotated in his head, a double helix, ribbons of information he was meant to pass on but couldn't.

Zooby came over and pressed his hands to Joseph's shoulders. "Calm down, mate."

Joseph concentrated on his friend's eyes, remembering the jeweller's shop and how CCTV had been put up after they'd robbed the place that time, how he'd panicked to the max, and Zooby had brought him down to earth, saying, "We robbed it when there *weren't* any cameras, fella, so as long as we don't go there again, we're golden."

Back then, Joseph had managed to get things in perspective, to sort out his manic breathing, to eventually think properly.

It wasn't working now.

"I . . . Fuck . . . She . . ." He pointed at the door.

"What's the matter?" Natasha came over and gripped the top of his arm.

The pinch of pain meant Joseph switched his attention to her. "Customer . . . Five . . . She's dead."

Everything seemed to happen at once. Natasha stepped away, her hands over her mouth. Anne threw her head back and laughed. And Zooby bolted into the corridor, while Joseph, he remained still, staring at a crying Natasha, the corner of his vision showing Anne clutching her stomach, awful, nasty chortles flowing out of her.

What was so funny about a customer being dead, for fuck's sake? They were in deep shit, even more now, and there she was, roaring.

"Oh my God," Natasha said. "I can't deal with this."

She stared at him, conveying something or other, but he was damned if he could work it out amidst all the panic, the emotions.

"Joseph." She leant in and whispered, "We should go. *Now.*"

"The money," he whispered back.

"Fuck."

They stood there, her arm around him, Joseph feeling pathetic, his mind nothing like it usually was — sharp, him on the ball — now cluttered and sluggish. He'd touched a *dead woman*, that was what he kept thinking, and she'd been cold and . . . *fucking hell, fucking hell.*

Zooby barged back in. "Shit!" He clenched his teeth and punched himself in the head.

Anne calmed a bit, letting out "Oh!" every now and then, and she moved to the door. "Do you want me to deal with this?" She cocked her head at Zooby. "I'll make it all go away. The rats can have her."

Rats? Hadn't Natasha mentioned those? Joseph couldn't grasp the memory hard enough, and it slipped away.

"And what a bloody bargain." Anne smiled. "We get to keep the money even though she isn't having a kid."

Joseph's mind cleared a little. Yes, the money was still there for them to share, and he could go elsewhere with Natasha, but the death of Five and that Vicky woman, that would follow them, in their heads.

Zooby paced, clutching his hair, his face pale. Anne stared at him as if his behaviour was alien, something he shouldn't be doing. Like *her* behaviour and reaction had been *normal.* Who laughed when someone was dead?

"What . . . what are you going to do with her?" Joseph asked Anne, immediately regretting it. If he knew, he'd have more guilt, more knowledge of another crime. "Doesn't matter. I don't want to know."

"No, you don't," she said, and it was ominous, that sentence holding the promise that she'd do something hideous.

"Zooby," she snapped, "Do you want me to do this or not? It means me not nicking the baby boy tonight, though."

Zooby nodded. Let go of his hair. Glanced around at them all in turn, then focused on Anne. "Nothing that can come back to any of us, right? This is still in with our original agreement. If anyone gets caught, we don't drop the others in it."

Anne nodded. "Of course. I already said that earlier. I'll just go and get her then." She tootled off up the corridor, whistling.

Joseph, Natasha, and Zooby stared at each other.

"This is too much," Joseph said.

"I killed her." Zooby. "I actually killed someone." He staggered to a chair at the table and sat. "What am I going to do?"

"She needs washing." Natasha closed her eyes for a moment. "You've touched her to do the injections."

Zooby moaned. "Ah, bollocks."

There was a pressure hose outside in the courtyard, which was a bloody relief given the circumstances. Zooby had rigged it up for when they left this place — their final time here would be spent cleaning the ground of the immediate parking area, then their vehicles, of any debris connected to the mill. He'd said he'd watched TV once, and some bloke had been convicted based on the dirt in the tyre treads.

Joseph reminded Zooby of it.

"Ugh. Cleaning a dead body, though . . ." Zooby paled even more.

"Better than being caught from your DNA," Natasha pointed out. "I'm sure Anne will do it for you. She seems to . . . like that sort of thing."

Joseph made a decision, sod what Zooby said about it. "Look, me and Nat, we're leaving. We'll come back tomorrow once Anne's picked up the baby girl."

"You're leaving me with her and Five?" Zooby shuddered.

"Sorry, mate, but I didn't sign up for murder." Joseph walked to the door and picked up his helmet. He still had the mask on, so he took it off and pushed it in his pocket.

He'd burn the damn thing come tomorrow. "See you in the morning for the payment."

"No way," Zooby said. "You need to be here with me while the kid's being taken, especially now Five is dead. What if one of the others dies as well and I'm here on my own with them?"

"How much shit have you been giving the women?" Joseph rammed his helmet on and flicked the visor up.

"Just a bit more than normal."

"Well, don't. If another one carks it . . ."

Zooby ran to the camp bed and kicked it, shouting about being fucking stupid by upping the meds. Joseph jerked his head at Natasha for her to go outside and get on the bike. She left, and Zooby turned to stare at the doorway she'd gone through.

"We didn't finish our meeting," Zooby said.

"I don't think now is the time to piss and moan about that. We'll be back tomorrow, end of. Unless you want to cough up the money now."

Zooby gave a wry laugh. "I'll dock you some, seeing as you're not fulfilling the agreement by staying here now."

"Fine by me — and anyway, I told you I had my own work to do, and you agreed I could do it. I'm not hanging around here while that nutty bitch drags the body in."

Joseph walked out, willing the next few hours to move quickly so he could do the same with Natasha.

CHAPTER THIRTEEN

Anne had bundled into her coat and stood outside. She loved the way the pressurised water affected Five's skin. It pushed at it, creating ripples, and she had so much pleasure moving the jet up and down the belly so the whole body seemed to shudder, as if the woman were alive. She hummed *Three Blind Mice* but substituted mice for rats, loving the bit about cutting their heads off with a carving knife. In her case, the knife was her teeth.

Rolling on floor laughing.

"Stop it, you daft woman," she muttered. "Laughing when someone's dead is inappropriate."

But Anne liked being inappropriate.

She stared at Five. Zooby had put a large plastic sheet down so Anne could place the body on it. Surprising how heavy she was to carry, which made manoeuvring her a tad awkward, and it was a pest flattening her out from the position she'd died in, which was on her side. He'd banged on about debris transference from here to wherever Anne was taking Five, and no, he didn't want to know any details of what the location would be. He was a boring bastard, keep worrying about forensics and shit. God, what happened to living on the edge, to taking chances?

She pointed the jet at Five's face. Water filled her mouth, puffing out her cheeks. Next came her ears — talk about getting them syringed.

Satisfied all traces of the scene, Zooby, and herself were off the body, Anne put on gloves then took a clean blanket out of the wrapper and draped it over Five. She tucked it beneath and lifted her, popping her in the boot, front down, ensuring none of the wet skin picked up fibres or whatever from the car. All for Zooby. All so he didn't soil his pants about it.

She stared at the black doctor's bag with holes in the side, which was at the back by Five's shrouded head.

"Loving your handbag, darling. Suits you," she told her. "Better than a Mulberry any day, eh? I mean, there's so much space inside for . . . Well, you'll find out, won't you."

She closed the boot and went back in to find Zooby, a spring in her step. She hadn't been this content in ages. "I'm off then." She put her mask on. While she knew how to avoid cameras on the roads, she loved the thrill the mask gave her. Anonymity. Her a beautiful monster living behind it. "I'll go straight from the dump site to the baby's place."

"Okay." Zooby didn't look too happy — what a mardy git. What was up with him? Why wasn't he excited about this?

Oh. Yes. He probably didn't like being a killer. Shame, but this was all on him, Five being dead, so he could damn well get on with it.

She left him and drove the short distance to Shadwell Hill, Zooby's voice in her head moaning: *It's too close to the mill. If they find her, they'll come here. So take her somewhere else, farther away.*

"Bollocks to you," she said back and guffawed at his reaction that played out in her head — mouth open in shock, eyes wide, cheeks going red to cover up that ever-present paleness he seemed to have.

He wasn't the same as he'd been in the Grapes during the planning stages. For some reason, he'd gone all maudlin.

She sobered while driving up the track to the top, shaking a bit from the memories of being up here with Raven when she'd called the rats to come out of the woods. Partway in on the walking track, she stopped where the evergreen trees either side gave her plenty of cover.

Mask off, hood up, she jumped out, leaving the headlights on low beam so they lit up the immediate area. She wanted to see what she was doing instead of working in the murk like she'd had to with Raven.

At the boot, she hefted Five out and carried her to in front of the car, then dropped her on the ground, bundling the blanket up in her arms. The naked woman didn't have an ounce of fat on her and probably worked out a lot — or ate salads all day long.

"Don't get up and go anywhere, will you. I just need to put this away." She walked to the boot, laughing about what she'd said, and stuffed the blanket beside the doctor's bag. A squeak came from it.

God, the things you did for fun.

She opened the bag. One of the two rats had suffocated. She shrugged and grabbed the live beastie, a smallish one. She wouldn't have too much trouble crunching down on the head. The animal didn't wriggle, didn't fear her — she'd tamed them all, just like Raven once had — and Anne took a lovely big breath then let it out. This was it, the moment, and she used her large penknife to cut a little slit to make the ripping easier, then opened her mouth and—

While the body twitched in her hand, it took her a while to chew, to crunch on bones, to swallow bit by bit, then she spat the skull into the bag — she'd break a tooth if she attempted to gobble that bugger. Her attention fell on Five, and Anne crouched, holding the rat over the woman's mouth, blood dripping into it.

"Yum, yum." She giggled and placed the rat down, close to the body. "Tastes so good, but then you wouldn't know, would you, seeing as you're dead." She stood and moved along to kick Five's foot, just because. The headlights lit the woman's pasty skin up so well. "Bet you didn't think this was how you'd end up, did you."

Five didn't answer, and that pissed Anne off. Some people were so rude, weren't they.

She stared at the face. It'd look so lovely with a slash on it.

Anne had the penknife at the ready. She knelt and drew the blade down from the temple, over the nose, and to the opposite jaw, heavy handed with it. Now Five looked like Raven had, and wasn't that just the best? A slice to the neck completed the picture, but there wasn't much blood, which didn't give the same effect. Five must have been dead a fair while prior to Joseph finding her. She scooped up the rat and squeezed it, deliriously happy that Five's face and neck were now a mess with the red stuff.

"Pretty." A sigh.

She dipped her gloved finger into the open end of the rat and left a little clue on Five's chest, then positioned her in the way she wanted her, to show how filthy Raven was.

"You be good here now. No scaring the dog walkers."

Rat dropped, she returned to the car, penknife in her pocket, and reversed out onto the parking area.

The drive home was uneventful, not that she'd expect anything to be going on at this time of night, but she did love listening to, and observing, the odd domestic that blew up in her street, usually in the early evenings, around dinnertime. The Henleys were a volatile pair who provided ample entertainment when she was bored. They lived opposite and never shut their curtains, so you could see him belting her one when she burnt the food or whatever. The resultant cries from the wife and the shouts from the husband were sweet music to Anne's ears.

She didn't have to wonder how she'd become so warped.

Well, whether she wanted to hear the tune of abuse or not, there was no such luck tonight, and she ought to be grateful really. No one to see her. No one to wonder why she'd come home then went straight out again.

She entered the house and ran upstairs, going into the rat room. Light switched on, she smiled at all of the nosy gits coming close to the wire in the doors to see her. There were too many of them, and she'd accidentally inbred a few, which was a pest, because people didn't want their pets to have club feet, did they, and a couple of them did.

She opened the door a little and reached inside to snatch one of the animals with deformed paws. She could get rid of them this way, each time she collected a baby. Why hadn't she thought of that before?

Out the front, she locked her house, put the small rat in the doctor's bag, and zoomed to her target's place, where she parked beside a large tree, its branches heavily laden with evergreen leaves, the canopy creating a shadow over her vehicle.

A quick glance at her phone showed the time — she had an hour to go. Mask on, she set her alarm and closed her eyes. A bit of sleep would work wonders. She was flagging.

* * *

The baby was out for the count in the cot, the space only big enough to hold that and a tallboy. No room to swing a cat. Anne did her thing again with the rat's head — two in one night, what a treat — then lobbed the rest of it on the windowsill. It came to rest against the scalloped bottom of a pink blind, and blood pooled on the sill. Some had dripped onto the baby's blanket while the body had been in motion, and the sheet beneath her had a few spatters. Nothing on the child, though. What a good aim Anne had.

She crept out of the room onto the landing where a night light was plugged in beside a gurgling radiator. What was it with mothers and those lights? Was it a requisite when having a child or what? There had been one at the top of the stairs in her childhood home, too. She'd check an online baby book just for shits and giggles to see if it was on the list of what to buy when having a sprog.

Anne almost laughed at her thoughts and bit her lip to stop it barking out. She peered inside the room next to the baby's. Oh. Oh dear. Now that wasn't supposed to happen. The mother had a bloke in bed with her, plain as day in the glow of another plug-in light by the wardrobe. Zooby had assured Anne that tonight was the night the woman didn't entertain, as it were, but he'd been wrong.

That had put a wrench in her plans.

Think about it rationally. You can still do it.

She took her penknife out, excitement flurrying inside her, and approached his side of the bed. One quick swipe, and his neck opened, blood gushing, him jolting and burbling a few times then . . . nothing. Good. He'd been considerate in death and hadn't woken the slapper. Either that or she was a heavy sleeper. Maybe they'd got drunk this evening and alcohol had sent her into a deep abyss.

Anne moved to the other side and stared down at her. She was just like Raven, going with lots of men, opening her legs to all and sundry, the filthy little cow. Did she even know who the father of the child was? Zooby had said to take the baby because his mate, the supposed dad, reckoned the mother didn't deserve her. So why wasn't he pushing for custody then? Or maybe he was.

Oops, he wouldn't be getting her.

"There now," she whispered, the urge to punch the penknife into the woman's face so strong she had to hold down her hand with the other by clutching her wrist. "You take a few final breaths. In and out. In and out."

The stench of the bloke's blood pungent in the air, she sniffed to get the full brunt of it. Gorgeous. Such a *nice* smell. The aroma meant the End, the finalisation of torment. *Crimson is the tide of death.* Raven was the first she'd ever had the pleasure of drawing into her lungs. It meant no more fear, no more looking at that woman who'd still come round for years, sitting at Mum's dining table, Tub tagging along with her, drinking that god-awful milkshake she loved so much.

Anne leant over so her red clown nose almost touched the target's. She listened to the mum's breathing, steady, peaceful, and wondered if she dreamed of beautiful things, like men buying her jewellery, taking her on holiday, or paying for a spa day, plus a new hairdo and acrylic nails.

She was apparently high maintenance, one of those mothers you saw congregating in a gaggle outside Superdrug when they were on the nappy and wet wipes run, all cooing over the babies while secretly thinking theirs were the best. Kids in the latest fashions, pushchairs high-end, mothers like Barbies, no Ken dolls in sight. Unless you counted this slapper here. She had Ken, Ben, Len, and more.

Nasty girl.

Anne stood straight. Snapped her hand out. The neck cut easily, then she carved across the face, adding pressure to get a marvellous gouge going on. That was better, the blood, the mess, the skin parting to expose a cheekbone, the nose cartilage, her molars, and finally, a peek of flesh-covered jawbone. The woman juddered a few times as well, her eyes opening in shock, pain, her mouth a huge, silent-O scream.

"You're a goner again," she told Raven. "Off to the Devil with you. No one likes a dirty-knickered woman."

A quick chuckle was all she allowed herself, then the penknife blade was secured in the handle, and she was prowling the rest of the house in case there were more man-beasts elsewhere. You couldn't be too careful. And who knew whether a filthy slag like her serviced a few at a time, all the blokes happy about it. Anne had heard she took money for doing it to top up her Universal Credit. It showed. The furniture was nifty, and the wallpaper appeared to be that expensive stuff.

More creeping. More skulking.

No one slept in the third bedroom or on the sofa.

Penknife in her pocket, she returned to the baby and scooped the sleeping dot up, the tiny body warm in her arms. "You're going to make your new mummy so happy. She's called Two, and the name she's chosen for you is Katalina. Get you, all fancy and everything. Now, let's go. And be quiet about it, or you'll be in so much trouble, and trust me, you really don't want that."

She snuck out via the back door, and in no time, she'd strapped Katalina into the baby seat. She glanced around to check the street — her mask would give anyone a shock if they peeked out, so more fool them if they did — then got in the car and took a leisurely drive to the old mill, this time singing *Humpty Dumpty*.

"They'll be putting your real mum back together again soon," she said, glancing in her rearview at Katalina. "They'll sew her face up but advise the family not to visit her in the coffin. She'll be a bit of a sight."

Katalina woke up once the engine had died outside the mill, so Anne hurried and took her in. Zooby could deal with the screeching thing while she made a cuppa and thought about the happenings of the night. The taste of rat was heavy on her tongue, and she licked her lips in case some had dried there. Waste not, want not.

"What have you bloody done to her?" Zooby came up to Anne, worry twisting his face, and relieved her of the squawking burden.

"Sod all, she's just a mardy fucker."

He fussed over her, cooing and all sorts, but the baby was having none of it. She balled her fists and scrunched her bright-red face up. Talk about ungrateful when he was trying to comfort her. Tub had been the same, always griping whether Raven saw to her straight away or not.

"Come on now, less of that." Zooby put her in the cot, leaving her to cry it out, and got a bottle ready.

He was so good at this sort of thing, Anne wondered if he had any kids of his own. If he did, he was weird for wanting to steal them. How would he feel if someone took his?

"Got children, have you?" she asked.

"Why d'you need to know?" Panic flooded his tone.

What did he think, she was going to kidnap it if he did? *Might do.*

"No reason. Just that you're great with them, that's all."

"I've got loads of younger brothers and sisters. I help my mum out."

"So won't she be missing you? You're always here lately."

He screwed the top on the bottle. "She thinks I've gone on a lads' holiday."

"Where to?"

"Magaluf."

"Right . . . So she'll be expecting lots of photos then, you with a suntanned bod and a cocktail held up. Most blokes would be putting them on Instagram daily."

He paled — seemed he was fond of doing that. "Crap. I didn't think about that part of it."

"Oh dear." *What a novice.* "You'll have to buy some fake tan."

Anne made them a coffee while he fed the brat, and she sat in the armchair, sipping and reliving the wondrous events.

The rats.

The slices.

The blood.

What a banging night. The man in the bed had been a bonus. A twofer.

Finally, the kid was settled, a new nappy on, and back to sleep, thank Jesus and his communion wafers. She burst out laughing at that. Such delightful nonsense.

Zooby gave her a funny look. "What the hell's so funny?"

"Nothing."

He picked up his cup and took a seat at the table, watching her warily. "So, how did it go tonight? And tell me the truth straight away, none of this hiding stuff like before."

"Ah . . . Now don't go getting all lairy, but there was a problem."

"Shit . . ."

"Calm down, Beardy, it's all good."

"Get on with it, will you?"

She sighed. "All right. I left Five in the woods, so that went fine, but at the house? I thought you said she didn't entertain tonight."

"She doesn't. She gets her nails done by some woman who comes round, then she does that pampering shit — face mask, foot spa, that sort of thing. It used to drive her ex mental because she turfed him out while it was going on."

"Well, she might have done all that, but she had a bloke in her bed."

"What?" His cheeks whitened even more. "Don't tell me you . . ." He swallowed, Adam's apple going apeshit.

"Yep. Had to. He got up, the man, and went to attack me. He had a baseball bat by the bed, and he grabbed it, swinging it right at my head. It was self-defence on my part. I slashed his neck, then she woke up an' all. I mean, what was I supposed to do? I had to shut her up before she even opened her mouth. I couldn't have her screaming."

"*Christ*, Anne! What the hell?"

She shrugged. "No need to get all silly about it. Panicking doesn't suit anybody. I put them back in bed like someone had come in and killed them there. The man was heavy, but I managed it by dragging him."

"You did what?"

"Oh, don't go on about transference again. If you do, I'm likely to lose the plot."

"You already have!"

Rude. "I'll let that slide. Next time, though . . ." She enjoyed how uncomfortable he seemed, how scared. If she shouted *boo!* he'd probably shit himself. "It'll all work out." A different subject was in order — this one was getting tedious. She'd changed her mind about staying here overnight, and he needed to know. "So when's Joseph coming back? I could really do with getting home for some sleep after all that hard work." She needed to sort the rats first thing as well. Their cages needed cleaning, the smelly devils.

"He isn't."

"Eh?"

"He'll be here in the morning."

"Suppose you want me to sleep on there, don't you?" She stared at the camp bed, giving it evils.

"I'd rather not be alone in case . . . in case one of the others dies as well." He scratched his beard. "Look, it doesn't matter. Go home if you want."

"Nah, it's fine. I'll nip off once he arrives — but I want my money first."

"No problem. And thanks. You know, for understanding."

"That's okay." *It isn't, but I'll have a think about how you can make up for it.*

* * *

"Do you have to go to Posh Nob's, Mum?"

The odd thing was, she looked forward to the rats now. Years had gone by, and Anne was twelve, a 'big girl' who didn't need to be so daft, not wanting her mum to go to work.

Anne had learnt to enjoy Raven's sadistic form of bullying rather than hate it — eating the rat heads, putting up with Raven in her face, the slaps — and Anne knew that wasn't right, but that was the way of it now. Although she'd never forget seeing the rats in the woods and how they'd done exactly what Raven wanted, if she could just grow older really quick, Anne could sort everything.

For now, she'd bide her time.

"You know I have to go." Mum stroked Anne's hair. "I'll be starting that new job full-time next week, so that means no more evenings for me once tonight's out of the way."

Anne couldn't wait. "Will Raven come round even then?"

"Of course she will. She's my best friend, and anyway, you'd miss not seeing Jess."

Jessica was Raven's daughter, Tub Belly. Anne wished she never had to see her again. Tub still guzzled lots of milk, although it was from a plastic beaker now and had Nesquik stirred in, that milkshake stuff, usually chocolate or strawberry.

Anne never got any. Raven brought it with her and only made enough for Tub.

"I don't like them." Anne had never told Mum that before.

"What, Raven and Jess?"

Anne nodded and looked up into Mum's eyes. "One day, I'm going to kill Raven.*"*

Mum gasped. "Anne!"

"It's true. I—"

The doorbell rang, so that put paid to finishing the conversation. Mum rushed to answer it, then she was gone in a flurry of hugs and kisses while Tub tromped into the kitchen to ferret in the fridge for milk.

Raven closed the door and moved towards Anne. She stopped, too close, and held up her doctor's bag. "I've brought a little friend for you."

"Good," Anne said. "Because I like eating them."

Raven widened her eyes. "What?"

"You heard me." It was so good yet frightening being bold, but she'd never be left alone with this woman again after tonight, so biting back was okay, wasn't it?

"You cheeky little bitch." Raven slapped Anne around the face.

It stung, and tears came, but Anne slapped her right back.

"Fuck off, you," she shouted, crazy angry, something taking over her, a loathing so deep she couldn't breathe for a moment. Then, "I hate you." She ran upstairs to the bathroom, locking herself in, and sat in front of the door, the lino cold beneath her bum.

Footsteps, such hard thuds, getting louder and louder with every stair.

A succession of thumps on the door.

"You'd better get out here right now," Raven said.

"What's Anne done, Mummy?" Tub must have come upstairs, too. What a nosy brat.

"None of your business, lard arse. Bugger off."

Tub wailed.

Anne closed her eyes. She'd stick it out here until Mum got back. It'd only be an hour and a half. "Go away."

The handle went up and down.

"I'm warning you, Anne."

"And I'm warning you. Leave me alone or—"

"Or what?"

Anne smiled at her reflection opposite on the sink pedestal and mouthed, "You'll see."

CHAPTER FOURTEEN

I knew it wouldn't be long before we were here again.

Bethany and Mike stood in the woods on Shadwell Hill, arriving at the same time as SOCO, who were busy doing their preliminary things. They stood a couple of metres away from the body while photos were being taken.

The place was notorious for dumping corpses, or at least it seemed that way. This site had featured in a few cases, and this one wasn't an exception.

"It's linked to Vicky, no doubt in my mind, given the evidence." She kept her sights on Mike and not the body. She'd had a quick glimpse, enough to know they were dealing with the same killer, and would study her better in a few, once she'd got her thudding heart under control.

"Yep." Mike's eyes shone above his face mask. "Except something isn't right."

"What's that?" She wondered if he was going to say what she'd clocked.

"Not enough blood. The face and neck slashes would produce more. There's not much on her skin, nor on the ground."

"They weren't done when she was alive."

He nodded. "That's what I'm getting at."

"Hmm."

"This case can go to Fuckyouville."

"I *knew* you were going to say that at some point."

She turned her back on the victim and surveyed the scene. SOCO between tree trunks close by and deeper into the woods, myriad pillar candles in their protective suits. Isabelle talking to one of her team halfway towards the entrance, their heads bent. Presley's red car appearing on the tarmac in the distance. Halogens on poles, lighting up the area, the true brightness of morning yet to come, the early hours giving everything an eerie slant.

She imagined what it would look like from the main road, all the vehicles parked on the tarmac, the lights from inside the cluster of trees a domed glow interspersed with shadowy tree trunks, speckles of illumination filtering through the leaves higher up, resembling a million white butterflies caught in the branches, flickering with the sigh of the wind weaving through them.

Drivers would know something was going on.

Tory Yates was down at the bottom of the track at the main road with Glen Underby, ready to stop traffic and ask questions: *Do you always come out here at this time? Where are you going? Have you been past already this morning, and if so, did you notice anything?*

"We'd best speak to this fella. He looks like a spare part." Bethany walked over to the 'finder', a jogger, who sat on a log a few metres from the immediate area, his pasty-white legs sticking out of black shorts.

A uniform standing beside him stepped away. Why had he been allowed to sit? The bloody killer could have taken a breather here. Evidence could have been compromised.

She introduced herself to the poor git who'd had the misfortune to see more that he'd probably bargained for this morning, although, to be fair, this was a known spot for discovering the dead, so wouldn't runners come here with the expectation of finding someone? Maybe it was a case of: *It won't happen to me.*

"What's your name, sir?" She lowered her face mask and smiled. It couldn't be nice having people surrounding you with only their eyes showing.

"Chris Choy."

"Can you tell me what happened?"

He stood, appearing a bit shaky. "I parked at the top of the track — that's my Focus out there — set off for my run, and didn't get far at all, obviously." His voice was thick, probably from an emotionally clogged throat. His Adam's apple was getting a fair bit of exercise. "I had my headlamp on" — he pointed to the one on his forehead, which wasn't lit now — "and it picked out the body. My blood ran cold, because I knew right away what it was, even though my head was telling me it was a mannequin or something."

"What did you do then?"

"Apart from swearing and crapping my pants?" He let out a wry laugh. "I rang the police. I always run with my phone because of . . . well, because of this sort of thing."

"Why jog here then?" She was curious as to why people still used this place.

He shrugged. "I'm asking myself the same question. There's no way I'm coming here again."

Another thing. The hour. Either he was dedicated to keeping fit prior to going to work or bloody mental to come out at that time. "Did you see anyone else around?"

"No. Nothing on the main road when I arrived, and I haven't heard any cars going past since until the police turned up. I didn't feel like anyone was watching me either. You know, that prickly feeling."

Uniforms had already scouted the area. No one had been found.

She sighed. Chris seemed genuine enough, just an unfortunate man, in the wrong place at the wrong time. "Do you feel up to driving?"

He nodded. "I just want to get home now."

"You've given your details to the officer here, I take it?"

"Yes."

"Okay, we'll be in touch. Go home. Thank you for your time."

He walked off with the uniform. Bethany and Mike moved back to their position near the body. She pondered on what Chris would go through now, seeing everything playing back inside his mind, experiencing the fear again and again, hoping for sleep to come easily at night, only to fall into the terrible scenario in his dreams.

Some people moved on; others never got over it.

"Wonder what that means on her chest?" Mike mused.

Bethany faced the body again. The killer had written 'Five' in blood, and to be honest, she was inclined to go with what it implied — this was victim number five. It stood to reason, didn't it?

Why then, didn't Vicky have a number on hers? And where are bodies two, three, and four?

She told Mike her theory. "So maybe this is a new thing they thought of, numbering the kills."

"Or they didn't have time at Vicky's," he said. "You know, more risk of being caught so they put a rush on."

Bethany nodded. "The thing with this one is, if we're going with our initial thoughts on those slashes being made after death, how did she die — I can't see any strangulation bruises — and why wasn't she cut at the original death site?"

"Might not have wanted the blood to spill there." Mike shrugged. "Maybe this one was murdered at the killer's home. She could have been suffocated."

Bethany crouched to study the woman's face. "Sorry to piss on the cornflakes you haven't even had a chance to eat yet. I don't need Presley here to tell me that's not the case. No petechiae present, and her eyes are closed naturally, as in, no scrunching from pain or struggling to breathe."

"Like she died in her sleep or something?"

"Yes. Her whole face, if you discount the slash, is relaxed." She stood. "And that rat — what the hell do they mean?"

It was minus a head again, and the body was misshapen, squashed, a bulge of innards spilling out at the neck. Its paws were claw-shaped, and to her, that said it had died in pain, unlike the woman. The tail, ramrod straight, gave the same impression.

"We don't know anything about this woman to know if she was a 'rat'," Mike said. "With Vicky, we know that's unlikely, so the animals must mean something else. Her being dumped up here is—"

"Ah," Presley said, coming to stand beside them. "Died in one position, placed in another, I see." He pointed to the victim's right. "Heavy lividity there."

Bethany hadn't thought of that, too engrossed in other aspects. "Poor thing."

"Poor thing indeed." Presley took a plastic sheet out of his bag and put it down beside the body, on the left, away from the rat. He knelt and got his temperature gadget out. "Let's see what time you died then. Oh, you're a bit on the stiff side."

Bethany studied the leaves above and wondered whether the body being naked was also significant. Vicky had been clothed in her pyjamas. Why change that pattern? Had this woman been violated in all the wrong ways? She'd avoided looking between her legs to find any evidence of a sexual assault.

"Ah, so she's been gone a while." Presley sighed. "We're talking around eight p.m., hence her stiffness. We're at the ten-hour mark of rigor, so at the twelfth, she'll be in the peak of it. I'm not going to be able to manipulate her until it's passed. With her legs being wide open, I can see already there's no trauma to her labia, but that could be a different story with the vagina. No semen in view, but again, that could be inside. She may have been cleaned up on the outside." He paused. "Vicky hadn't been tampered with, by the way. I'll send you my PM report a bit later, once I've dealt with this young lady."

"So no rape," Bethany said, more to cement that in her mind than stating the obvious.

"No sexual intercourse at all recently," Presley said. "As to how this one died — tox will give us the answer as there are no obvious signs. Those slashes weren't the culprits, and

I'd say she wasn't strangled. Going by the pattern of lividity, though, she was on her right side, legs drawn up, hands possibly in prayer by her face, so the foetal position. Look at the back of her right hand, the palm of her left. Both are mottled. With how she's been posed here, it would have to have been done prior to rigor, obviously, as there's no indication to my eye that she was broken into this star shape. However, to further complicate things, the layman may think she also died on her back, because if you look closely, you'll also see lividity there."

"Explain, please?" Bethany asked.

"The short version is: She died on her side and remained there for around two hours, which is when lividity becomes apparent. She was then moved, giving the clotting blood time to gather on her back, the backs of her thighs, arms et cetera."

"Right, and if she was moved after two hours, someone kept her dead wherever, possibly because, if she died about eight, there was a risk of the killer being seen carrying a body. Would you say she was moved about ten if she died at eight?"

"Thereabouts." Presley stood. "I'm intrigued to know what killed her."

And I'm intrigued as to who. "Yes, it may give us some sort of clue." With no ID, they had no idea who this woman was, and perhaps that was the killer's intention. "The chief will have to deal with the public on this one. Press conference and whatnot. Someone's got to be missing her, surely."

She thanked Presley and turned to Isabelle, who now stood chatting close by with the SOCO she'd been talking to earlier. Two more were putting up a rectangular cordon.

"This looks like an intent convo you're having," Bethany said as more officers came by to erect a tent over the body.

"Tyres," Isabelle said. "There are four marks where a vehicle was static here for a while. Given the weather, the recent rainfall from the storm we had before you went to Spain, it's incredibly damp here, so the weight of the car or whatever made divots, plus, if you look farther along, you'll see tracks where it was driven in here." She frowned and said to the cordon officers, "Actually, string that up from here, right to the entrance, two lines of it, then we know where to concentrate a search, especially in the area where someone got out of the driver's or passenger sides, also the boot — the body might have been in there."

Bethany had a look for footprints. There was a patch where the ground and leaves had been disturbed. "Someone's been there."

Isabelle nodded and moved along, outside the main area, and stared down. "And here, the boot. Actually, there's a double line of sorts where someone's walked from the boot to the body, maybe a couple of times."

Bethany shivered at the image that conjured. A killer dressed in black, striding back and forth in the darkness, the trees the only witnesses to what they were doing. The rustling of the fallen leaves and the faint periodic whoosh of a car going past on the main road, if anyone else had come past at that ungodly hour. Thank God the woman had already been dead and hadn't had to see it. With the absence of bruising, indicating torture, she'd perhaps died peacefully, and Bethany clung on to that so it eclipsed the knowledge that Vicky had experienced the opposite. Pain, fear, maybe knowing her child would be taken.

"Okay, I'll message Kribbs now, let him know what's on his plate when he rolls up at the station."

Bethany: HI, SIR. SORRY TO MESSAGE SO EARLY. WE NEED A PRESS CONFERENCE. BODY FOUND IN THE WOODS ON SHADWELL HILL, THE USUAL DUMP SITE. FEMALE, BETWEEN TWENTY TO THIRTY, SLIM BUILD, NO DISCERNING MARKS, BLONDE. NO IDEA ON THE EYES — THEY'RE CLOSED; SHE'S IN RIGOR. DIED AROUND EIGHT LAST NIGHT. SLASH TO THE FACE AND NECK AFTER DEATH, THE WORD 'FIVE' WRITTEN IN BLOOD

ON HER CHEST. NO SIGNS OF SEXUAL TRAUMA SO FAR OR STRANGULATION OR BEATING. NO ID, HENCE ME NEEDING THE PUBLIC'S HELP HERE. WILL LOOK INTO MISSING PERSONS ASAP.

Kribbs: WHAT A WAKE-UP MESSAGE.

Bethany: SORRY, SIR.

She phoned Ursula Fringwell, the nighttime desk sergeant. "Hi, it's Bethany. Can you start looking into missing women for me before Rob takes over on his shift? Body here in the woods. Died about eight last night." She gave the description.

"Two seconds." The clacking of a keyboard, then, "No females reported missing yesterday, although there are a couple who have been gone for around a week, reported two days ago. Sisters, actually. Both blonde, both slim like you said. One has a tattoo on her ankle, though, a bumble bee."

Bethany turned to check the victim, just to make doubly sure. "No, this lady doesn't have one. No piercings either. Do you have pictures of them?"

"Yep."

"Send them, please."

"Doing it now."

Bethany's phone chimed shortly after, and she accessed her email. "Oh. Fuck. From what I can tell, given the state of the victim's face, this is one of them. She looks more like the sister with shorter hair."

"That's Fay Elliot. The other is Tammy. I'll send you their address — they live together. I'll also send you one for the parents. They rang in about their girls going missing."

"Thanks. Can you put in for a search on the women's financial records, please, and their phones. Let Rob know what's going on when he arrives. I'll text Fran and Leona now. They can fill Tammy in."

"You do know she won't be in, don't you?"

"Damn, I forgot. She has an interview."

Tammy was leaving them — she'd decided policing in Shadwell wasn't for her. She'd tried to fit in here, but her old stomping grounds of Oxfordshire were calling her. It was sad, the woman was brilliant at her job, but Bethany had told her she needed to follow her dreams and be happy. If that meant being elsewhere, then so be it.

"Okay, well, if you can get on with that, I'd be grateful, thank you." Bethany cut the call and looked at Mike. "Two women missing for a week. Sisters, one of them the same description as this lady. I'd say I've positively identified her from a photo. Fay Elliot."

"Doesn't sound good. If this is one of them, where's the other?"

"That's what I thought." She quickly messaged Kribbs to get him to hold off on the press conference until she'd spoken to the Elliots. No point in alarming the public unless they had to. Then she snapped a photo of the victim's face in case one of the parents were strong enough to look at it and confirm or deny whether she was their daughter. "Right, we need to get going. We have a mum and dad to possibly devastate."

CHAPTER FIFTEEN

Goodbyes said, Bethany and Mike undressed and gave their protectives to a SOCO who manned the entrance to the woods. She signed out of the log, hoping she wouldn't need to come back here for years.

Chance would be a fine thing.

On her way across the tarmac, which was freckled with SOCO looking for evidence, she accessed her emails to get the address she needed, and in the car, put it into the satnav. A new estate had sprung up on the outskirts, Kingly Eco Village, full of homes with solar panels and environmentally good things apparently. What they were she had no idea, but the houses were ridiculously expensive. She hadn't been there before, so the satnav had the job of guiding her.

"Mr Choy has the unfortunate task of scrubbing this from his mind, and I don't think he'll be successful," Mike said.

"Me neither. If we see it often, to the point it becomes 'normal' as such, and yet we can't forget it, what chance does he have?"

"Killers don't give a stuff about the other lives they wreck."

"No. I've said it before. A murder creates emotional ripples in the living." She started the engine and drove down the track, waving to Tory and Glen as she pulled out onto the road, going left.

The satnav protested.

"Where are you going?" he asked.

"Just a quick detour past Wind Energy, then a bit farther up."

"Checking for what?"

"People."

While she didn't believe the killer was anywhere close, it was best to check, not only for the paperwork but her peace of mind.

Wind Energy stood in darkness to the right, as did the empty mill a mile or so along on the left. She obeyed the satnav woman, who sounded close to having a coronary at the direction being wrong, and did a U-turn, continuing back to Shadwell.

They didn't chat much on the journey, Bethany stuck inside her head at the thought of two sisters going missing at the same time. Abduction? If so, were they dealing with more than one killer here? Or one killer and an accomplice who helped lure the women in? That didn't make sense in Vicky's case, as she was murdered in her home, so what the hell was the deal here? Did Fay and Tammy have children? Had they been taken, too? Ursula hadn't mentioned any, so that was a small mercy.

God, we're here. Bethany's stomach rolled over.

She let out a long breath, hating the fact she'd be waking people up in a minute. No lights shone from the large ultra-modern house, and only one other in the street had a yellow glow downstairs, a kitchen, in full view with someone making a cuppa inside it. How lovely to be them, oblivious, carrying on with the business of getting ready for the day when two women were dead at the hands of a sadistic bastard.

"Here we go," she said and popped her seat belt buckle.

"How are we playing this?" Mike asked, doing the same.

"Ask questions first, reveal later. The usual."

They got out and walked to the front door, the air chilly. She idly wondered what kind of day it would turn out to be.

The sun had yet to make an appearance, kept hidden by the dark six a.m. sky.

Bethany pressed the bell push. It took a while for a light to go on, the one on the landing, she reckoned. A rumpled-looking brown-haired man in striped cotton pyjamas answered. Late forties. Bloodshot eyes. Grey shadows beneath, wrinkles with the air of defeat about them, deep and craggy, showing how much strain he was under. A broken father then, one likely teetering on the cusp of madness: *Where are my girls? Does anyone have them? Are they hurt? Alive? Dead?*

"Mr Elliot?" She produced her ID.

His face paled, and he closed his eyes momentarily. "No. Please, no . . ."

She ploughed on. "DI Bethany Smith and DS Mike Wilkins. We need to come in, sir."

He staggered backwards, bumping into a telephone table. A silver-based lamp wobbled, the white shade loose, swinging pendulum-like.

A blonde woman bent over the banisters at the top of the stairs. "John? Who is it?"

Bethany took the opportunity to go inside and take control of the situation so things didn't deteriorate. She needed answers before these two crumpled — if the victim was even their daughter. She introduced them, and the wife came downstairs, a fluffy pink dressing gown on, the belt hanging loose. Her red fleece pyjamas had Bethany wishing she was still in her own bed. Sock slippers covered the lady's feet, a cat's eyes and nose on the fronts. She stood by John and clutched his arm.

"What's your name, love?" Bethany asked while Mike shut the door.

"Rebecca." A posh voice. Her plucked eyebrows met in the middle. "What's going on?"

"Let's go into the kitchen, shall we?" Bethany smiled. "Looks like we got you out of bed, so that calls for the kettle being put on, yes?"

Rebecca nodded, and John swiped at his wet cheeks — his mind had gone to the worst-case scenario then. The couple walked down the hallway, John putting an arm around his wife. To comfort her or himself? Bethany and Mike followed. Rebecca switched on the light, and the large kitchen flooded with brightness. Wooden stools positioned around an island must have beckoned John, as he slumped onto one, elbows propped on the marble top, head in his hands.

Rebecca turned to Bethany and implored her silently, wringing her hands, her bottom lip caught between her teeth.

"We're here about your daughters," Bethany explained. "We'd like to ask you some questions."

Rebecca's shoulders relaxed somewhat — she probably thought everything was sort of okay now, or as okay as a missing daughters' situation could be. No asking if they'd been found. No mention of bodies.

Yet.

"At this time of day?" Rebecca went to a fancy coffee machine that belonged behind a Costa counter and entered the job of drink-making without enthusiasm, going the through the motions, nothing more.

"Yes, it is early. Sorry about that."

The ensuing silence while Rebecca continued with her task was awkward.

Once they were all seated around the island, Mike took his notebook out then sipped his coffee. John cradled his cup as if for support, the square ends of his long fingers overlapping. Clean nails, no sign of scratches on his skin. How awful to be looking at a father like that, checking if he was the one they were after. Still, it had to be done.

Rebecca stared at Bethany, anticipation shining in her tear-filled eyes. Her mind must be going ten to the dozen. To put a stop to the somewhat prolonged agony, Bethany began.

"You reported your daughters missing two days ago, but they've been gone for a week. Why the delay?" That was what had been bugging her the most. Then again, the women were adults, they lived together, so why would the parents know their every move? Bethany had to remind herself that although Fay and Tammy were the Elliots' children, they *weren't* children anymore.

Rebecca pill-rolled with her pointer fingers and thumbs. Early onset Parkinson's? A nervous or comforting habit? "We didn't realise it was a week until they didn't show up here for a celebration dinner we'd arranged."

"What was the celebration?"

"They were at the end of the adoption process. We moved to Shadwell to be closer to our daughters for when the babies were taken home. All of us used to live in Essex."

Bethany's stomach plummeted, and her mind went *there* — Maisie North had been abducted. Could it be . . . ? Was that too fantastical? Was she jumping the gun? She glanced at Mike, who didn't appear to have caught on to what Rebecca's statement might mean.

"Adoption process?"

Rebecca blushed. "This is going to sound conceited, dreadful maybe, and you might not be wrong in thinking that. I don't understand it myself, and neither does John, do you, love."

John shook his head. "It's all a bit . . . well, it's the body image rubbish I can't get my head around."

What are they on about? "What is it you don't understand?"

Rebecca sighed. "This is no reflection on me, okay?"

Ah, a woman who cared too much about what other people thought. Maybe, what with living in a house like this, they were well-to-do and had certain standards they expected their daughters to uphold. Sounded like Fay and Tammy had their own minds, though.

"Please continue," Bethany said. "We really do need some answers, quickly."

Rebecca sniffed. "Neither of them want to actually carry a child — they're rather, um, precious about their bodies, getting stretch marks and that sort of thing." She blushed as if her daughters' decisions embarrassed her. "They've always been that way, body conscious. I personally don't understand it, I loved being pregnant, but they wanted children and decided to do it together. They're also big on there already being too many unwanted children in the world, so taking care of those is better than adding to the population. They don't even . . . Oh God, they don't even have *husbands*." She shuddered, as if that was the most hideous thing on the planet. "We brought them up the *right* way, to meet someone, marry, and have children, but society and its radical views changed all that, took our teachings and threw them out of the window. I'm afraid our daughters have gone off the rails."

Hardly. Bethany didn't understand why Rebecca seemed so disgusted. Okay, keeping their bodies perfect was a bit vain, but the rest? The adoptions? Admirable. And who said you needed a husband anyway? "So have they got the children yet?"

Rebecca shook her head. "That's what's puzzling. It took me a while to accept the idea of having cuckoos in the nest, but I'd come to terms with it after a fashion and suggested the meal to show them I wasn't so set in my ways, even though it would have been torture, you know, pretending to like grandchildren that aren't truly mine. The idea of even calling them grandchildren is anathema to me, but I'd decided to do it for our girls."

Magnanimous of you. "And?"

"They'd gone to collect them, wouldn't say where, and we didn't pry. We don't like to do that."

Bethany almost choked on a sip of coffee. From what Rebecca had said, she sounded like a world-class prier.

"They were bringing the babies to us that evening," Rebecca said. "They'd chosen girls."

Maisie . . . ? If so, she was taken too late for one of the daughters to have her on the night of the celebration. "What was the adoption agency? Was it abroad?"

"Oh no, here."

Mike got his phone out and tapped in a message. Alarm bells must be going off for him, too. Bethany felt better that she wasn't alone in her thinking, but how terrible that they'd even had to entertain such a thing. Had they become so cynical that no scenario was too 'out there'?

"If it's through the proper channels, that'll be easy to trace," Bethany said.

"Proper channels?" Rebecca looked appalled. "Are you suggesting our girls *wouldn't* go to a proper agency?"

"It's a new one," John said morosely. "Not the usual place you'd go for babies, Tammy said."

Bethany frowned. That didn't sound right at all. "Do you know the name of it?"

"My mind's gone blank." He shook his head. "She said it was on the internet. She'd found a questionnaire, filled it out, and she was accepted. Then Fay did the same. They were sent official papers to sign — I saw them, looked them over, and everything seemed legitimate." He paused and released a ragged sigh. "Now they're missing, I'm worried out of my mind. What if it isn't an adoption agency? What if they went to collect the babies and something else happened instead? What if it was really some . . . some bloke who . . ."

To stop him from panicking, Bethany asked a few more questions about the website.

"I don't know what it is," John said, "but I bloody wish I'd pushed for them to tell me."

"What about the papers?" Mike asked, off his phone now. "Was there a letterhead at the top?"

John scrunched his eyebrows. "Um, there was one of those things, like the royals have. Kind of a crest. Maybe dragons or lions? I can't remember. Ah, now it's coming to me. I'm sure it said Silver Lining Adoption Agency above it, and below the crest, there was some kind of motto. It was off, now I'm thinking about it."

"What did it say?" Bethany asked.

"We take then we give." John blinked. "I thought it was literally them taking babies from one mother and giving it to another, but isn't that a weird sort of thing to put?"

Weird was right, considering Maisie had been 'taken'. Had she been destined for Fay or Tammy? If so, was another baby going to be abducted for the other sister?

"How did the agency work, do you know?" Bethany needed more information to go on.

"They paid cash," Rebecca said. "I know that because they asked us for the money." She pressed a hand to her chest. "We were buying grandchildren who weren't even real, weren't ours in the proper sense, for goodness' sake."

Money changing hands means it's sus. "How much?"

"Twenty thousand each." Rebecca snorted. "That was our house extension gone."

"Why did you agree to give them the cash if you weren't truly on board with the situation?" Mike asked.

Rebecca rolled her eyes. "John can't say no to the girls. Oh, and before I forget, I recall something about a 'handler'. That was how they'd described the person who would give them the children."

The agency had to be a ruse. Cash for the babies — not a good sign — and meeting with the 'handler' to collect them . . . That was last week. So, Fay and Tammy had gone together and hadn't been seen since.

"I have something distressing to ask of you," Bethany said to stop them all going around in circles, discussing the same things over and over.

"Oh God," John moaned.

"A body was found earlier in the woods." Bethany pushed on so they didn't interrupt. "The female fits the description and a photo I've seen of Fay. Now, I have a picture of the woman . . ."

"I'll do it," Rebecca said. "I'll look at it. I can't stand this limbo anymore."

"It may well not be your daughter," Bethany reminded her, "so seeing someone else's may prove just as traumatic."

"I need to know, don't you see? *We* need to know." She gripped John's wrist and squeezed hard.

John sat silent, tears streaming.

Bethany took her phone out and accessed the image.

John closed his eyes.

Bethany held her mobile up.

And Rebecca screamed.

CHAPTER SIXTEEN

Joseph's eyes itched. He hadn't had much sleep. Worrying about him and Natasha scarpering without being caught had played heavily on his mind all night, and now, with everything he needed packed into two small rucksacks, ready to go into his saddlebags, he was finally finished here. He'd stay at the mill until it was time to go. One o'clock couldn't come soon enough.

He gave all his things one last glance, told himself they were only items, nothing to get attached to, and walked out of his place, into the dark morning.

Key pushed inside a gap where the outside windowsill was rotting, he ensured a bit of the end stuck out. He'd ring the landlord on a ten-quid burner once he'd got to his destination, tell him there was next month's rent on the kitchen table and he was welcome to keep the furniture because he wasn't coming back. Then he'd phone the police, give them Anne's name.

Bike packed up, he drove to Natasha's, taking in the lamppost-lit roads as if for the first time, seeing them and the houses as they really were instead of what he'd got used to and had learnt to ignore — ragged, in need of an overhaul, a sight a newcomer might recoil from. Shadwell was tired, and so was Joseph. He needed to get out.

Natasha waited for him on the kerb beneath a streetlight, her backpack on. So she'd chosen not to return here after they'd collected their money, too? Her face was stained with tears. He supposed it would be a wrench for her, leaving what she knew if she wasn't quite ready for it, moving to the unknown, starting all over again. He'd help her settle in York, and they'd make new friends. Failing that, they had each other.

It had to be better than staying here where they could get caught any minute.

He cut the engine and took his helmet off. Didn't matter if anyone saw him without it now, did it, not that anyone was nosing out of their windows at this hour. He'd grow a longer beard in York. Zooby looked totally different with his fake one. Joseph could blend, disappear in a sea of faces even, become no one.

"You sure you're up for this?" he asked quietly.

She nodded, appearing *un*sure. "I think so. Actually, no, it's a big step, but we *really* can't stay here now." She leant forward to whisper, "Anne must have put Five on the hill."

Joseph's legs numbed, then the feeling shot back, but they were wobbly, no strength in them. "What?"

"It's online. A bit vague, only a headline and a short paragraph, but a body is up there, face and neck slashed. Says more news to come. I'd show you, but I took my SIM out and buried it in the garden."

"What a stupid cow she is. Why there when it's so close to the fucking mill?"

"I don't know. We should get our money and go early." She pushed the spare helmet down over her head and got on the back, arms around Joseph's middle.

He started the engine, the headlight beam splashing over a red car, then he was off, his guts twisting. Anne was a serious problem, a rash thinker, someone he could do without in his life. As for Zooby, they were mates, but Joseph was prepared to forego that relationship in order to distance himself from this bullshit. If Anne hadn't killed that woman, things would be different, but they weren't, they were a mess, and he didn't want any part of it.

He made the journey on autopilot then realised his mistake. Shadwell Hill stood in the distance, light seeping between the trees. Another illuminated the parking area, showing up cars and a white Transit. He couldn't drive past, not when he reckoned there was another car at the bottom of the track and the shapes of two people. It had to be the police, didn't it? What if they saw his headlamp and came after him?

Lungs constricting, he made a swift U-turn in a lay-by, his heart banging hard, and took another route where he'd come out farther down, way past Wind Energy, and him exiting a country lane would be too far up for the police at the track to spot him. Those on the hill might, his headlamp but a speck in the darkness, so he'd switch it off, then continue to the mill.

They arrived without incident, and Joseph braced himself for seeing Anne. His anger at her putting them all in such danger threatened to come out in the form of his fist landing on her face, so he held his arms by his sides, telling himself not to rock the boat when he was so close to getting out of here.

The money, he was here for that and nothing else.

The door was locked — not surprising, given the time — so he knocked, Natasha standing beside him.

"Who is it?" Zooby asked from behind it.

"Joseph and Nat. Turn the light off before you open the door. It'll be seen otherwise."

The sound of the bolts scraping across, ones Zooby had put on when they'd taken over the place, then the door opened. Joseph and Natasha entered, and Zooby locked up and put the light back on. Anne sat up on the camp bed, her hair tidy, as if she'd had no trouble sleeping. Joseph thought it should be the opposite, guilt keeping her awake over what she'd done, but it seemed she didn't have a conscience. He ignored her and sat at the table, lifting his helmet off. Natasha did the same, taking a seat opposite him. Zooby walked over to the kettle and poured bottled water into it from one of the massive flagons.

"The police are on the hill," Natasha said. "We had to come here the long way round."

"Ooh, that was quick," Anne chirruped. "Someone must have found her."

"D'you think?" Joseph blurted. Fuck, and he so hadn't wanted to interact with her anymore. Seemed his sarcasm needed an airing. "Really clever to leave her there."

"I thought so." She smiled, clearly not twigging what he was getting at. "So near yet so far. Us here, them there."

Did she like living dangerously or something? What was *wrong* with her?

"Don't even worry about it. The rats will have eaten Five already." Anne mimed a mouth opening and shutting with her hand. "Chomp-chomp."

Joseph stared. What the hell was she *on*?

Fucked in the head, that's what she is. "What rats?"

"The ones that come out in the dark." She frowned. "Raven calls them."

"Who's Raven?" Zooby asked, panic wrenching his features. "Don't tell me you've let someone else in on this? Christ, Anne, it's supposed to just be us."

"Calm your tits. Raven's dead." Anne shrugged. "I topped her years ago."

Joseph went cold. "You've killed before now?"

"What of it? God, I'm off to check the customers. You lot are so boring it's unreal. No sense of adventure." Anne slid her mask on and sloped across the room, disappearing into the corridor.

Joseph had the mad thought she'd gone down there to murder one of the women. He pushed it away — surely she wouldn't be *that* stupid, would she? But who knew how Five had died. Maybe *Anne* had offed her, not the drugs.

Zooby stared after her, mouth hanging. "Fuck." He whispered, "She's off her bloody trolley. I'm telling you, she's not all there. She was *laughing* in the night. And that's not all of it. She only went and killed a second mum — *and* her fella."

Joseph shot up, his thighs whacking into the table edge. Natasha gave him a warning by widening her eyes: *Don't kick off. Wait for the money.*

Joseph offered her a short nod and retook his seat. "Zoobs, you need to get Two home — *now*, while it's still pretty dark. Another hour, and you're going to be spotted. Use the long route like I did, headlights off until you're out of sight of the hill. There are coppers everywhere." All right, that was an exaggeration, they were concentrated at the hill, but he wanted to make sure Zooby was aware of how easily he could get caught.

"I need to bath the kid, get this place off her," Zooby said.

"No time." Natasha shook her head. "Seriously, get rid of them."

Zooby nodded then handed out the coffees. "Right. I'm just putting it out there that I'm not happy about sending the baby off with no wash or new clothes. She could have evidence on her. Put your masks on in case Two gets funny about putting the blindfold on." He strode into the corridor, coming back with a doll, which he switched for the real deal, a baby from one of the cots. He took her through the doorway.

Joseph and Natasha covered their faces with the masks.

"She's out of control," Natasha whispered.

"Don't I know it."

Zooby appeared, guiding Two into the room, the woman clutching the baby. He'd managed to put her blindfold on then. Joseph found the correct documents on the table and handed them to Zooby. Then they were gone, out of the main door, thank God.

A few seconds passed with Joseph and Natasha staring at each other. It was so weird looking at a clown, and he absently wondered if she felt the same way.

"I didn't look in the cot on purpose when we came in," he said.

"Me neither. Sort of like pretending this isn't happening. If I didn't see her, I didn't have to admit we've done wrong."

"Exactly that."

Anne returned, grabbing a coffee from by the kettle and sitting in the armchair, legs stretched in front of her as if she didn't have a care in the world. The atmosphere tensed immediately.

"They're all so out of it." She laughed. "I mean, he must be giving them a fair whack of the gear if they can't tell they're holding dolls. Did you hear about my antics last night, by the way?"

Antics. So that was how she saw it. Like a joke.

"I was attacked by the woman's fella." Anne sipped her drink. "He shouldn't have even been there, so Zooby needs to buck up when it comes to gathering intel. I had to defend myself, then she woke up an' all. Bloody inconvenience, that was."

Joseph didn't have it in him to respond. If he did, he'd say stuff that might set her off, and who knew if she'd go for him next.

"Rat got your tongue?" she asked.

What was up with her and rats?

"They taste nice, you know," she went on.

Natasha got up and tidied the already tidy Pampers boxes. Joseph wished he hadn't left his laptop in one of the saddlebags so he could pretend to work.

Anne leant forward and whispered to him, "I don't like you. I don't trust you. Someone to keep an eye on, you are. What are you up to? I know it's something. I can feel it."

Her words were so spot on he panicked. "Look, I'm here to do a job, not make friends with you, all right? I want to get it done, and when it's over, pretend it didn't happen. You've risked us all with the shit you've got up to, and the sooner we can stop this the better."

"It'll be a while. We have rounds of snatching to do yet."

Zooby can't have told her he's changing the plan yet. "Yeah, well, leave me alone while we're at it."

She narrowed her eyes. "We don't even need you now. You've done your part with the website and the documents." She glanced at the pile of them in front of her. "Why don't you just fuck off? It's not like you're keeping watch here with Zooby now, is it? Your *real* job is taking precedence. I seem to recall you saying, in the Grapes one time, you wouldn't do that. Still, we can all change our minds, can't we."

That last bit was loaded with a totally different meaning, he was sure of it. She'd referred to herself, that *she* could also change her mind from whatever the hell she'd previously decided.

"Yep, we can," he said.

She nodded. "Hmmm. I'm going to enjoy it."

Her expression was so sinister he had to get up, away from her, worrying about what she'd meant. He changed the cot sheet the baby had rested on and replaced it with a clean one. Then he checked on the customers to make sure Anne hadn't bumped one off. They were all sleeping apart from one of them, who sat on her bed rocking her doll.

He stood in the doorway and stared at her, wanting to tell her to leave, to forget the money she'd spent, and the baby she thought was real.

"What's the tattoo mean?" He pointed to her ankle.

She frowned, as if the answer to his question was too hard to find in her fogged-up head. "I forgot. How's my sister?"

He didn't know what to tell her. Lie and say she was here somewhere? Say she was dead? He opted to remain silent. This wasn't his problem, it was Zooby's.

Joseph closed the door and stayed in the corridor for a while, anything so he didn't have to see Anne anytime soon. The minutes ticked by slowly.

The rumble of an engine had his guts cramping. Zooby? Or the police?

Breath held, he waited.

"Where's Joseph?" Zooby's voice.

Relieved, Joseph entered the room. "All done?"

"Yeah." Zooby nodded. "Natasha, you go round there about twelve, all right?"

She nodded, still in her mask. "I need my money. I want to get my debts off my back as soon as possible."

Zooby walked over to a small safe hidden beneath a cot. He dragged it out, inputted the code, and opened it up. Money counted on the floor, he scooped each pile up and handed them out. Joseph shoved his into an inside pocket of his jacket. Natasha placed hers in her back pocket. Anne watched them intently, the creepy cow.

"I need to get home and finish some work I started yesterday," Joseph said. "And if you're up for taking a suggestion, you two hide your cars in the warehouse part of the building. The police are far too close and might come sniffing round."

"Right." Zooby played with the beard. "Come here later for the usual meeting."

Joseph nodded, put his helmet on over his mask, and walked outside, Natasha on his heels. He drove them past the outskirts then stopped in a lay-by. Raised his visor and looked over his shoulder.

"We shouldn't wait until one, like we planned," he said. "We don't need to now the mother and baby have gone home early and we have our money."

"Agreed. I brought my stuff anyway, didn't want to go back to my place and wait. I'd planned to hang around at the mill if he didn't pay us until later."

He faced ahead, and in the side mirror, caught sight of a car coming. So the driver didn't spot his mask, he flipped his visor down and sped off.

The car sped, too.

Fuck, was it undercover coppers or something? He should have changed his plates before they'd set off. If they stopped him for whatever reason, he'd be in the shit if they ran them through the database.

The car drew closer, gaining on him.

He went full throttle, and Natasha's squeal and the tightening of her arms around him said she was scared. So was he, truth be told. They couldn't get caught, not now they were on their way to freedom.

* * *

Anne floored the accelerator and managed to get right up the bike's arse. Something was going on with those two — why weren't they heading to Shadwell? She'd planned to follow them, get rid of Joseph at his place once he'd dropped Natasha off at hers, but this route was heading north.

They had to be on the run.

The crunch of her front bumper ramming into the back of the bike sounded glorious, the sight of it falling to the side and the riders coming off even better, especially the thud of their bodies on the road. They were flung to the right, and she drove over them, enjoying the lumps beneath the tyres and how the car jostled. Brakes on, she lurched forward, almost nutting the windscreen, then reversed over them, keeping going so she could get a good run up when she went forward again.

A superb burst of speed, and she crushed them to the road, a glance in her rearview telling her all she needed to know. Those fuckers were dead. Shame about Natasha, she was an all right sort, despite not wanting to know about the rats, but Joseph? He'd got on her nerves right from the start, and getting rid of him was epic.

She backed up again and got out. Took the money from their pockets.

Rich as eff.

She'd visit Two and the baby at noon, in place of Natasha. It was the least she could do.

CHAPTER SEVENTEEN

Carla woke at the sound of Lily mewling. Thank God. The drugs they'd given her must have worn off at last. The baby had been dozy all of last evening, enough for Mum to query it around ten o'clock, three lines of concern across her brow. Carla had lied, hopefully convincingly, saying Lily had a cold last week and the last knockings of it were hanging about.

Once she'd gone upstairs, Carla had tucked Lily into her side in the single bed, worrying she'd roll on top of her during the night, considering she didn't have that particular maternal instinct that would alert her, even in sleep, the moment danger presented itself. But she'd left the Moses basket in Shadwell in her haste to leave, and there was nowhere else to put the little dot. Mum had followed behind her, coming in to pull the quilt down like she had every night Carla was small. It was sweet but annoying at the same time. Mum suggested using a drawer, like in the olden days, with blankets inside for cushioning, but really, Carla wasn't up for that.

She yawned and checked the clock, leaning over to switch the lamp on, delaying looking at Lily in case she stared up at her, eyes going wide at the realisation that Carla wasn't Vicky. The baby might scream the house down, and Mum was bound to come in, fussing and asking if she could help, clucking around in mild panic, wanting to fix everything and make life easier for Carla.

Bless her and everything, but . . . no. Carla wanted to do this by herself.

"Good morning," she said to test the waters.

Surely Lily would blart now she'd heard her? Carla held her breath.

A coo.

Carla dared to roll onto her side and peer down at Lily nestled by her belly. And oh, the tiny darling gave a gummy smile, nose scrunched, her blue eyes alight with trust, and everything bad faded away. No more past, no baby theft, no murder. They were here, together in their bubble, and Lily would never know who Carla really was. Mother and daughter, that was the long and short of it, a secret only Carla and the organisation would know.

An arrow of guilt came, with the name of Vicky North, a dead woman, poisoning the tip, the venom of it seeping into her blood and infecting the nice moment.

What was the antidote?

She sang to Lily, and that eased her conscience for a while, but soon the child fretted, whimpering and stuffing her fist into her mouth. She'd be hungry, so Carla reached over her shoulder and felt around for one of the bottles she'd made prior to coming to bed. The milk would be cold, and it was apparently bad to give it to a baby if it wasn't freshly made, but Mum had said Carla survived it, and all this newfangled parenting was a load of rubbish anyway.

Lily took the teat greedily, and Carla had to remember to stop the feed halfway through to burp her. She'd done the same while in that grotty room but hardly remembered any of her time there now — it was as if what she'd learnt there, Weird Glasses teaching her, hadn't happened.

Maybe her mind had the idea of wiping it.

Carla should tell herself that time didn't exist, and the story she'd given her parents was true. If she believed it, other people would, too.

Lily emitted a big belch, and Carla sat up to feed her the rest. The baby fell asleep afterwards, so Carla crept out to have a shower, thanking whoever was up there looking out for her that Mum and Dad were still asleep. She returned to the room, thinking this child-rearing business was a lot easier than some of the chapters in the manual suggested. Perhaps Lily was one of those rare children who settled easily in any situation, not a moment's trouble, although a vague recollection of her crying a lot in the manky room sprang to mind.

It was that place then, which had set her off. Everything would be okay now.

A creaking floorboard denoted Mum or Dad rising.

Carla dressed, even put some make-up on, but she took it off. It didn't do to resemble her old self, a woman who'd been part of stealing a baby. She left her hair in its natural waves instead of drying and straightening it, consciously altering her appearance, as if her seeing her basic look in the mirror meant she wasn't the Carla pre-Lily. She felt human again, clean and clear-minded, ready to move on.

Until thoughts of the news intruded.

She went to access the internet on her phone and wondered whether she really should. She'd maybe see more than she had yesterday. The police were bound to have more information by now, the way they rooted around in their investigations and unearthed hidden gems that revealed all. And did seeing the news marry with her previous decision to stick to her story and continue with the fabricated version of events? No, it didn't.

But what if someone in the organisation had come forward, blowing it all wide open? What if Carla had been identified, despite them promising everything would remain anonymous?

Lily snuffled, drawing Carla away from her fears and into protective mode. At least that side of her maternal urges was working.

She had to be strong for both of them. A life of lying waited ahead of her, but it would be worth it, so long as she had that baby.

* * *

Mum had cooked a full English, although Carla declined the black pudding. Dad entertained a laughing Lily in his sturdy arms while Carla ate. She wanted nothing more than to stay here, cocooned by her parents' support in their lovely kitchen, but drawing them into this mess more than they already were, well, it wasn't something she could handle. She needed to leave, much as it pained her.

"Did you get enough sleep, love?" Dad asked, jiggling Lily.

"Yes, she went right through."

"Well, aren't you the lucky one." Mum plunged her hands into the mountain of soap suds in the washing-up bowl. She didn't use the dishwasher until the evening meal. "Or are the sleepless nights in the past now? There's so much we've missed out on."

"They seem to be." But hadn't Lily woken relentlessly when she'd first taken over her care? The memory floated just out of reach, smoke in the wind, and Carla was glad of it.

"Getting them into a routine is always best, I say." Mum added a frying pan to the bowl. It sizzled from still being hot, and she got on with the business of scrubbing it. "Is that what you did?"

"Yes, the health visitor told me how to do it." Well, the baby manual had, but she didn't need to divulge that snippet.

"How do you find them, the health visitors?" Dad asked. "They used to get on your mum's nerves back in the day. Always prying."

"Oh, mine's okay. Nice enough."

"Do you remember," Mum said, "when she tried to tell me I should hold our Carla all the time as a baby can't be spoilt? I'd seen enough of my friends with their children to know they bloody can, and while it's lovely to have a good cuddle, carting them around in your arm while you're doing the hoovering wasn't my idea of fun. You were quick to realise, Carla, that it was okay to be in your Moses basket crying while I went about the house." She turned, a wire soap pad in one hand. "I shouldn't have held Lily all that time yesterday. Practise what I preach."

"It's okay." Carla popped a mushroom in her mouth. *I wanted you to have that, because we won't be here for much longer.*

The doorbell pealed, and Carla instantly went on alert, her body taking over her mind. She sprang to her feet and had to stop herself from snatching Lily off her father and running upstairs to hide. Her cheeks flushed with guilt and terror, her skin erupting with goosebumps, her heart missing beats. And all the while, Dad carried on tickling the baby under the chin, Lily laughed even more, and Mum smiled.

"I'll get that," Mum said and dropped the scouring pad to whip a tea towel off the side.

"I'm not here," Carla blurted. "I mean, if it's Lily's dad. He knows where you live, and I—"

"Oh, it won't be *him*." Mum winked and bustled out into the hallway, drying her hands along the way.

Carla had taken a seat with the door to her left so couldn't see out there. It was frustrating yet also a comfort. That meant whoever had rung the bell couldn't see her either.

"Morning!" Mum's bright and cheery voice floated in.

"Get out of the way so I can have a cuddle with the little love, Karen."

Oh God, it was Sandra Drivet from across the road, the nosy woman Mum thought was amazing. Carla had known her all her life and detested the way she knew everyone's business, including theirs. Mum must have told her Carla was here, or Sandra had spotted her car. But that couldn't be right. She'd hardly see Carla as a 'little love' and certainly wouldn't want to cuddle her.

Definitely Mum then. What was she thinking?

There was nothing for it but to play out the charade, just this last one before she got out of England for good. Carla cut a slice of now cold fried egg and almost gagged at the texture of it in her mouth. She glanced at Dad, who studied her with concern, as if he'd picked up on her panic. He rolled his eyes good-naturedly, a swift change from his previous expression — he'd never liked Sandra either and had moaned about her for years.

"Just grit your teeth and smile," he said. "You know the drill."

Then Sandra was there, by Dad's side, in all her leopard-print coat and beehive hair glory, grabbing Lily as if she had the right. Weren't people supposed to ask permission to hold your baby first? Carla experienced such a surge of anger she didn't know what to do with herself so swallowed the egg and attacked a Cumberland sausage, cutting it into several pieces.

"Oh, what a gorgeous little thing," Sandra gushed, high spots of colour on her cheeks, or that could be the copious amounts of pink blusher she daubed on top of the thick powder that didn't match the rest of her skin — she was one for the tanning beds.

Sandra all but threw Lily onto her shoulder and patted her back a tad too hard for Carla's liking. She had the childish urge to tell her Lily had already been winded, thanks very much, but chose to spear a chunk of sausage instead, stuffing it into her mouth to stop the words coming out. Was this how it would be, forever biting her tongue regarding Lily to save people's feelings, when Carla's were pushed to the wayside by doing so? Should she stand up for the innocent baby's rights or allow Sandra *carte blanche*, gritting her teeth like Dad had said?

The woman herself flung Lily into the crook of her arm, curling her palm around the baby's bum, her scarlet nails stark against the white of the sleepsuit Lily had slept in. Carla winced, thinking the stupid cow might drop her, and even Mum and Dad appeared concerned.

"Be gentle then," Mum said.

"Oh, they're not china dolls," Sandra admonished. "They're hardier than you think."

"I realise that." Mum bristled. "But she's not long got over a cold, so you being rough like that . . ."

All Mum's bluster about not spoiling a baby didn't seem to apply to Lily.

The sausage stuck in Carla's throat, along with emotion. Mum was in Carla and Lily's corner, her motherly and grandmotherly instinct coming to the fore, sticking up for Carla and the baby when they couldn't do it for themselves in the face of someone like Sandra. She managed to get the food down and concentrated on cutting a bacon rasher which had gone tough as old boots.

"I do see what you mean, though," Sandra said.

"Good. I'd prefer my granddaughter to remain in one piece," Dad muttered, his fingers fluttering as if he resisted claiming Lily back.

"Oh, not about that, Eric." Sandra peered hard at Lily. "I'm talking about what Karen said earlier this morning. She rang me, you know, so terribly excited."

Dad frowned and gave Mum a look that said everything. He was annoyed, probably thinking Mum had shared things with Sandra that he'd prefer remained private — things Carla wanted to remain private. Like her business with the father of the baby, not that he knew it was all made up.

"What's that then?" he asked.

"That Lily is like that Maisie baby who was snatched." Sandra inspected the child even more, as though searching for confirmation that Lily *was* Maisie.

Oh my God. Carla had to force herself not to get up and go over there, Lily being snatched for a second time in her short life with Carla's need to hold her close. Dad seemed on the verge of doing similar, and Mum, she appeared just the same, if a bit shamefaced about discussing Lily and Maisie in the same conversation again. The likeness must be playing on Mum's mind if she'd said something about it to Sandra. Maybe it hadn't been in a way that meant Mum believed Lily was that other child, but more a passing comment that they resembled each other. Knowing Sandra, she'd let that idea run riot in her mind, and soon, everyone around here would know her feelings on the subject.

The bacon was tough and cold on Carla's tongue.

"What are you going on about?" Dad moved closer to Sandra. "Of course the babies look the same. They all do at that age. Unless they've got different hair colours."

"But not all of them have a strawberry birthmark behind their ear, do they?" Sandra was triumphant, that much was clear. "Look, here you are, see?" She pulled Lily's ear back to display her find.

A red splotch in the shape of an ice-cream cone.

"It was in a news update this morning," Sandra prattled.

Fear enveloped Carla. Why hadn't she noticed that? She was sure Lily hadn't had a birthmark in the filthy room — she'd checked every part of her when Weird Glasses handed her over for the first time, toes, fingers, the lot. But could she trust her recollection of events? She'd already acknowledged earlier that those memories were hazy.

"A coincidence," she managed around the chewed-up bacon. "There's another baby with that sort of birthmark behind her ear. I met the mother on weighing days." Too much? Trying too hard to cover the blunder up?

"A bloody big coincidence." Sandra let Lily's ear go. It was red on the top curve where she must have pinched it, although Lily remained content. "So, the father. Where is he in this rather vague picture?"

"What do you mean, vague?" Dad harrumphed.

"Well, Karen didn't say much about how Lily came to be. Okay, I know how babies *get* here, of course I do, but the circumstances . . . I wasn't even aware Carla *had* a man." Sandra rocked Lily, who grabbed at her red bottom lip and squeezed. Karma for the ear. "Ow, tha hurs, you lil monney." She prised the hand away. "Monkey."

Mum pulled a wet wipe out of a packet on the table and cleaned Lily's fingers as if the lipstick would damage her granddaughter. "I didn't tell you anything because it's Carla's story to share if she wishes to." She glanced at Dad, as if to tell him yes, she *could* keep her mouth shut sometimes.

"That's so unlike you, though, Karen." Sandra raised her eyebrows. "You love to gossip."

"Not in this case." Mum had a hard time taking Lily away from Sandra, but she managed it in the end. She gently held her against her shoulder and rubbed her back.

"Well, I'll be off then." Sandra, clearly affronted, did an about-face and strutted from the room. "I'll see myself out. I can tell you're busy and have no time for me."

The door slammed. The noise of it seemed like an echo of a parallel life, the other side of this where Carla could be in prison, and her cell door was the one making that racket. She swallowed the bacon at last and pushed her plate away, all desire for food gone. What set up home inside her was a vast need to get away from here, go to France, now, and never come back.

"That woman grates on my bloody nerves," Dad said. "I wish you didn't have anything to do with her, Karen."

Carla agreed with that, especially now the image of that birthmark was undoubtedly stitched into Sandra's mind so tightly it'd never go away. Had the newspapers printed a picture of Maisie, the mark clearly visible? Would thousands of people now be surreptitiously checking behind random babies' ears in search of it so they could call the police?

What should she do? Book a ticket to France, not telling her parents until she'd done it? A trail would be created, one the police could follow if they ever got wind she was involved in this god-awful mess.

She rose as casually as she could and walked over to kiss Lily on the head. "Can I use your computer, Dad?"

"You know where it is, love," he said.

Her mind made up, she went into the study, closing the door and leaning on it. She stood there for a moment, calming her nerves, wishing Sandra hadn't come round. Somewhat on a more even keel, she sat at the desk and secured her flight to a new life, hacked off she hadn't been able to obtain a way out until this afternoon. By tonight, she'd be at Nice Côte d'Azur airport, waiting for a taxi to take her and Lily to Antibes where her parents' holiday home was. She could visit Saint-Tropez and Cannes, giving her daughter such a special upbringing, more than she'd have had in Shadwell with Vicky North, she was sure. With the money Carla had at her disposal, Lily would want for nothing, and the amount of love Carla had inside her was enough for a hundred children.

It'll be fine. Just get out of England. Become someone else. She repeated that in her head all the way to the kitchen.

Much to her parents' astonishment, she announced her plans.

Mum's face fell. "So soon? But I've only just met her." She brushed her lips over Lily's head.

Dad narrowed his eyes for a brief moment, then disguised it by closing them and stretching, as if that was what he'd been doing all along. Or maybe he was, and Carla was seeing things that weren't there. When he looked at her again, he was his normal self. But Carla hadn't imagined it. She knew. Dad had cottoned on to what she'd done, all this talk of Maisie tipping him off.

"Yes, go," he said. "England isn't the place for you, not if Lily's dad turns up and causes trouble."

She exchanged 'dad' for 'police' in her mind and understood him loud and clear.

Leave, before you get caught.

CHAPTER EIGHTEEN

Bethany and Mike had left Alice Jacobs, the FLO, to deal with the Elliots. John and Rebecca were in no fit state to continue their day without professional emotional support. Rebecca had agreed to formally identify Fay tomorrow after the post-mortem. It was a relief to leave them, to be honest, and they had a lot to talk about on the way back to the station.

"That mother . . ." Mike scratched his head.

"Oh, I know. Fancy being so bothered about what other people think that it controls your life."

"I'm surprised she agreed with John about handing the money over. *And* about having 'cuckoos' in the nest. My estimation went down regarding her as soon as she said that bit. While I find Fay and Tammy's reasons for not wanting to get pregnant weird, adopting is a decent thing to do. Rebecca should be proud of them."

"She's not seeing it that way. It's more like the babies will taint her precious and perfect life. If they're not of their 'stock', she's reticent to welcome them into the family."

Mike's phone went off, and he read the message. "That's Fran. There's no such agency registered as Silver Lining."

"Didn't think there would be. Is it nuts to think Maisie was taken for Fay or Tammy? I keep telling myself it's too far-fetched, it's a coincidence, but a little voice is waffling on that we should go down that road."

"With no sign of Silver Lining anywhere, and payment being made to basically buy kids, it's certainly pointing to a fake agency. What harm can it do, looking into this angle? We've got sod all else."

"Oh balls. Answer my phone, will you?" The ring was muffled in her pocket. She handed her mobile over.

He slid it to speaker. "Mike here, Rob. Bethany's driving."

"Just had a call come in about a road traffic accident. Wouldn't normally bother you, but the check I ran on the plate of the motorbike involved brought up the fact that a search on it was already made — by you lot."

Bethany's interest had piqued the second he'd said 'motorbike'. "Go on."

"Two fatalities, a man and a woman. It wasn't the accident that killed them, though. An early report from Glen, who was already nearby at the hill scene, says they were run over, possibly a few times."

Murder. "Blimey."

"I've run some checks on the IDs for Glen, so he can tell you the info."

"Brilliant."

"A member of the public was driving by and spotted the bike and bodies, called it in."

"Okay, we're out and about anyway so will take this one," she said. "Sounds like it's our man who made the phone call saying he knew who'd killed Vicky North and took Maisie."

"That's a turn up, although him being alive would have been preferable."

She couldn't argue there. "Where do we need to go?"

"Two miles past the old mill, heading out of Shadwell."

"Let Fran know the names of the deceased, please." She changed direction and headed that way. "Tell her it's a possible on the bike rider. She'll know who you mean. Thanks. Speak soon."

Mike swiped her screen. "What the fucking hell?"

"I know. So, what about this. The killer somehow found out the bloke rang us. He decided to leg it, and the killer ran him over."

"But who's the woman?"

"A girlfriend?"

"Let's hope they have ID on them."

It didn't take long to reach the road in question, an ambulance and patrol cars clustered ahead. Presley's was there, too, him probably coming straight here from the woods. She parked, got out, and walked towards Glen.

"Bit of a mess over there." He waved at the cordon.

"I gathered as much. You think they've been run over?"

He nodded. "A few times. I checked for signs of life anyway. ID are passports — one in a saddlebag, another in the woman's backpack. There's also a laptop, blank passports, and birth certificates. He's Neil Bennett, she's Heidi Jones. No employment details — I asked Rob to help me out there, and he couldn't find anything. A bit weird."

"It is." She glanced at the parked cars. "I take it the driver who found them is in that yellow Honda."

"Yes," Glen said, "although there isn't much to tell. There were no cars on her journey along here, so whoever drove over them was long gone. She stopped, didn't get out of her car, and phoned us."

"I won't bother speaking to her then. You can tell her to go home." She cast her gaze about. Had the bikers been coming into Shadwell or leaving it? "Didn't you or Tory notice the bike go past when you were standing at the bottom of the track?"

Glen shook his head. "No. Didn't see a car either. If we did, we'd have stopped them."

"So if they were leaving, they had to have been on the road that curves around Wind Energy and comes out on this one. That country lane."

"Bit out of the way if they were only leaving Shadwell," Mike said. "Everyone uses this road if going north."

"Obviously not," she said and caught sight of the old mill in the distance to the right. "Should we check up there just in case?" She pointed to it. "We came out here earlier and saw nothing but didn't go right up to it."

Mike scrubbed his chin. "Can't hurt, although I'm betting it's just as abandoned as it always is."

Her phone rang. Rob's name filled the bar across the screen. "Yep."

"Just got a call. A neighbour has found a man and woman, dead. No baby in the cot."

"Christ. Where?" She motioned for Mike to get his notebook out and repeated the info as Rob gave it to her. "Sixteen Lemon Grove Gardens, Oriana Blake, twenty-eight. Damien Tipton, five Lemon Grove Gardens. Missing baby, Elsie Blake, six months old." She sighed. "We'll go there now. Can you tell Isabelle? I'll let Presley know as he's here with us."

She shoved her phone away and walked to the cordon.

"Pres?" she called.

He turned from standing over the male rider, helmet in his hands, and peered her way. "Yes?"

"Sixteen Lemon Grove Gardens. You're needed."

He nodded. "There's nothing left for me to do here anyway. I'm done. This man has a mask on, by the way. A clown."

What? "Okay, thanks." She popped some booties on and went over there, taking a picture of the mask. "Can you lift it so I can see his face?"

Presley did so, placing it in an evidence bag. Bethany took a picture of the man. Young, in his twenties. A stubble beard. Wide, bloodshot eyes, a bloodied mouth.

"Thanks," she said. "See you at the next scene."

She returned to Mike, and they got in the car.

"Elsie is meant for Tammy?" Mike said.

"It's looking likely." She shot off back the way they'd come, taking the country lane into Shadwell. "While we undoubtedly have Fay, where is Tammy, Maisie, and now Elsie?"

"What I can't work out is, why take the babies if you're going to kill the adoptive parents anyway? Why was Fay murdered and left in the woods if Maisie had been stolen for her?"

"Think about it, yes? Maybe, in order for Fay to believe a baby was coming, they nicked Maisie and showed her the news. She kicked off, what with Vicky being dead, and the killer needed to shut her up. No one's going to take a child and run off into the sunset happily, not when someone's been murdered, are they?"

"Depends how desperate they are for a child," Mike said.

"True. Maybe I don't get it because my desire to have kids died with Vinny." A dash of grief stabbed her, as it always did when she thought of what might have been.

While Bethany and her husband had been dedicated to their careers, a baby wasn't even in the picture, but they may have had one at some point — if he hadn't been suffocated by smoke from that bloody fire. Now, she wasn't interested. If it couldn't be Vinny's, she didn't want one at all.

She entered Shadwell, lowering her speed. "Right, so say what I said is true, and Fay caused a fuss. Did Tammy witness it? Is she now stuck wherever she is, unable to leave? If so, and the killer is risking Tammy opening her mouth once she's let go, why bother taking Elsie Blake?"

"If they're pretending to be an adoption agency, they might have lured other desperate women in."

"Now *that* is a nasty scenario. Ah, uniforms are here already."

She parked in the middle of the street, in front of a cordon streaking across the road. Officers were at front doors asking questions, and Penny Dickens stood outside number sixteen. A SOCO van trundled along and stopped behind Bethany's car, then Presley came up the rear.

A SOCO jumped out of the passenger side and approached. "Isabelle said to wait. She'll be about five minutes."

"Fine by me. I'll go and speak to those officers over there." Bethany dipped beneath the cordon and walked to Nicola Eccles who was just leaving number two across the road. "Any luck?"

"Unfortunately not. Even the neighbour who found the bodies didn't hear anything during the night."

"Who went in the murder house, you or Penny?"

"Penny. I stayed outside with the neighbour. She's in number twelve, a Sally Michaels."

"We'll nip there then while we wait for Isabelle." She strode over to Mike, bending under the cordon again. "We'll chat to the lady who found the bodies."

At the front door, Bethany knocked. It was opened quickly by a young woman with mascara-stained cheeks and blonde hair.

"Sally Michaels?" Bethany held up her ID and introduced them. "Can we come in?"

Sally nodded.

The living room was small, colourful toys dotting the carpet. A baby boy sat chewing on a plastic brick. Sally sat on the sofa closest to him while Bethany and Mike remained standing.

"Can you go through what happened this morning?" Bethany asked.

Sally gulped. "Me and Oriana were meant to get together for a play date. She was coming here at half eight."

"That's early, isn't it?"

"Not really. Both our kids get us up about five, so by eight thirty, it seems like lunchtime to us. Anyway, we were going to have breakfast then go into town. I texted her at twenty to nine because she's never late, and by ten to, I went round there. She didn't answer, so I used the spare key she gave me and went in." She closed her eyes and shuddered.

"What happened then?"

"I called out, and my son decided to cry at that point, so I couldn't hear if Oriana answered me. I looked around downstairs, she wasn't there, so I went up. Elsie wasn't in her room in the cot, and I just thought Oriana had taken her into her bed or something, you know, they'd had a rough night and had fallen back to sleep. That's unusual for her, but it's the kind of thing you think, isn't it."

"It is. Carry on."

"I walked in there and . . . and she was . . . she was in bed with Damien, and that's unusual as well. He normally stays at his place when she's having her pamper night, down the road at his mum's. Number five."

"Right." Bethany asked the usual questions about any grudges and whatnot.

"Elsie's dad can be a bit funny."

"What do you mean?"

"He's always saying Oriana doesn't look after her properly. Keeps threatening to take the baby off her."

While that was interesting, how could Bethany suspect him when Vicky had been killed in the same manner? Why would he have even killed Vicky? "What's his name?"

"Phillip Stockley. He actually lives next door to Damien at number six. Awkward."

Bethany thanked her and left. They walked to Stockley's house. He answered, face streaked with tears, skin blotchy. She told him who they were, and he let them in.

"What the fuck's going on?" he demanded. "Where's my kid?"

"Do you mind my colleague having a look around?" she asked.

"Do what you like. I'm just interested in Elsie."

Mike left the room.

"We've only just become aware of the incident, but I can assure you, as with Maisie North, officers will now also be concentrating on finding your daughter. Where were you last night?"

He laughed. "Oh, fuck me. Here we go. You think *I* took Elsie?"

"It's something we have to consider, yes."

"I was here. Ask my mum and dad — they're at work, by the way." He gave the place of their employment. "Ask for Carol and Wesley."

"Thank you. Do you know of anyone who would want to murder Oriana and—"

"What?" He stared, wild-eyed. "What the hell are you on about?"

"You haven't been informed?"

"Have I fuck. I was just told Elsie was missing when I went round there to see what the chuff was happening. I saw the police, got worried. I told them it was my kid. They said I had to go home until someone came to speak to me. It'll be that prick, Damien."

"Damien is also deceased."

"Shit." He sank onto the sofa. "Jesus Christ, this wasn't supposed to happen."

"Excuse me?"

"I can't do this." He dropped his head into his hands. "I thought I'd be able to go through with it, but . . . Look, Oriana wasn't supposed to be involved, and Damien, he should have been at home."

"Mike?" she called. Then to Phillip, "You might want to explain what you're talking about."

Mike came in and stood in the doorway.

"Phillip has something to tell us," she said and raised her eyebrows.

Phillip flung himself backwards, arms out by his sides. No threat then.

"Listen, Oriana's a really shite mother, okay? I want to get that straight right off the bat. We weren't really a couple. I got her up the duff after a three-night stand. Now I know what she does with herself to make money, I'm wondering if the kid's even mine. I love Elsie whatever, but I'm not the best parent for her either. I need to grow up, and I'm skint, can't give her what she needs, know what I mean? So I told my mate about her, how she needed to be away from Oriana. I mean, come on, what kind of mum lets all sorts of men in and has it off with them while the baby's kipping? Damien's only one of a long line, I can tell you."

"Okay . . . So this mate of yours. I'm guessing he has something to do with this?"

Phillip wiped at his eyes, mopping up tears. "Yeah. He runs this adoption agency — don't even bother asking me what it is or how someone like him is in charge, because I don't know. He showed me his paperwork and everything. All legit. I just thought he'd turned over a new leaf. Anyway, he said he could find a decent mother for Elsie, it'd just take a few weeks to set up. Then he gives me a bell about ten days ago, says it was happening last night. Elsie would be taken. She'd have a new birth certificate, a passport, and some fella he had working for him knew how to hack systems so a fake birth could be recorded. It sounded perfect. No one would know who my littlun was. It was for the best. She'd have a better life with the new woman."

"Do you know anything about who the woman is?"

"Someone from Essex, that's all I know. I remember it because I asked if she was a typical Essex girl and whether my Elsie would be brought up using fake eyelashes by the time she was ten. I felt right bad about saying that afterwards, but it was just a joke."

Essex. Fay and Tammy. She steadied her breathing. "Where was Elsie being taken?"

"I didn't ask. Thought it best I didn't know anything so I didn't have to hide it from you lot, but it turns out I'm weak, because I couldn't even go through with lying."

"You do realise you're probably going to face time for this, don't you?" she asked. "You've aided and abetted a kidnap."

"Shit."

Mike walked out into the hallway and opened the front door. "Uniforms here, please," he shouted.

Phillip stood, hands out, wrists together. "You'll get no trouble from me."

Bethany stared at him. "Good. What's this friend called?"

"I just know him as Zooby."

She knew that name. It cropped up from time to time regarding petty thefts. His real one was Bevan Zooblavich.

And I know all about you.

CHAPTER NINETEEN

Bethany rang for Leona to come out and take a uniform with her to speak to Oriana's and Damien's next of kin. Fran would stay in the incident room and do what she did best regarding Bevan Zooblavich — finding his family, friends, his usual haunts. Bethany couldn't go inside Oriana's house even though Isabelle had arrived. There were more pressing matters to attend to than seeing dead bodies. She had a feeling it would be a similar scene to Vicky North's anyway, complete with a headless rat.

Fran's message came through with details once Phillip Stockley had been cuffed and taken to the station. He'd muttered that he was sorry more times than she cared to count, and while she understood him wanting a better life for Elsie, his method of getting it for her was low down on the scale of good fatherly things to do.

> Fran: ZOOBLAVICH'S ADDRESS, TWENTY-FOUR SHADOWS RISE.

> Bethany: NEVER HEARD OF IT. WHERE THE HELL IS IT?

Fran: ONE OF THE COUNCIL HOMES ON THAT NEW ECO VILLAGE.

Bethany: BLIMEY, WE WERE ONLY THERE EARLIER THIS MORNING. I DIDN'T KNOW THE COUNCIL HAD SNAGGED SOME.

Now, she admired the beautiful homes and gardens as she looked for the right street.

"This is it." Mike pointed to the road sign.

She turned into Shadows Rise, where the buildings were all the same, terraced with white front doors and windows. Each slim residence butted the pavement, and she supposed having no front garden meant less work but more chance of people nosing in while they walked past. Cars parked against kerbs that hadn't had the chance to be pushed down by the weight of the vehicles yet. The road was dark tarmac and, given time, would become grey with the weather and use.

Twenty-four had smeared windows, maybe from a dog pressing its nose to it or children with mucky fingers. Either way, it stood out compared to the shiny ones in other houses.

They knocked on the door that had mud splatter on it, and she wondered whether the inside would be dirty. Shame, since it was a new build.

A woman of about fifty opened the door, harassed-looking with grey-blonde hair hanging loose. "Yeah?"

"Mrs Zooblavich?"

"Who wants ter know?" She squinted at them, hiding her brown irises.

Bethany produced her ID and gave their names. "Is Bevan in?"

Mrs Zooblavich laughed, flashing off manky teeth with brown curves hugging the gums. "Oh, here to pin something on him, are yer? Well, yer can scuttle back off into yer little hole, because he's not even in the country."

Shit. "Where is he?"

"Magaluf. One of them lads' holidays. Gone to have some sea and sun. He's earnt the rest. Always helping me with the kids, he is."

"When did he go?"

"Week before last, not that it's any of your beeswax."

It fits with Fay and Tammy going missing. "Do you know how he booked it?"

"That Tui place. Online. Got a late deal, half price."

"That's great. Thanks."

Mrs Zooblavich slammed the door, and the knocker rattled.

In the car, Bethany sent a message to Fran for her to check whether Bevan's passport had been used and also to contact Tui — hopefully, if they were aware it was a murder inquiry, they might reveal whether Bevan had booked with them. If not, Fran could sort a warrant.

Fran: WILL DO. I HAVE SOME INFO. ZOOBLAVICH HANGS AROUND WITH A LAD CALLED JOSEPH HUNT — WHO OWNS A MOTORBIKE, THE SAME TYPE AND COLOUR THAT WAS IN THE CRASH THIS MORNING.

Bethany: HAS HE GOT ANY PREVIOUS?

Fran: PETTY THEFT.

Bethany: DO YOU HAVE A PICTURE?

Fran: AN OLD ONE FROM WHEN HE WAS NINETEEN.

Bethany: THAT'LL DO. HIS ADDRESS AS WELL. WHAT ABOUT EMPLOYMENT?

Fran: JOBSEEKERS.

While she waited for the image to come through, she accessed her photo folder and stared at the picture of the man at the accident. Fran's arrived, and Bethany compared the faces.

She leant over to show Mike. "Would you say this is the same person?"

"Not sure."

"Right, I've got his address, so we'll go there in case it isn't him who's dead. If he's not in, we'll pop and see Ken Corby again. He might recognise him from when he bought the moped."

She drove to Hunt's, but there was no answer, and all the curtains were shut. A young woman came out of the next place along and frowned at them while hefting a tufty-haired toddler up her hip.

"Do you know Mr Hunt who lives here?" Bethany held up her ID and wafted a hand in the direction of Hunt's.

She tucked a strand of blonde hair behind her ear. "Not as such. He nods if I see him, I smile. He doesn't seem like he wants to make friends."

"When did you see him last?"

"He went out really early this morning. I heard his bike revving. Really gets me down as it wakes Timmy." She kissed the child's head.

"Does he get many visitors?"

"Loads. They knock, he answers and hands them an envelope, then they leave. I've watched him do it and almost rang the police once. I don't want all sorts of people turning up here. Look, I have to go. Timmy has nursery." She walked off and deposited the kid in the back of a white car.

"Thoughts?" she asked Mike.

"He works from home?"

"Doing what, though? Got to be cash in hand as Fran said he's on Jobseekers."

"Something iffy most likely."

"Come on, off we go. It seems like we haven't stopped today."

"We haven't."

A quick jaunt took them to the car showroom, and Ken Corby was out the front, giving his all to persuade some middle-aged woman to buy a clapped-out silver Fiesta. He waved his hands, his tie getting caught around his wrist.

"But three hundred quid is a bargain," he said. "Especially if it's only to nip about in town. I can give you a three-month warranty on that. New exhaust. Cheap as chips."

The woman shook her head, laughing. "Why don't you just let me look? I have to see a few before I make up my mind." She wandered along to another vehicle.

Corby spotted them and rushed over, one hand up, finger pointing to the sky. "See something you like last time, did you, and came back to get a deal?"

"Afraid not," Bethany said and showed him Hunt's picture.

"Hey, that's the fella with the white trainers, the one who bought the moped."

She thanked him and returned to the car. "So he must have bought the moped for the plates, like we thought."

Mike nodded. "Thing is, checks have already been done on CCTV to find him. Nothing, so he uses roads without any cameras, apart from when he rang in."

"Deliberately hiding? If he's the bloke Phillip Stockley mentioned, the one who does passports and whatever — and it makes sense with his neighbour mentioning the envelopes — are these people who're buying the babies planning to leave the country?"

That spurred her on to message Rob, asking him to alert all airports and ports. It could be too late if the mother had already left with the child, but logs could be gone over to see if any babies were on board and what their destination had been. Maybe Tammy had decided to run with Maisie now Fay couldn't. If so, who was Elsie destined for? With Fay dead, was there another woman waiting in the wings, or was Tammy taking both girls, seeing as they'd been paid for?

She checked in with Tracy Collier.

Bethany: AIRPORT AND PORTS ARE BEING CONTACTED. JUST KEEPING YOU IN THE LOOP.

Tracy: WANT ME TO HANDLE THAT SIDE OF THINGS?

Bethany: PLEASE. THANKS.

Tracy: OKAY, I'LL RING ROB AND LIAISE.

"Right. We should go to Heidi Jones' because she was in the crash with Hunt," Mike said. "I'll get the address off Rob."

"He's going to be pulling his hair out. I just got hold of him as well about flights."

Her phone blipped.

Rob: DID YOU KNOW MAISIE NORTH HAS A BIRTHMARK BEHIND HER EAR?

Bethany: NO!

Rob: I'VE JUST HAD A CALL FROM ONE OF THE WOMEN VICKY USED TO HAVE COFFEE WITH AFTER GOING TO THE HEALTH CENTRE. SHE SAW THE NEWS AND THOUGHT SHE'D BETTER RING IN —AFTER SHE CONTACTED THE *HERALD*.

Bethany: UGH. OKAY, DISTRIBUTE THAT INFO TO ALL RELEVANT PARTIES, PLEASE.

Rob: YEP. JUST GOT MIKE'S MESSAGE AS WELL. THE ADDRESS DOWN FOR HEIDI

JONES IS THIRTY-FIVE BENSON AVENUE, ALTHOUGH THE ELECTORAL ROLL HAS SOMEONE ENTIRELY DIFFERENT. KIRSTY AND STEVE LONG, PLUS THEIR DAUGHTER, RACHEL. THEY'VE BEEN THERE FOR THIRTEEN YEARS.

Bethany: HEIDI COULD BE A LODGER. WE'LL GO THERE NOW. COLLIER IS GOING TO GET HOLD OF YOU ABOUT AIRPORTS ETC.

Rob: PHONE'S RINGING NOW.

She told Mike what was going on while she drove. Once there, it was clear the Longs had no idea who Heidi was. So, a fake address to go along with the fake agency. It made sense. If Joseph Hunt was a forger, a hacker like Phillip had said Zooblavich's friend was, it was easy enough for him to lay a false address down in the system. Digi forensics would be able to tell if they dug deep enough, though.

"What now?" Mike asked, back in the car.

Bethany took her phone out to read the message that had just come in. "Hang on."

Fran: ZOOBLAVICH HASN'T BOOKED WITH TUI AND DIDN'T LEAVE THE COUNTRY USING A PASSPORT IN THAT NAME.

She turned to Mike. "I'll tell you what's next. Finding where Zooblavich hangs out — I doubt Fran has had time without Leona and Tammy there to help her. He's in the UK — unless he left using a fake passport."

She drove back to the station, eager to help Fran, getting on a computer and searching Zooblavich's records for any other friends they could question. It took minutes to discover a list of people, plus Fran supplied some from Instagram, where Zooblavich had an account.

"No holiday pics on there?" Bethany asked.

"No," Fran said.

"What a surprise . . . Right, Mike, we're off again. There's someone I really don't want to see, but we have to." She cringed at the thought.

"Who?"

"Uncle Crack, a known associate of Zooblavich."

"Aww, fuck."

* * *

Heights had never agreed with Bethany, and standing on the walkway outside Crack's high-rise flat while his goons went inside to see if they were allowed an audience just proved it. Mike, however, placed his forearms on the top rail and all but hung over, watching the people below.

"I don't know how you can do that," she said.

A skinny youth came out of Crack's and gave her the nod. "He said he'll see you because it involves the babies, innit. Only you, though, blud, not him." He poked the air at Mike.

She looked at him and nodded: *It's okay.*

He nodded back.

"Thank you." Conscious of the toady staring at her as she entered the flat, Bethany tried not to let her unease show. Going in here alone was a stupid idea, but the babies, they needed her to find them. She doubted very much Crack would do her any harm, not while she was here in an official capacity.

She walked to the room she'd seen Crack in before, and he sat at the table, same as previously, his navy-blue suit sharp, his white shirt crisp. No Primark or Burtons for him. He stared at her with those unsettling eyes of his, and she put the shutters over her face so he couldn't read her. He bent his head to tell her to close the door.

She obeyed and hated herself for doing it straight away.

"Have a seat." He held his palm out.

She sat. Felt on show. Scrutinised.

"What can I do for you, Mrs Smith?" He put the end of a pen in his mouth and closed his lips around it.

"Like I told your . . . colleague out there, it's about the abducted children. Any information as to the whereabouts of Bevan Zooblavich would be greatly appreciated."

"How appreciated?" he asked around the pen.

"If you're suggesting we turn a blind eye if you're caught—"

"I wasn't." A long stare. "Dinner. Me and you."

She blinked. *What* had he just said? Her cheeks flamed. If he wasn't so damn appealing, his offer wouldn't bother her. She was confused. How could she find him attractive when she still loved Vinny and always would?

"Um, how about a no on that," she said, regaining her usual poise. "These are *babies*, not bargaining chips."

Crack put the pen on the table and spun it. "Shame. It would have been nice to get to know you."

"I'm afraid I'm not for getting to know. Look, if you're going to fuck me about, I'll get my information elsewhere."

He laughed. "Oh, I do like you. Feisty. Got some fire in you." He allowed a small smile. "You take no shit." He rose and walked to the window to peer out over Shadwell, a lord surveying his drug manor. "You think Zooby's got the babies?"

She swallowed down a sarcastic retort of: *Why else would I mention his bloody name?* "I might."

"So you do then. What does he want with them?" He looked at her over his shoulder.

Fuck you and your bastard eyes. "I can't divulge—"

"Then neither can I."

She got up and walked to the door. "Thank you for your time — and wasting mine while two innocent children are fuck knows where having fuck knows what done to them." God, she was so angry. Why did he always have to play games?

"He's got a place he goes to."

She stopped immediately and spun to look at him.

He came over to stand an inch or so away from her. "Forget dinner. One drink. In the Lamb Shank. Next Saturday. Eight o'clock."

Yes. "No."

"Fair enough." Another pause. "Try the old steel mill."

"Past the hill?"

"The very same. He uses it for parties and such. Surprised you lot haven't had any callouts to go and tell them to turn down the noise. It's quite the place to hide a couple of nippers."

"Thank you," she said. "Seriously, thank you."

"You know where I am if you change your mind about getting together."

Bethany rushed out, elated at the information yet rattled by Crack. She couldn't go out for a drink with a criminal, and as she ran down the hallway towards the front door, she hated herself for thinking: *If only we weren't on opposite sides of the law.*

CHAPTER TWENTY

Raven came to the house every week on a Friday. She had a few drinks with Mum, and Anne still hated her guts, although the fear of her had completely gone. Raven was just a bully in the guise of a piss artist, a bottle of alcohol never far away these days. She was a washed-up prosser, although she apparently took no money for her 'work'. If that were the case, psychologists would say she must be searching for something or hate herself. Whatever, she was a bitch just the same.

The rat-eating had stopped once she didn't have to look after Anne anymore but, proverbial elephant that Anne was, she never forgot — and she never would. She'd forever remember what Raven had put her through. How could she put years of abuse behind her as if it had never happened? It didn't matter that time had passed. At seventeen, Anne still suffered with the hurt of it all.

Tub Belly was in the living room with her, while Mum and Raven drank white wine in the kitchen, cheap plonk from the offie down the road. The occasional giggle drifted through between murmured conversation, Anne gritting her teeth whenever Raven cackled. What did Mum like about Raven to have remained friends with her for so long? Couldn't she see what a shallow trollop she was? Since the night Anne had admitted it, Mum never had asked her why she hated Raven and Tub, why she wanted to kill Raven. It was as if Anne hadn't said anything of the sort, the outburst gently forgotten.

Anne wasn't sure she'd tell her anyway, not now she'd formed her plans. She'd mulled them over for years after she'd hidden in the bathroom that time, playing out the scenario in her head on repeat, getting thrills at the moment she killed her abuser. It was coming closer, that need to act it out for real. It hovered beneath the surface of her outwardly calm sea. Beneath, it raged and boiled.

Especially as Tub slurped her milkshake through a straw and looked at Raven, waiting for a reaction. She always did that. Anne wasn't about to give her one, though, much as the urge was there. The stupid fat cow could swivel. What she wouldn't give to punch Tub in the face, or push her thumbs into her eye sockets, or maybe even slit her throat with the penknife she'd stolen today from the bloke at work who used it to open the packing boxes.

Restraint was sometimes hard to maintain while looking normal on the outside.

Raven roared again, bellowing so loudly Anne had to force herself to remain seated. Her body stiffened with the need to do something to her. Punch, kick, pinch. She pretended to watch the telly, some soap opera Tub loved, but in her mind, she saw Raven lifting a glass of wine to her lips, guzzling the contents down, getting drunker and drunker with each gulp. She'd been half cut when she'd turned up earlier.

Anger surged. It would have to be tonight, seeing as Raven was so pissed up. It'd be easier to bring her down. Anne couldn't take this crap anymore. Imagining was no longer enough.

Time passed, as did a couple more programmes, Tub leaving the room and returning with her milkshake replenished for around the fourth time. When would those two in the kitchen call it a night?

Raven appeared at the living room doorway, leaning on the jamb. "Come on, lard arse," she slurred at Tub, blinking in slow motion. "Get your backside up off that sofa. We're going home." She gave Anne what she must have thought was a frightening glare.

Shame it was wasted on her. It didn't affect her now. Anne sent one right back: I'm coming for you.

Raven and Tub left, and Mum weaved up the stairs, calling a wonky goodnight over her shoulder. Anne waited for the bedroom door to close, grabbed her handbag from the cupboard under the stairs, and exited the house. Raven and Tub would be walking home, their place was only up the road, but Anne got in Mum's car anyway — she'd need it for what she had in mind.

Was this really happening? Was she actually doing it? It felt as if she was watching one of her scenarios instead of acting it out. She was outside herself looking in, removed somehow, an observer to her own actions.

She started the engine, a bit nervous — she'd only recently passed her test — and drove down the street. There they were, Raven stumbling along, Tub somehow managing to hold her up. Anne sailed past them and took a spin around the block, and by the time she came back, the pair were nowhere to be seen. The hallway light was on in their house, though, and a shadow in the shape of a skinny person stood behind the leaf-patterned glass in the front door. A second one went up the stairs, and Anne presumed Tub was on her way to bed, going by the size of the figure, seemingly as wide as she was tall. Tub had developed a love of cream horns, crisps, and Minstrels, the gannet.

Butterflies of delight batted their wings in Anne's chest, and she ferreted in her handbag and brought out what she needed, something she'd had in the inside pocket for such a long time now, ready for this moment. She pulled the cut-off leg of a pair of black tights over her head and studied herself in the rearview. Her features were all squashed to one side, and she didn't look like herself at all. She could be mistaken for a robber, a rapist, someone bad.

She put leather gloves on, flexing her fingers so they became a second skin. So she didn't bottle it, letting nerves get the better of her, she got out and approached the front door, glancing left and right to check for other neighbours. It was well past midnight, though, and only a couple of homes had lights on, thin strips of cream round the edges of curtains.

The world had become a strange dark place behind the nylon.

Music sounded, probably Tub playing it in her bedroom. Inconsiderate at this time of night. Anne tapped on the front door with a knuckle, creating thuds instead of outright raps, and the Raven shadow turned, wavering for a moment where the silly bitch probably couldn't stand straight. Wine had replaced her blood she'd imbibed so much. She opened up and stared, blinking, probably trying to come to terms with what she was looking at. Had someone come to attack her? Steal her money?

Anne punched her in the face. Raven staggered back, landing on her arse, and Anne entered, flashing her boot out to kick the nasty pleb in the mouth. That was satisfying, more so as a tooth pinged out and landed on the grubby carpet. Blood dribbled over her lips.

"Whut the fuh?" Raven struggled to get up, drunk as arseholes.

Anne spotted a steel ornament of a naked woman on the telephone table beside a suede-covered address book. She grabbed the head in a tight fist and arced her arm. The heavy square base corner whacked into Raven's forehead, splitting the skin, but surprisingly, she wasn't knocked cold, just stunned. As Anne knew from eating rats' heads, skulls were made of strong stuff.

The music changed to another song, and the ceiling creaked. Anne imagined Tub dancing in her bedroom, thinking she was a popstar.

What a dilbert.

Anne walked farther in and stood behind Raven, grabbing her beneath the armpits, scooting around so she could drag her out backwards. It took a couple of minutes to get her down the path and to the car, Raven's shoes coming off on the garden path, and a few more to heft her into the boot. Raven mumbled complaints, and Anne slammed the lid down, shutting out the sight of her.

Back inside the house, she crept to the dining room at the back, which was used for the rats Raven bred. It stank, the stench of creature urine souring the air, and sawdust, droppings, and the whiff of dried pet food. Raven's black doctor's bag was on the floor, the one she used to take to Anne's house and to transport rats to buyers. Anne opened one of the cages and grabbed a beastie, shoving it in the bag and locking the clasp on top.

She left the house, closing the front door quietly, and smiled at the thought of Tub going to live with relatives or with strangers from the foster system. The little brat deserved everything that was coming to her, and hopefully, as an especially satisfying twist, she wouldn't be allowed to chug Nesquik like it was going out of fashion. Plain water would be Anne's choice for her, and dry stale bread instead of the cream horns. She used to want Tub to have a better mum, but not anymore. Not after years of suffering her presence while their mothers got together, wine their best friend.

She drove towards the hill. Raven could scream all she liked up there, and Anne intended to do horrible things to her so she did just that. Excitement pounced on her again, and she laughed from the thrill of it. God, who needed drugs when the prospect of killing gave you such a high?

"You'll get what's coming to you," she shouted, hoping Raven heard her. "You'll wish you never fucked about with me, I can tell you."

A thud came in response.

"You'll get a taste of your own medicine," Anne called out. "Rats taste yummy once you get used to them. You won't have time to, though. Only one head for you, missus, then it's lights out."

She parked close to the tree line at the top of the track and took a moment to inhale the fresh air. It was so peaceful up here, the stars bright, the darkness sending the trees black with white moonlight frosting. Anne moved to the boot, and Raven stared up at her drunkenly, her forehead bleeding, the gash unsightly to some, beautiful to Anne. More blood had come out of the gum, courtesy of the missing tooth, and that annoyed her. She'd have to clean the carpet of the boot so Mum didn't see it and ask questions. What a palaver.

"Come on, out you get." She snatched at Raven's spindly arms and dragged her out, her feet catching on the lip, and threw her onto the ground just because she could. "Stand up."

Raven rose on unsteady legs, flinging her arms out to her sides then slapping them down again. "What are you playing at?" It sounded funny. Probably because of the tooth issue, the alcohol, and the knock to the head.

"I'm not playing. This is serious." Anne grabbed the rat bag and held it up. "This might give you a clue."

Raven's eyes bulged, just about seen in the darkness. "Oh, knob off, will you? What are you going to do, get me to eat it? Whatever, shithead."

She doesn't get it. I'm older, able to hurt her back. Does she still see me as some stupid little kid who's scared of her?

"Go into the woods." Anne picked up a tyre iron from the boot and waved it.

"Piss off." Raven lurched to and fro, hiccoughing.

"Are you seriously thinking of ignoring me?" Anne swiped the weapon downwards and across. It connected with the side of Raven's twiggy lower leg. She was surprised it hadn't broken it.

Down she went, screaming, onto her side, clutching the affected limb, her knee to her chin. She whimpered for ages, sounding like she choked on blood. Quite the gargle going on there.

"Now, fucking do as you're told," Anne snarled.

She gripped Raven's skinny upper arm and hauled her up, then marched the limping, crying woman into the woods. The creature chittered in the bag.

"You can come out soon enough," Anne said. "Patience, Ratty."

"You're nuts," Raven said, the words elongated.

"I wonder why."

"Fucking . . . hate you."

"The feeling's mutual. Shut up now. You're boring me." She dug her fingers into Raven's skin, and the resulting squeal brought her pleasure. She swung Raven then let go so the lousy woman flew forward and fell on the ground. "Okay, here will do."

She placed the rat bag down, took her belt off, and straddled Raven, who flailed her arms and pummelled her heels on the ground, wailing about her 'poorly leg'. Anne caught her wrists one after the other, holding them against Raven's chest, feeding the belt beneath. She pushed the arrowhead end into the buckle and drew it tight. The skin had probably concertinaed. Shame Anne couldn't see it.

"Ouch, you bloody bitch!" Raven spat at her.

Spittle landed on Anne's cheek. "Oh. You really shouldn't have done that."

Another punch to the face had Raven screaming again.

Anne opened the bag and took the rat out. "I hope you're hungry."

* * *

Deeper into the woods, a ditch waited to claim Raven. Anne had spied it on a recent visit here, and she'd added it to her murder plan and the daydreams about killing her. The walk there had been fraught with tension, Anne reining in her temper on several occasions. Raven alternated between heaving, shouting obscenities, and crying. It seemed receiving this kind of treatment wasn't as nice as dishing it out. Funny, that.

Raven stumbled about in front of her, unbalanced from alcohol, probably a concussion, and the fact her wrists were secured. Anne called out for her to stop. Raven ignored her, speeding up, probably thinking she could make it to the nearby field and leg it to the farmhouse about two miles away.

Anne chased her and brought the tyre iron down on the back of her head. Raven flopped to the ground, and Anne followed her down, sitting on the backs of her thighs. The iron did a stupendous job of turning Raven's head into a big old mess. Wet heat splashed Anne's face, blood of the Raven, and with her anger spent, Anne rose slightly and turned the body over.

Raven's eyes, scrunched shut, told the tale that she'd died in pain.

Good. She deserved that.

Anne dug her thumb and forefinger into her front jeans pocket and brought out the penknife. She flicked the blade out and slashed a diagonal across Raven's face, and in her mind, this act showed what Anne had always thought and what Raven was — a two-faced bitch, one side a nice person in front of Mum, the other a vicious wretch when alone with Anne. The slice to the neck was to ensure she was dead, no other reason. Blood oozed, thick and black in the night.

Anne stood and stared down at the woman who'd ruined her, sent her on this path. She presented as a shadow, and Anne kicked her so she rolled, repeating it over and over until the body fell into the ditch. It was about a metre deep, and it took her a while to gather enough forest debris to cover the body. Back and forth she went, scooping up leaves and twigs and mulch. The ditch was level with the ground in that spot now she'd filled it, but as it was near the edge of the woods, she doubted anyone would come this far out and notice.

And even if they did, no one could prove she'd been here.

She picked the rest of the rat up and lobbed it onto the leaves.

It was done. Anne expected to experience the sensation of being free, but disappointingly, she didn't. There was no lightening of her troubled mind, no shoulders lifting from a heavy emotional weight being removed. She trudged back to the car and drove down the track with her headlights off — another vehicle was coming along the main road at a clip, probably a boy racer, his mates laughing in the back. She pulled over and waited for it to pass, then went home.

Maybe tomorrow things would seem better.

* * *

Tomorrow came, and Mum was in a right old state. Tub, in all her milk-shake-moustache glory, had turned up at the front door, her face wet with tears. She must have had a Nesquik prior to discovering Raven wasn't there. She said a tooth was in the hallway, and blood, and Raven's shoes were in the front garden.

Unfortunately, Mum said Tub could stay with them for now, and after the hours passed and nighttime rolled around, still no sign of Raven, the police were called, Mum telling them she was worried one of Raven's boyfriends had done something to her.

The day after, Raven's body was found in the woods by a nosy dog who'd wandered off the central track. Its owner rushed to get him back, and the hound stood proudly beside the ditch, barking its head off at a headless rat on the leaves. It had then dug deeper, and Raven had been revealed.

Anne, being nice for the next week or so, put on her acting head and comforted Mum. Tub had gone to stay with relatives, thank God.

Time meandered on. A week. A month. A year. A few more.

Seemed the police couldn't find the killer.

Anne smiled at that.

CHAPTER TWENTY-ONE

Zooby had checked the customers and, as all was well, he made a coffee and sat at the table to browse the news on his burner phone. It was best to keep tabs, considering what Anne had done. What was he supposed to do about her? He could hardly tell her off in case she turned on him.

His heart stopped beating for a few seconds at the sight of his screen.

SECOND CHILD KIDNAPPED!
MOTHER AND HER BOYFRIEND DEAD!
PETER UXBRIDGE — REGIONAL CRIME

Shadwell is in uproar at the news of a second child being abducted overnight. Elsie Blake, six months old, was taken under the cover of darkness, just like Maisie North. Her mother, Oriana Blake, was found with her face and neck slashed, the same as Miss Vicky North. Damien Tipton also had his throat cut. The couple lived in Lemon Grove Gardens and had been seeing each other for two months.

Neighbours fear one of Miss Blake's 'customers' did this, although why he'd take the baby is anyone's guess. Blake is known to entertain men for a living. The baby's father, Phillip Stockley, was unavailable for comment, but there is talk of him wanting Elsie removed from such a damaging environment. He is helping police with their enquiries.

Is that term just a ruse? Did he kill his ex-girlfriend, her lover, and kidnap his own child? Did he also abduct Maisie and murder Vicky North? So far, no one saw a thing in either street, so conformation on that may come later.

Where are the babies? Police from many counties have joined together to search for them. Fields are being walked through yet again, old ground covered despite it already being done for Maisie. Elsie's kidnap means everything has to be checked again. Officers are on alert at airports and ports as evidence suggests fake passports may have been created, and systems have been hacked. The idea of babies being taken out of the country is chilling, isn't it?

Keep on the lookout, folks. Someone had to have had blood on them after committing these terrible murders. Someone may be acting differently. Can you help? Call us here in our offices or contact Shadwell police. As always, Crimestoppers is invaluable if you wish to remain anonymous.

Stay safe out there. Shadwell is once again a minefield.

Fuck. How did they know about the passports and Joseph hacking? One of the gang must have talked, told a friend, sworn them to secrecy, except it wasn't a bloody secret anymore, was it.

Zooby shook all over, alarmed at the blip of an incoming text message. It was his mum. She knew to only contact him on this burner if something was going down.

Mum: ONLY JUST HAD A CHANCE TO TELL YOU. COPPERS WERE HERE. HILARIOUS THAT YOU'RE AWAY AND THEY CAN'T PIN ANYTHING ON YOU.

"What?" Fear crept inside him, insidious and all-consuming, seeming to fill his bones instead of marrow.

He grabbed his cup to drink some coffee, trying to still his racing mind. There were too many questions dancing in flurries, as hard to catch as swirling snowflakes, melting, more taking their place until a blizzard raged.

"Fucking *hell*," he said, throwing his cup.

It hit the wall above the camp bed, brown fluid staining the blanket. The sound of a car had him all but shitting his pants, and he rushed over towards the cots, moving one so he could stand on a metal beer keg left over from one of his parties and peer out of the dirty, narrow window high up. It was only Anne, and she stopped the car, got out to open the large door across the way, then drove it inside. Zooby got down and paced. At least she'd had the sense to hide the fucking thing instead of leaving it outside, an obvious beacon for the police. Joseph had been right in suggesting they do that.

She tapped on the door, and he went over to open it, sick with fear — everything was unravelling, his mind still jam-packed with questions and worries. She smiled wide, as if she was pleased with herself, and stepped inside like nothing was wrong. She must have showered when she'd nipped home as her hair was damp and she had different clothes on.

He bolted the door and turned to face her, angry she could be so blasé about it all when he was slowly going mad.

Why the hell did I start this? If Phillip hadn't moaned about little Elsie needing a new mum months ago, I wouldn't have thought about the adoption agency. None of this would have happened, and now he's been taken down the nick. He must have blabbed. That was why the police went round to Mum's.

"That's a bit of a mess," Anne said, staring at the camp bed. "Have a paddy party, did you?"

"I had every right to have one." He stomped over there, grabbing the corners of the blanket and creating a sack to carry all the mess to the bin. He dumped it inside. "You've seen the news?"

"Haven't had time. I had an errand to run over. I mean, run." She laughed her crazy laugh, head tipped back.

Fuck me sideways, she's so weird.

"The police are still at the woods." She flicked the kettle on and got busy with two cups, spooning instant coffee in. "And guess what?"

He couldn't take any more. "What?"

"They stopped me at the bottom of the track on my way here. Asked if I travelled that road a lot. Of course, I said no, I was just on my way to Doncaster to do a bit of shopping, maybe go bowling and to Dunkin' Donuts. The apple ones are piff."

"Piff?"

"Yeah, it means good."

"Right, I knew that." He didn't, but whatever. "What did the police say?"

"They told me I couldn't continue on that road as there'd been an accident. I knew that already, though."

"An accident?" God, what the hell had been going on while he'd been here by himself?

"Yeah, I mowed Joseph and Natasha down, then ran them over. Three times."

Zooby's legs couldn't hold him up any longer. He staggered to the armchair and sat, his skin seeming like it wanted to peel itself off, goosebumps pulling it tight. The beard itched, and he longed to strip it off, the glue hard around the edges, but he'd only bought one so couldn't replace it.

"You . . . you ran . . . them over?" he managed to get out, voice cracking.

"Yeah. Made for a bumpy ride." She chuckled and poured boiled water into the cups, then added milk granules and stirred as if they were only discussing the damn weather. "Here, get this down your hairy neck." She gave him a cup. "Try not to smash this one, eh?"

He curled his hands around the china, a cold chill streaking through him until he shivered. "Why? Why would you do that?"

"They were legging it," she said. "Leaving us to deal with the rest of the kidnaps."

"How do you know?"

"I followed them earlier. They were heading out of Shadwell."

"They could have gone that way to avoid the police at the hill."

"What, driving past the country lane that would take them to Shadwell? Not bloody likely."

"How far up did you kill them?"

"Far enough so we can't be seen coming and going here."

"Thank God we haven't got a kid lined up for tonight."

"Well, since you brought it up . . . I need to go and collect my old boss' grandson, Dominic, the boy I couldn't get because Five died."

"No. Leave it until this shit dies down. In fact, we should get the customers out of here, dump them in the middle of nowhere, and call it quits." He still hadn't got to grips with what Anne had done. She'd killed one of his best mates, and poor Natasha, she was just someone drawn into this mess, wouldn't harm a fly. He thought about how she was supposed to have visited Two and Elsie/Katalina later. She wasn't a threat, just some kid who needed money. Should he send Anne to do a check now or do what he said and just abandon ship? "Fuck it," he muttered.

"Okay, we'll leave it," she said, seemingly happy with what he'd said.

He didn't believe that was the case. Far from it. She'd bloody go and steal that baby boy later, and there was nothing he could do to stop her. But if he wasn't here to help her when she delivered it, if there were no customers because he'd set them all free . . . He could do it now, just open the door and tell them to go.

Before he could change his mind, panic taking over, Zooby rushed into the corridor and flung open all the doors. "Get out. Go on, leave. You can't stay here anymore."

The customers all came out, staring at each other in dazed shock. The dolls cried, some whimpering, others outright bawling. The women headed for the door to the main room. Zooby watched them shuffle in there, and Anne laughed as if she was about to wet herself.

"Look at the state of you scabby mares," she said.

Zooby shook his head and followed, staring at the congregation in front of him — women who were in desperate need of a bath, all holding dolls close to their chests. He ran to the main door and slid the bolts back.

"Go."

He'd drink that damn coffee quickly then leave before the police at the hill or the crash site spotted the customers wandering about, or even people in their cars. And he'd never come back, not even for the parties he usually held here, despite how much he made from ticket sales. He'd pocket the money from the safe, keep it for himself. As for Anne, she could go and screw herself. If it wasn't for her, they wouldn't be in this mess.

* * *

Tammy squinted at the bright light. Her body ached so much, her new baby suddenly heavy in her arms. She'd have to be careful she didn't drop her.

The other women — *Who the hell are they? Where is Fay?* — wandered down a track, then turned left, zombies following one another into a field. Tammy continued ahead, spotting a road below, but she didn't go down there. Not yet. She needed to go back to the filthy place and ask the man where her sister was. Where the other baby was.

She stumbled, grit biting into the soles of her feet, and managed to push the door open. The man was there, sitting at a table, but the lady who'd been laughing wasn't. He jumped up and came towards her, pointing.

"What are you doing here? Fuck off. Just leave, will you?"

The baby cried, and Tammy rocked her as best she could, one of her arms especially weighty. She'd seen spots on it earlier at the inner elbow. "My sister. I need to find my sister. She was with me when you picked us up."

"She left," he said. "So sod off."

Laughing Lady came back in. "You heard him. Get lost." She breezed past her through the main doorway.

Tammy wandered outside, so lost, her legs leaden, her head cloudy. The woman was at a large door in a warehouse, dragging it open. Tammy pushed herself to walk over there, to beg for a lift, but she was told to bugger off. She turned, determined, moving faster, heading down the track so she could flag a passing motorist, but if she had to walk to the nearest town — Shadwell, she hoped — she'd do it.

Anything to get away from this terrible place.

CHAPTER TWENTY-TWO

Bethany drove along the main road and stared in shock at people walking in the fields up by the old mill. They appeared dazed, even from this distance, with no apparent destination in mind.

"What the hell are they doing up there?" she said. "This is the middle of nowhere, for Pete's sake."

"Bloody hell, are they holding *babies*?" Mike leant forward to peer through the windscreen. "Jesus Christ, watch out!"

A car barrelled out of the track turning and headed straight for them. Bethany debated forcing it to stop by continuing on but in the end swerved out of the way, catching a glimpse of the driver in a clown mask, the same as the one at the scene of the accident, then a baby seat in the back.

"Shit, get on to control. Did you see that? They had a mask on." She glanced in her rearview and recited the number plate, repeating it over and over.

Mike grabbed his phone and rang it in while Bethany did a U-turn to give chase, adrenaline pitching a tent inside her and camping for the duration.

"Tell them about these bloody women as well," she said and sped back towards the hill. It hurt her to leave the wanderers behind, but what could she do? She needed to apprehend the suspect before someone else was killed and another child snatched. But they had babies with them. The dilemma was a tough one. Should she go back?

"Tory and Glen have jumped in the car at the hill and are following," Mike said. "They've got the driver in their sights. Go back for the women."

Someone 'up there' had sorted the quandary for her. Vinny?

Bethany executed a swift three-point turn, belting it down the road, her grip on the steering wheel tight, and careened onto the track. She put her foot down, hurtling towards a female near the top who stumbled holding a baby, her hair bedraggled and in need of a wash. Was the baby Maisie? Elsie? She cursed not coming up here to check this building out sooner.

She came to an abrupt halt beside the lady and wound her window down, panic fluttering in her chest. She got her ID out and showed it to her, debating whether to get out of the car or not — she might spook her if she did, and the baby might be dropped. "DI Bethany Smith. We need to check that baby is okay."

"She's fine. Quiet now. I need to find Fay," she said. "That man in there said she'd left."

Oh God. "Are you Tammy Elliot?" Bethany glanced down at the woman's ankle. *A bumble bee tattoo.*

"How do you know my name?" Tammy slurred. She seemed out of it, on drugs or something. She swayed, the baby's face smothered in her top.

Bethany's heart lurched. "The baby can't breathe like that, Tammy."

"Oh." She put it up by her shoulder and absently rubbed its back.

Bethany said, "What man do you mean?"

"The one with the beard."

Shit. "Did he just drive away?"

"No, that was Laughing Lady."

Who? There's a lady involved in this? Bethany couldn't stay in the car any longer. She got out slowly with the intention of ushering Tammy into the back seat, but the sight of the baby's head gave her pause. She reached out and stroked the head. It had a rubbery feel to it. Christ, was it dead? The child cried, startling her. She hadn't expected it to make a noise.

"Can I just make sure your baby is okay?" she asked gently. "Let me see her face?"

Tammy lowered it and cradled it in one arm. A doll, with creepy staring eyes, not Maisie or Elsie.

"Please, get in the car," Bethany urged, her attention drawn to the main road.

A police car shot towards them up the track.

"On second thought, go with the police." She jumped back in the car, zoomed to the mill, and parked, tyres screeching.

A bearded man with floppy hair and large glasses opened the door and ran out, heading to another part of the building that had a massive wooden door, much like one on a home garage. She drove forward, closer, wanting to cut him off, but he swung the door open and went in. A car was at the back. She stopped again, her and Mike tipping themselves outside immediately. They ran towards him, into the building, just as he was about to get in his vehicle.

"Stop, police!" Mike shouted. "Do *not* get in there!"

The man obeyed but darted at them, his face screwed up with determination to get past them and away. Bethany stuck her foot out, tripping him. He tumbled down, then scrabbled to get back up, running out. She chased after him, grabbing his T-shirt at the back and giving it a good tug. He bent over, and the momentum took her with him. They both landed on the ground, Bethany grunting at the pain lancing her knees, but she was damned if she'd let him go. They rolled over, him attempting to get away, growling, her trying hard to stop him. Mike joined in, throwing himself onto the man and pinning him in place.

Bethany scooted away a bit and took cuffs out of Mike's back pocket. She secured the man's wrists, and together they lifted him to his feet. Bethany walked around to look at his face and recognised the eyes from an arrest photo.

"The weather in Magaluf is a bit shit today, isn't it?" she said. "Oh, I forgot, we're in the UK. What the fuck have you been up to, Bevan? Who was that other person who just drove away?" She was out of breath, her lungs tight.

"She's a bloody nutter," Zooblavich said. "This is sod all to do with me. She organised all this. I'm just the bloke who sat in there and watched the customers."

Customers. Women who'd been conned into parting with their money for a baby? "Who is 'she'?"

"Anne Lown. Crazy cow. Kidnapping babies and killing people. The mothers. Some boyfriend of one of them. *And* she ran my mate and Natasha over."

"Who is your mate? Joseph Hunt by any chance?"

Zooblavich paled, as if he hadn't expected her to know.

"Bevan Zooblavich, I'm arresting you on suspicion of abduction, murder, and defrauding . . ."

While she said the rest, he stared at the sky, which chose that moment to spew rain on them. It hit his face, dribbling down his cheeks, and she wondered if he took the chance to cry as his eyes were glassy. Another patrol car arrived, and two uniforms ran over and took control of Zooblavich, a third waiting by the car.

"I want to talk to this Anne Lown," Bethany said and got her phone out to get an update from Rob.

"I'll check inside the mill first," Mike said.

"Be careful," she told him, grateful the third uniform went with him. "Ah, Rob, what's the latest on the car chase?"

"Tory's got her," he said.

"Where?"

"On the other side of the woods on the hill. She drove up there over the fields. She's apparently waffling on about rats coming out of the trees to eat Tory and Glen."

"Bloody hell. We're going there in a sec. Mike's just looking inside the mill. We need an ambulance here and transportation." She glanced around, thankful the first set of officers had rounded up the women. "You're going to be seeing some females soon. One of them is Tammy Elliot, and she has a doll — I'm assuming the other women have, too, as none of the officers here have called me over to say they have actual children. So, no sign of Maisie or Elsie yet."

"Fucking hell. Sorry for swearing. I'm just . . . this is getting to me."

"Don't apologise for giving a shit, love. Anyway, I need to go."

Zooblavich was being put inside the back of a police car, so she strode over there.

"Where are the babies?" she demanded, leaning over to peer inside at him, anger rising.

"With their new mothers. That's what Anne told me anyway." He shrugged, playing the part of an innocent so well.

"Where, though? I need addresses."

He acted as though he thought about that for a minute, dragging the seconds out. "I heard her say Blenheim Crest and Jester Avenue, but don't quote me on it."

"I'll quote you all I like, you scummy piece of shit." She stormed off towards the building he'd run out of and rang Rob again. "Get uniforms to Blenheim Crest and Jester Avenue. I want them knocking on every single door until they find those babies."

"Doing it now."

She walked inside, shoving her phone in her pocket, and stared around at a large room containing cots, a table and chairs, a camp bed, an armchair, and boxes of Pampers. A small kitchen unit stood at the back, a package of milk formula beside a kettle and some cups, bottles, and a sterilising unit. She swept her gaze back to the table. A stack of red books with plastic-type covers. A pile of passports. She stepped closer. Beneath them were birth certificates.

She had a look through them. A few different surnames, two of them Elliot. So Fay hadn't been given a child if the passport for it was still here. And there was a piece of paper with something written on it:

They cry. They scream. Those dolls are rarely quiet.

"You bastards," she muttered and jumped, on alert, at an internal door opening.

Mike and the uniform came in.

"There's a corridor with rooms off it," Mike said. "Camp beds and cots in each. Baby bottles, some toys, wet wipes and the like. The women must have been incarcerated here for a while." He shook his head. "They're filthy, mouldy, in no condition for people to live in them. At the end is a toilet and a sink. No shower."

"Okay. I have possible addresses for Maisie and Elsie from Zooblavich."

"Thank God. Two of the rooms have dolls in the cots, so I'm assuming one was for whoever had Maisie, the other for Fay?" Mike sighed. "Because the amount of rooms are enough for those two plus the women outside, and they all have dolls with them."

Bethany went into the corridor to look. The place was foul, and the air stank of mould, which lived on the walls in place of paint, some areas so thick she reckoned they were about an inch in depth. The toilet at the end had stains inside it and hadn't seen any loo cleaner for ages. The seat was cracked, wooden, and faded with dubious marks on it.

Her phone rang, and she took it out, swiping the screen quickly. "Rob? Anything?"

"Elsie has been found in Blenheim Crest. A woman is with her. Says she adopted the baby."

"And Maisie?"

"Nothing, although a neighbour in Jester Avenue said a woman moved in and had a baby with her on the day after Maisie went missing. She left with her in a car."

"Dare I ask if we've got a plate? A make?" She ran into the main room.

"No, sorry."

"Shit!" She kicked one of the chairs around the table. "Okay, thanks." She stared at Mike, cutting the call. "Elsie's safe. Maisie's . . ." She bent over from the emotion of it all, bracing a palm on her knee, and sucked in deep breaths to stop herself from crying. A hand touched her back and rubbed, had to be Mike's, and she stood upright, looking him in the eye. "What if the new mother has taken her away? How the hell will we find her?"

"I don't know, but we will. I won't rest until we do. Police are at the airports and whatnot, don't forget. Tracy will see that part through."

She swallowed, nodded, and walked towards the front door, throwing over her shoulder, "We're going to the woods. I want answers from this Anne woman."

* * *

Anne Lown stared at Bethany as if she were shit on her shoe. "Fuck off." She leant on the police car and smirked, hands behind her back where they were cuffed. "Like I'd tell you where she was, even if I knew."

"And do you?" Bethany asked.

"No. The stupid woman legged it with the kid. Ask Zooby. He's the brains behind this."

"He said *you* are." Bethany was so desperate to find Maisie she'd beat it out of Anne if she was allowed. Sadly, she'd get in trouble for it.

Mike cleared his throat.

I know, stay calm. I'm trying!

"He would say that." Anne rolled her eyes. "He drugged the customers, you know. No idea what he injected them with, but one of them *died*. He took her and buried her in there." She nodded at the woods. "Came and told us what he'd done an' all, well proud of it."

"Us?"

"Yeah. Me, Joseph, and Natasha. He killed those two as well by the way. That's why I sped out of there. He was about to kill me."

Bethany didn't know which one to believe, but her main priority, now they were under arrest, was to find Maisie.

"Why would he tell us where the babies went then? Why allow us to find Elsie, which we did, if he thought the new mothers would identify him as being the one to drug them? He told us he basically just watched them for you."

"The cheeky bastard!" Anne said. "He *did* drug them, and he *is* the one who set this all up."

"How?" Bethany spied the meat wagon from the corner of her eye, coming to collect Anne.

"He got Joseph to set up a website and all that shit, and I applied for my job online. So did Natasha."

"What was her role?"

"Visiting the new mothers after they took the babies home to make sure they'd settled okay. Zooby gave the kids Phenergan to shut them up on the journey so they didn't make a noise in the street and wake the neighbours when he dropped them off. Natasha had to check them in case Zooby gave the kids too much. The customers could rat on us to you lot if the babies died on them."

This just kept getting worse.

"Why were the women held in such disgusting conditions?"

"Again, ask him. Christ, I just poked my head in on the women every once in a while, wearing this mask." She indicated it hanging below her chin. "That was my only job, all right?"

"Do you know anything about rats?"

"They taste nice." Anne clamped her mouth shut as if she hadn't meant to say that.

"Excuse me?"

"Nothing."

"Why did you tell these officers here that rats would come out of the woods and eat them?" The rats were a connection to her — could *she* be the killer?

"They live in there, everyone knows that." Anne cocked her head and glared as if to say: *Are you thick or what?*

Bethany had a feeling she wasn't going to get anywhere with her yet. "I'll be speaking to you and Zooblavich at the station. We'll be putting in for warrants to search your properties." She nodded at the officers coming forward from the meat wagon. "We'll see which one of you cracks first, shall we?"

"Won't be me. I was only a babysitter, just like Raven."

"Who's that?"

"None of your business. Ah, shame to cut our chat short, but it looks like I have to go."

"There's something I need to do before that. Anne Lown, I am arresting you on suspicion . . ."

CHAPTER TWENTY-THREE

Carla shook so hard she wondered whether anyone at Doncaster Sheffield Airport could spot it. There weren't that many people about in this area where she waited, and most of them were eyes deep in their phones.

She'd arrived early, needing to be here, closer to getting away. Dad had been eager for her to leave anyway, helping her pack her few belongings, Mum wondering what all the rush was about.

Once Mum had gone to make up some bottles for Lily, Dad had whispered, "I don't know what you're involved in or why, but I'll never say a word. It's wrong, what's happened, but you're my daughter, and I can't see you arrested and—" He'd stopped, too emotional.

Carla sighed, close to tears. Should she allow her dad to carry the burden of this as well? It wasn't fair to him, yet she'd basically signed his guilt warrant for the rest of his life. And should she have given Lily up the minute she'd seen the news? Could she do it now?

She glanced down at her daughter. Lily was in the pushchair, looking pretty in the lilac-flowered dress and white lacy tights, a thick pink cardigan keeping her warm as well as a teddy bear fleece covering her. Carla had put a white woolly hat on her as well, tugging it down to hide the birthmark. She didn't need the worry of people nosing at the child to catch a glimpse of behind her ear. With Lily bundled up this way, she was less exposed. Did it look obvious that was what Carla was doing, especially them being inside with the heating on?

A nervous tic had her foot jerking into the luggage beside her where she sat — Dad had insisted she take one of their posh cases. She was unable to do anything for another couple of hours as the check-in wasn't open for her flight yet. Still, with Lily settled after having a bottle — another cold one, and the guilt would *not* go away over it — she could try to relax. She was almost there, almost tasting freedom and the life of a mother she was desperate to live.

A woman with ginger hair entered and walked past with a man. She peered over, obviously staring at Lily, making no bones about it. News had spread nationally, Carla had seen another report an hour ago on the BBC website, so people were bound to be on the lookout. If Carla were a stronger person, she'd act more like nothing was wrong, but she wasn't, and this had all become far too dangerous now. Murder. Kidnap. Buying a baby. It all amounted to breaking the law. Even her handing money over for Lily might be illegal. She didn't know for sure, and that was what got to her the most. She'd entered into it innocently, not aware of what was allowed and what wasn't. How was she to know Lily would be Maisie, stolen out of her cot? The adoption papers she'd signed had looked legit, but they obviously weren't. It was wrong, all of it.

It hasn't stopped you bringing her here, though, has it? You're still willing to run away with her. You're taking a baby from her real family.

But what if that family was awful? What if they didn't treat Lily right once they had her? No, she couldn't allow it. Carla already loved her so much from the short time they'd been together, so giving her up now wasn't an option.

And to top it all off, she probably looked scared.

More people came in and milled about, and some sat nearby, others choosing chairs across the way. Carla concentrated on them, watching for signs that they knew who she was, what she'd done, and what she planned to do. But that was just silly, her thinking like that. How could they possibly know? It was her paranoia talking.

But was it, though? She checked her surroundings, and if she had to run, all exits had folks at them and she'd easily be snagged by an outstretched hand.

The woman and man came back, maybe strolling for exercise out of boredom, and the redhead stared at Carla again.

A shiver ran up her spine, the hairs on the back of her neck rising.

Please, just let me get on that plane, through customs at the other end, and then it'll all be over.

She wanted to keep an eye on the couple now they'd passed but didn't dare. It might look obvious she was terrified if they turned and caught her gawping. She bounced her legs, holding her hands in her lap to prevent picking at her nails or fiddling with her hair, both signs her nerves were going through the roof. And the leg bouncing — what was she thinking? She may as well have a sign over her head saying BABY STEALER HERE!

Oh God, Oh God, they're coming back.

They chose the seats beside her, the woman right next to Carla.

Shit. Fuck.

"Hello! Going on holiday, are you?" She held out her hand. "I'm Tracy."

Carla swallowed and shook it. "Hello. Yes, going on holiday." Just what she didn't need, someone poking into her business. There was a risk she'd slip up owing to anxiety, and she wanted to grab the buggy and escape. "Fancied a break. A bit of sun."

"Where are you off to then?" Tracy asked.

"France." Carla could kick herself, but it was too late to take it back now. Hadn't she just told herself she'd slip up? She should have said Spain or Italy, anything other than her real destination. How could she have been so *stupid*?

"Don't be nosy." Her husband, if that was who he was, shook his head. He didn't have a wedding ring on, so maybe he was just her boyfriend. "Sorry, Tracy has a habit of yakking." He gave an apologetic smile.

Relieved they were just an ordinary pair, Carla smiled. "It's okay." It wasn't, far from it, but she'd have to ride this out until they got up and left her alone.

"What's her name?" Tracy gazed at Lily, a smile in place, although it seemed forced. Tight, like she was angry. Didn't she like babies?

Carla was uncomfortable, her earlier relief gone. "Um, Lily."

Tracy slapped a hand to her chest. "Oh, how beautiful. And how old is she?"

"Six months. She was premature, that's why she's so small." *Stop justifying her size. Stop adding more information than you need to.*

"Goodness. That must have been frightening, going into labour early."

"Hmm."

"I bet your old man was a support, though, wasn't he?" Tracy peered around, searching the other passengers. "Where is he then? In the loo? Or are you going on holiday just with the baby?"

Carla blushed, sensing a judging moment coming from Tracy about having a child without a father in tow. "I'm not married. Single parent here."

"Oh, I'm sorry."

"It's fine. I prefer it this way."

"Did he bugger off then? You know, get all excited about having a kid then decided, when she arrived, it wasn't all it was cracked up to be? Or were you left once you got pregnant? God, some men, eh?"

Carla couldn't work out if this was an average conversation or not. Did people ask such intrusive and personal questions as a general rule, or had she been stuck with a woman who spoke her mind no matter what?

"Lily's dad isn't . . . he isn't around, and that's all right. I manage okay, and I have my mum and dad if I need them."

"Always good to have family support, not that I'd know anything about it, but that's a whole other story." Tracy leant towards the pushchair. "Oh, she's waking up, look. Can I hold her?"

"Tracy!" the man who could be her husband snapped. "Honestly. You're a stranger. You can't expect people to just hand over their kids."

"A little cuddle won't hurt." As Carla said it, she cursed herself, but the same as earlier, it was too late now. If she got up and walked away like she wanted to, it would be weird. Carla took Lily out and secured her hat lower, almost covering her eyes, then placed her in Tracy's arms, all the while asking herself if she'd taken leave of her senses. "There you go."

"Oh, would you just look at her, Damon. Isn't she so sweet?" Tracy moved Lily around to her other arm, farther away from Carla, and the hat went wonky.

Shit. Shit! I should have put make-up on the birthmark!

Carla reached out to right the hat, but Tracy got there first, taking it off completely.

"It's so warm in here," Tracy said. "They must have the heating whacked up. No need for all that wool, is there?" She stroked the baby's head, looking down, her little finger tugging the ear forward.

Carla stifled a gasp.

Tracy stared at the birthmark then looked up and made eye contact with her.

Damon stood, putting his hand in his pocket and drawing something out. He held it up. "Detective Sergeant Damon Hanks. We'd like you to come with us and discuss that birthmark behind the baby's ear."

"Maisie North, isn't it?" Tracy asked sternly, eyebrows raised.

Carla's lack of a response gave her away, she knew it. She tried to speak, to deny it, but no words came out.

It was over, just like that.

"No, please, no. You don't understand," Carla finally said, making a grab for Lily.

Tracy stood with her and moved out of reach. "I don't think so, love."

"I adopted her. She's mine." Carla couldn't see for the tears. "I'm her mummy now. Please, please, give her back."

"*Is* she Maisie North?" Damon asked.

Tears ran down Carla's face. "I didn't know it was her. Not until after. Oh God, please don't make me live without her. I can't . . ."

Damon raised a hand, and people came running out of nowhere. They took Lily, rushing off with her to where an ambulance crew stood by one of the doors. Where had they come from? How had they known she'd be here?

Carla's heart broke, and she screamed, so hard and for so long, she lost her voice. Her happiness. Her baby. And her beautiful new life.

CHAPTER TWENTY-FOUR

Bethany and Mike paced the incident room after eating some lunch, waiting for Bevan's and Anne's solicitors so they could get on and interview them. One of them was lying about being the main player, and she intended to find out who it was.

Her phone rang. Tracy's name popped up on the screen.

"Hello?" Bethany said.

"Maisie North is secure," Tracy said.

"Oh, thank God!" Tears stung Bethany's eyes, and she called out to her team, "We've got Maisie."

Cheers went up, Fran dabbing at her eyes, Leona beaming, and Mike swallowed, blinking rapidly.

"I'll let Rob know," Fran said, "so he can pull officers from other airports and the search areas."

"Good idea," Tracy said. "I haven't had time."

"So what happened?" Bethany asked her.

"We took a punt and went to Doncaster Sheffield Airport," Tracy said. "I thought of someone desperate to leave wanting to get to the closest one — I'd do that, wouldn't you? We'd put officers in place at the others anyway — glad I wasn't at Gatwick or Heathrow. Can you imagine the amount of babies we'd have to nose at? Anyway, turns out, after we walked through the various areas, I spotted a woman with a pushchair. And did she look dodgy or *what*? Nervous as fuck. So, you know me, I sat next to her."

"Bloody hell, and?"

"We had a little chat. Amazing how much you can find out. Going to France, single parent. Well, alarm bells went off, especially because, in a warm waiting area, the kid had a blanket and a woolly had on so you couldn't see much of her. I had to find a way of checking behind her ear."

"Why didn't you just ask to look? You're a copper, you have the right."

"Where's the fun in that?"

"Blimey, woman."

Tracy laughed. "The kid was waking up anyway, so I ask to hold her, just happened to take her hat off, and oh, what do you know, my finger pulled her ear down. Exact same birthmark as Maisie."

"What did the woman do?"

"Crumpled. Said she'd adopted her and didn't know it was Maisie until afterwards. She screamed, had a right mare once the baby was taken away. It was a bit difficult to watch, to be honest. I don't *ever* want a kid, and if that's what it's like to lose one, I'll never change my mind on that."

"Aww. You've kind of got to feel sorry for her really. So what's happening with her now?"

"She's in a holding cell at my station. The ride back there wasn't pleasant. Lots of crying. You know the sort, where you think your heart's going to burst."

Bethany understood that, and Tracy would, too, with what she'd been through in her life. "Poor cow."

"Want in on the interview?"

"I have to speak to the pair we picked up first. They're blaming each other for this mess. I have no clue at the minute which one the killer is." She glanced at Mike, who twirled his hand round in a 'wind it up' motion. "I have to go now, actually. Can we nip over afterwards? Will it be too late, plus awful, to leave her for that length of time? I just want to do an initial interview with my two, nothing in-depth until tomorrow. That okay?"

"Yeah, she can do with having some time to herself. She's still crying a lot. Doctor's been in to see her, cleared her for questioning, and besides, her solicitor can't get here for two hours anyway, then they'll have a chat and whatever beforehand."

"Brilliant. Got to go. See you soon." She pushed her phone in her pocket. "Is one of them ready for us?"

Mike nodded. "Zooblavich."

"Okay then, off we go. We're going to speak to the woman who had Maisie after we've finished here, so let's keep these interviews short and sweet for now." She addressed Fran and Leona. "If we're not back by seven, call it a night, okay?"

They left the incident room and went downstairs.

Rob looked up from behind the front desk. "Ah, there you are. Zooblavich is in Interview One. Solicitor and a uniform present."

"Thanks."

"He had a lot of money on him. Thousands."

"Probably what he'd got off the sale of babies. Bastard."

She led the way down the corridor and took a deep breath. "You ready for this?"

Mike shrugged. "It's all a bit . . . I don't know. The whole thing makes me feel unclean. Make sense?"

"Yep. Let's get it over with then."

They entered. Zooblavich appeared chastised, as if he may well spill some delicious beans. Maybe his solicitor had advised him to plead guilty and be done with it. His beard had gone, which was odd, and his skin was pink. No glasses. Bethany sat opposite him and his brief, Mike beside her, and did all she had to do regarding the recording. All the while, Zooblavich twiddled his thumbs.

"My client wishes to clear some things up." The solicitor, a man in his fifties with black hair and almost white sideburns, gave the impression he'd walked out of the past, especially with his old-fashioned, musty-smelling suit.

"Right." Bethany gave Zooblavich her attention. "Have a shave or something, did you? This isn't a bloody hotel."

Zooblavich shrugged. "It was fake. I picked it off. Bloody thing was itchy."

"And there was me thinking you were just being trendy these days. And itches are the least of your problems. Okay, what have you got to say?"

He hugged himself. "Look, I set up the agency, all right? It was for Stockley's benefit at first."

"For the tape, his full name, please."

"Phillip Stockley."

"Zooblavich is referring to the father of Elsie Blake. Continue, please, Mr Zooblavich."

"Well, it's like this. He said he needed a new mum for the kid because Oriana—" he turned to the recording machine like it was a person, leaning forward to speak to it — "that's Elsie's mum, by the way. She wasn't doing so well in looking after her. It got me thinking how I could make money from it, and before I knew it, I was talking to my mate, Joseph Hunt, and I asked what he thought of us taking a few babies and selling them on." He moved away from the machine and settled back.

Bethany's disgust button had well and truly been pressed. He'd spoken as if it was an everyday thing to discuss abducting kids.

"Go on."

"So my plan was to keep stealing the same six babies, over and over, then, once I'd made a fair whack, give them back to the original mothers. I didn't tell the others that, though. They thought the babies would stay with one of the new mothers come the end. We couldn't keep handing the babies to other customers once they got older, people would recognise them as belonging to whoever we originally sold them to. I mean, they'd be introducing the nippers to their family and everything, wouldn't they."

All those people with the wool pulled over their eyes. All those hearts broken when the babies went missing again. Zooblavich is sick in the head.

"Who do you mean by not telling 'the others'?" she asked.

"Joseph Hunt, Natasha Otter, and that mad tart, Anne Lown."

He went on to explain the sickening plan. So many women devastated — the original mothers plus the new ones who were desperate to have children. Didn't any of the 'gang', as he'd called them, have a conscience? Did money prove such a lure they were willing to do anything for it? Seemed so.

"But Anne fucked it all up, didn't she," he went on. "Stupid twat. Joseph warned me there was something off about her, but I didn't take any notice, and it was too late by the time he'd said. Anne knew too much. So, she goes off to nick Maisie, right, without us knowing she was doing it, because that kid was *never* on our radar, and comes back with her after. We find out she bloody killed the mother, and I *shit* myself. I thought she'd turn on me if I went against her, like, so I kept my feelings to myself about it, but I *did* tell her not to murder anyone else."

Bethany snorted. "That was magnanimous of you, but she clearly didn't take your advice."

"No. One of the customers died, and Anne dumped her. Then she snatched Elsie and did what she did to the mum and that bloke. That was it for me. I told her we were stopping it. *Then* she says she ran Joseph and Natasha over." He picked at a hangnail. "What the hell is *wrong* with her?"

"You are aware there's something wrong with you as well, aren't you?" Anger flared, her pulse throbbing in her neck. "Why were you even doing this in the first place? What kind of person thinks it's okay to kidnap babies?"

"My mum. I wanted the money for her, so she wouldn't have to struggle with my brothers and sisters."

Okay, he could be classed as a good son in wanting to help his old dear out, but there were legitimate ways to go about it, for God's sake. "Tell me everything."

He did. Natasha, while she must have been a strange one to even want anything to do with a scheme like this, had needed money to clear debts. She was in it up to her eyeballs. She'd been in on all the meetings and WhatsApp chats, but her role had only been to drop in on the new mothers and ensure the babies were okay. Bethany had the idea that was so the children were monitored for the subsequent snatches, ensuring the 'goods' were healthy enough to be resold.

Joseph had been the one to set up the website, create the questionnaire, do the hacking, and falsify passports, birth certificates, and those red books she'd seen, which were apparently health diaries, something like that, issued by health visitors. Earlier, Fran had discovered an open investigation ticket regarding fake documents, and it seemed they'd found the one doing it in Joseph, but he was doing his time in Hell now instead of a cell. Digi were looking at his laptop, found at the crash scene in a saddlebag, searching for clues as to how he'd set things up.

Zooblavich was, indeed, the baby and customer sitter, like he'd originally said, but also the one to collect the customers, incarcerate them, inject them — he wouldn't say which drug and where he'd got it from, he had 'standards' when it came to grassing his mates up — and deliver the customers and babies home.

Standards, my arse. He got the gear from Crack and hasn't got the balls to dob him in.

Once again, the drug lord would get away with supplying. They had no solid proof he'd been involved with this, and considering his reaction about the babies and Zooblavich being the one to orchestrate it all, plus Crack giving her the location of the steel mill, Crack wasn't happy with what his drugs had been used for. She thought about taking him up on his offer for a drink, if only to try to catch him out.

Anne, though . . . If Zooblavich was to be believed, she was the kidnapper and killer.

Satisfied she'd got as much out of him as she could, she ended the interview and, unable to stand talking to him any longer, or watching his tears of self-pity and listening to his whimpering excuses, she walked out with Mike.

In the corridor, away from Interview One, she said, "What an utter whiner. That was a case of him trying to justify what he'd started, as if we'd go lenient on him because he wanted his mum and siblings to have a better life. Bugger off."

"Yep. Classic 'It was me, but I don't want to take full responsibility for it'."

She poked her head around the door to speak to Rob in reception. "Lown?"

"Interview Three," he said. "They've been in there a while. Solicitor has let me know they're ready."

Ready to talk or ready to piss me about? "Thanks."

She walked towards room three with Mike, thinking about the 'customers' and how they were faring. All of them had been through a medical assessment as well as mental, bloods taken to determine what they'd been drugged with, and would be returning tomorrow to give their statements. It'd be a long old day. How had they reacted once they'd discovered the babies were dolls? What kind of emotional scarring would that leave? Had Tammy been told Fay was dead?

She snapped out of her thoughts and walked into the room, incensed at the sight of Anne Lown, who sat with her solicitor, a blonde woman of about thirty. A new uniform, Jack Moller, stood beside the door. Bethany and Mike sat, and once again, she did what she needed for the recording, then leant forward, hands in her lap, holding her phone in one of them.

"What's your client's standing at present?" she asked the solicitor.

The woman wrote on a notebook, ripped the page off, folded it, and passed it to Bethany.

May require a psychological evaluation. Play it by ear.

Bethany passed it to Mike beneath the table and nodded at the solicitor, who gave her a look as if to say she wasn't happy representing Anne.

Who would be?

"Anne, please can you talk us through how you came to know Bevan Zooblavich," Bethany said.

Anne, as Bethany had predicted she would, gave the same guff about applying online for the job as a babysitter for women.

"So you weren't, as we've been informed, employed to kidnap babies?"

Anne shrugged.

Bethany's phone warbled. "Excuse me one moment. For the benefit of the tape, DI Bethany Smith has received a message." She glanced down at her screen.

> Fran: LOWN MENTIONED A BABYSITTER CALLED RAVEN, YES? I'VE DONE A SEARCH ON RATS ON THE HILL, JUST IN CASE THEY LIVED UP THERE AT ANY TIME IN THE PAST, AND A MURDER CASE CAME UP INSTEAD. A HEADLESS RAT HAD BEEN LEFT AT THE SCENE, IN THE WOODS AT THE HILL, AND A RAVEN HIDDLESTON WAS FOUND WITH HER FACE SLASHED DIAGONALLY AND HER THROAT CUT.

Bethany's heart skipped a beat, and she forced herself not to smile at having a tight lead to go on regarding Anne.

> Bethany: THANK YOU.

> Fran: A SEARCH OF ZOOBLAVICH'S HOME ADDRESS FOUND NOTHING EXCEPT A PHONE IN HIS ROOM — THE ONE HE HAD ON HIM WAS A BURNER AND APPEARS TO ONLY HAVE BEEN USED FOR THE ADOPTION STUFF AND HIS MUM GETTING HOLD OF HIM. MAYBE HE GAVE HER THAT NUMBER IN CASE OF EMERGENCIES. LOWN'S PLACE . . . A ROOM FULL OF RATS IN CAGES.

> Bethany: CHEERS.

She stared at Anne, schooling her features blank. "Who is Raven Hiddleston?"

The woman's face screwed up, then she bared her teeth. "You can fuck off talking about *her*."

"Why? Painful, is it?"

"Get lost."

"Did her murder upset you, too?"

No answer. Arms folded. Bottom lip sticking out. Eyes narrowed. What was she thinking? About Raven? How to get out of this mess?

Bethany pushed harder. "Funny how her face and neck were slashed, the same as Vicky North and Oriana Blake. Also funny how a headless rat was found at Raven's scene, too."

"Yeah, it *is* funny." Anne roared with laughter, eyes now alight with hilarity — or was that mania, madness, delight in what she'd done?

"I didn't mean in the amusing sense."

Anne stopped immediately, her expression empty as if she hadn't just laughed. "Oh."

Bethany changed tack. "I see, from records, that you previously worked for Franklin Insurance Services Limited."

"Yeah. What of it?"

"A call was placed by Vicky North about a burst pipe."

"And? Happens all the time. That's why you get insurance."

"The ticket was supposedly dealt with by a Jolene Lyme, only . . . she swears she didn't take it. Now, officers have been to Franklin's and spoken to the boss, a Mr Knight, who informed them that while you were training Jolene at the time, you had access to her ticket sheet and could input data. I'm putting it to you that *you* took that call and found out Vicky had a baby. Zooblavich, while chatting about *everything*, I might add, said Maisie wasn't even on the list of babies to kidnap."

"Bog off."

"Why do you have a room full of rats?"

Anne's head snapped up. "You leave my snacks alone."

Oh my God. "Snacks?"

"Nothing wrong with eating them, is there?"

The solicitor made an *eek* face.

"You do realise, don't you," Bethany said, "that we will extract the DNA from the rats at your house to see if they match those left at Vicky North's and Oriana Blake's houses, plus the one in the woods with Fay Elliot. We will also check the saliva from the rats left at the scenes — they *were* bitten off, yes?"

Anne cocked her head. "Do you like Nesquik?"

"Excuse me?"

"Strawberry or chocolate? What's your favourite?"

Where is she going with this? "I don't drink it."

"Tub does."

"Who's Tub?"

"She was a baby who grew into an annoying little cow."

"Is she relevant to this investigation?"

"Who knows? Do your detective thing and find out. D'you know, I really fancy a cream horn. Never did have one. I'd like to see what all the fuss was about."

"What significance does a cake have here?"

Anne sighed. "Tub again. Old Lard Arse. Her and her Minstrels."

The chocolate sort?

Bethany's phone tinkled.

Fran: A CORDELIA LOWN, ANNE'S MOTHER, REPORTED RAVEN HIDDLESTON MISSING.

Bethany: EXCELLENT.

She smiled at Anne. "So, was your mum good friends with Raven then? Only, she reported her missing."

"Don't you bring my mum into this. You can just naff right off on that one. She did the best she could, although I do resent her for not realising what was going on, what I went through." Anne leant forward and headbutted the table, over and over, growling as well as letting out squeaks, like a rat or mouse, then she hummed *Three Blind Mice*.

"The interviewee is banging her head on the table," Bethany said as the uniform shot over to lift Anne so she didn't do herself some damage. "The interviewee is now being held back by PC Jack Moller for her own safety."

Anne's forehead was red.

"Why did you feel the need to do that, Anne?" Bethany asked. Her mother was a sore subject, it seemed.

"Oh, just go and do one, will you, woman? Stop trying to get me to tell you stuff. What went on back then is in the past."

"Not if it affected what's been going on here."

Another message.

Fran: PENKNIFE FOUND AT ANNE'S. BLOOD ON IT. DIGI HAVE BEEN THROUGH HER PHONE. SHE'S IN THE WHATSAPP CHAT, AS IS ZOOBLAVICH AND OTTER. ALTHOUGH JOSEPH IS DOWN AS BEING IN THE CHAT GROUP, HE NEVER WROTE ANYTHING.

Bethany smiled at Anne. "Actually, *you* can go and do one. We have proof of a WhatsApp conversation regarding the 'jobs' you all had. I think you'll find, along with blood on a penknife we've found, that we have enough evidence to send you off on a nice holiday at Her Majesty's pleasure. Interview suspended at . . ."

Anne stared at her solicitor. "Aren't you going to do anything? I need to go home, feed the rats. Want to stop off at Tesco first, though, buy a cream horn."

"You'll have to remain here, I'm afraid," the solicitor said. "We'll have another chat in private to discuss your options. Have a cup of tea and perhaps some food?" She tilted her head at Bethany.

"We'll provide a sandwich. Cream horns aren't on the menu, though. This isn't the Ritz."

CHAPTER TWENTY-FIVE

On the way to the next town over, Bethany pondered on where Maisie would live now. Fran had informed her prior to them leaving that the father, Greg Walker, didn't want her, and neither did Vicky's parents. That news wasn't a surprise. Other relatives were being asked if they'd be willing to take her on, but for now, she remained in the care of Social Services, fostered by a couple who already had four other children. Elsie was with Oriana's parents. Her father, Phillip Stockley, was still in custody facing charges of conspiracy to kidnap, so the poor little dot wouldn't be seeing him anytime soon. Not that he'd expressed any interest in a visit with her. What was wrong with Greg and Phillip that they didn't want to look after their own flesh and blood? What message would that send to Maisie and Elsie as they grew up, possibly into confused girls?

Now, Bethany sat at an interview table beside Tracy instead of Mike, and it felt odd without her wingman. The woman who'd purchased Maisie, renamed by her as Lily, was beside an austere-looking solicitor who appeared as if he wouldn't take any shit. A play-it-by-the-book type. He'd introduced himself to the tape as Jeremy Adams, sounding officious and full of himself. Damon and Mike were watching on monitors in another room.

"My client wishes to comply with the police in all matters," Adams said, pompous. "Apart from illegally obtaining a child and parting with money for said child, which she didn't know was illegal, and entering into what she thought was a legitimate adoption, Carla has done nothing wrong."

Tracy barked out a laugh.

"Apart from planning to take the baby out of the country," she pointed out, acerbic as anything, "*after* she knew it was Maisie North, a kidnapped infant whose mother had been killed in order for the abduction to be successful."

"Yes, that as well." Adams cleared his throat, suitably chastised. "But that is another matter, relating to the bond she'd developed with Lily."

"Maisie," Tracy snapped.

Bethany stepped in, armed with information from Zooblavich. "Your client had a bond with a *doll* for the duration of her stay at the steel mill. She only received Maisie the morning after the kidnap. Maisie was given Phenergan to keep her quiet while a Mr Bevan Zooblavich took her, and Miss Yearson here, home."

"What?" Carla blinked. "No, you've got it wrong. I had Lily all that time, and the man with the weird glasses took her away for a bath and brought her back with her hair cut."

Bethany shook her head. "The doll had curly hair — it was left in a cot when we visited the mill — and you were then given Maisie North, who *didn't* have hair quite like that. Mr Zooblavich said he cut Maisie's, but it was nowhere near as curly as the doll's."

"I've loved Lily for *days*," Carla said. "I won't believe I had a doll."

"How would you know anyway?" Tracy asked. "You were drugged as well."

Carla rubbed her inner elbow, fingertips skating over scabbed holes. "But she cried. She took milk from a bottle. Dolls can't do that."

"Special ones were used, the type to teach people what it's like to have a real baby," Bethany said. "I'm sorry, but you were conned right from the start and lost a lot of money in the process." She sighed. "Why did you decide to take Maisie out of the country anyway when you knew she'd been kidnapped and her mother murdered?"

A story tumbled out. A car accident. An operation. Carla unable to have children. Her boyfriend leaving her as she was 'barren' and 'useless' to him. Her depression. Her filling out the questionnaire. Zooblavich telling her she had to move to Shadwell in order to adopt and remain there for six months afterwards. Bethany kept it to herself that Zooblavich had told her Maisie would then be kidnapped again from Carla and given to someone else, repeat, repeat, repeat until the baby was returned to Vicky. It would be rubbing salt in a massive wound if she let that info out.

The account ended with Carla sobbing, saying all she'd wanted was a baby, her desperation to keep Maisie so strong she was willing to kidnap her and take her abroad. She'd mentioned her parents also getting attached to the child, and Tracy used her phone at that point, showing Bethany beneath the table what she'd written.

Officers were being sent over there to question them.

Bethany nodded her agreement.

"This carries a serious charge, what you've done," Tracy said to Carla. "You'll be bailed, no doubt, and might get lucky and be presented to a judge who has empathy in your situation. You might only serve a few months if they feel sorry for you."

Carla cried harder, her head bowed. Adams patted her back awkwardly.

She raised her head. "I don't want to go to prison. Please, don't send me there."

Tracy coughed and straightened up. Bethany's eyes stung.

Carla stared at each of them in turn. It was hard to be looked at by such a despondent woman. Bethany had to pull on her reserves to cope with it.

"Where is Lily now?" Carla asked.

Tracy let out a breath which gave away the fact she was agitated with the use of the name Lily. "*Maisie* is with Social Services."

"Oh God," Carla wailed.

"Interview suspended . . ."

Bethany couldn't help but feel sorry for this woman, but it seemed Tracy didn't. They left the room, and in the hallway outside, Tracy leant against the wall, tipped her head back, and closed her eyes. A tear trickled down her cheek.

"Is it wrong of me to want Carla to have Maisie back?" she asked. She opened her eyes and turned her head towards Bethany. "Don't you go telling anyone I'm crying."

Bethany laughed, despite the situation. "I won't. And no, you're not wrong. I feel the same. She loves the baby, would give her a decent life. What she did was selfish, granted, but with the best intentions. Maisie being with either her father or Vicky's parents . . ." She shuddered. "Let's just say she'd have a shitty life."

"Could be just as shitty if she's placed with dodgy foster carers." Tracy paused.

"The couple she's with are nice. I've met them before."

"Don't make out bad ones don't exist, because they do. We only find out once a kid blabs or a school informs us things don't seem right. Maisie's so innocent, and she doesn't deserve to be in the system."

"What can we do, though, but hope for the best?" Bethany leant on the wall, too. "I thought you felt the opposite way in there. You were tetchy."

"I was trying to keep it together. I'm not the hard-hearted cow people think I am, told you that before. All right, I give that impression, but that's for my own safety. I can't go gadding about, throwing vulnerable emotions everywhere. It wouldn't be good for my colleagues."

"Or for you?"

"No, especially not for me." Tracy pushed off the wall. "I've built barriers. No fucker can bring them down except Damon, and he knows not to try. It wouldn't be worth the shit I'd give him." She wiped her face with her palms and laughed. "So, onwards and all that. Fancy some dinner? There's a nice Indian up the road. My shout."

Bethany nodded, and they walked up the hallway side by side, two women joined by their jobs, and who knew, one day they might even become friends if Tracy allowed her in.

Tracy slung her arm across Bethany's shoulder. "D'you know, I quite like you."

Bethany smiled. "Funny, that."

"Funny indeed. I don't usually like anybody, so count yourself lucky. Or unlucky, depending on your outlook."

"I'll take lucky. And you can do the same, because I quite like you, too."

They pushed through into the reception area, where Mike and Damon were gassing.

"We're all off to the Indian," Tracy said, approaching them. She winked at Damon. "Don't piss your pants when I say I'm paying for it, will you. Come on." She nudged him in the ribs and escorted him outside.

Bethany and Mike stared at each other as the door swung shut.

"You all right?" he asked, his hand on her shoulder.

"Yeah, you?"

"It was tough to watch."

"I bet."

"So, you've broken down Tracy's wall, have you?"

"Looks like it, but I prefer to say she's let me take a few bricks out of it, enough for me to climb though when she allows it, and not so many of them missing that she can't put them back in if I get too close."

"You're probably right. So, an Indian, eh?" Mike opened the door and raised his arm for her to go out first. "Good, because I'm starving. I could eat a scabby donkey."

"Glad you didn't say rat. I got the distinct impression Anne eats them."

"Gross."

"Hang on a sec. Message." She stopped walking to read it.

Tammy: I GOT THE JOB. KRIBBS HAS AGREED I CAN START AS SOON AS I'VE MOVED BACK DOWN SOUTH. THANKS FOR TAKING ME UNDER YOUR WING. I'LL NEVER FORGET IT.

Bethany's eyes leaked.

> Bethany: AH, I WISH IT DIDN'T HAVE TO BE LIKE THIS, BUT GOOD LUCK, LOVE.

Tammy: THANKS!

Bethany sighed. She was losing a damn good officer.

"Everything okay?" Mike asked.

"Tammy got the job."

"Bollocks."

"I know."

They walked towards the car, Bethany glad for the suggestion of going for a meal. She needed to decompress. Tomorrow would be another day of working out exactly what had gone on regarding this case, so an evening of kicking back would do her the world of good.

No, this wasn't the same as relaxing in Spain, and their holiday seemed a distant memory now, but she was ready to see this through to its conclusion, and she'd be happy once she'd closed the file for the last time.

Onwards, like Tracy had said. It was all Bethany knew to do these days.

THE END

THE JOFFE BOOKS STORY

We began in 2014 when Jasper agreed to publish his mum's much-rejected romance novel and it became a bestseller.

Since then we've grown into the largest independent publisher in the UK. We're extremely proud to publish some of the very best writers in the world, including Joy Ellis, Faith Martin, Caro Ramsay, Helen Forrester, Simon Brett and Robert Goddard. Everyone at Joffe Books loves reading and we never forget that it all begins with the magic of an author telling a story.

We are proud to publish talented first-time authors, as well as established writers whose books we love introducing to a new generation of readers.

We won Trade Publisher of the Year at the Independent Publishing Awards in 2023. We have been shortlisted for Independent Publisher of the Year at the British Book Awards for the last four years, and were shortlisted for the Diversity and Inclusivity Award at the 2022 Independent Publishing Awards. In 2023 we were shortlisted for Publisher of the Year at the RNA Industry Awards.

We built this company with your help, and we love to hear from you, so please email us about absolutely anything bookish at: feedback@joffebooks.com.

If you want to receive free books every Friday and hear about all our new releases, join our mailing list: www.joffebooks.com/contact

And when you tell your friends about us, just remember: it's pronounced Joffe as in coffee or toffee!

ALSO BY EMMY ELLIS

DI BETHANY SMITH

Book 1: THE COLD CALL KILLER
Book 2: THE CREEPY-CRAWLY KILLER
Book 3: THE SCREWDRIVER KILLER
Book 4: THE SCORCHED SKIN KILLER
Book 5: THE STREET PARTY KILLER
Book 6: THE CANDY CANE KILLER
Book 6.5: THE SECRET SANTA KILLER
Book 7: THE MEAT HOOK KILLER
Book 8: THE BLADE KILLER

DETECTIVE CAROL WREN MYSTERIES

Book 1: SPITE YOUR FACE
Book 2: HOLD YOUR BREATH
Book 3: GUILT BURNS HOLES
Book 4: BEST SERVED COLD
Book 5: BLOOD RUNS DEEP

Printed in Dunstable, United Kingdom

64598799R00139